Iris
ROOTED

THE FLOWER LADIES TRILOGY 3

D. A. SPRUZEN

Published By: 4 Horsemen Publications, Inc.

4 Horsemen Publications, Inc.
PO Box 419
Sylva, NC 28779
4horsemenpublications.com
info@4horsemenpublications.com

Cover Illustration by CD Corrigan
Typesetting by Autumn Skye
Edited by Kris Cotter

Library of Congress Control Number: 2025948201

Paperback ISBN-13: 979-8-8232-1024-9
Hardcover ISBN-13: 979-8-8232-1025-6
Ebook ISBN-13: 979-8-8232-1026-3

Contents

Part II

Prologue

Shifted and cracked by old roots and neglect, the paving stones made for hazardous walking. So as she hobbled around the corner, she focused only on her feet — it wouldn't do to trip at this point. She straightened a little and looked around as if searching for a building number, her eyes sweeping over splitting siding, crumbling mortar, and flaking paint, blemishes almost disguised by shadow in the rapidly darkening twilight. To think this neighborhood was only a ten-minute bus ride away from her lovely home. She passed the corner store, whose plump little owner, an Indian man whose family was probably unwelcome in these parts, slowly lowered a rusty grate over the front window and door, its mechanism groaning while he spat out syncopated gibberish as if trying to come up with the right epithet. As he stretched for a moment, he noticed her approach.

"Better get home now, lady. You know about the recent unpleasantness, don't you? I myself am a bit later than I like to be."

"Oh, my, yes. Thank you, young man. I'm going straight home. Not much farther now." Her voice sounded convincingly feeble. He probably wasn't much over fifty, but even his thinning oiled hair looked too dispirited to hang on much longer. And he clearly hadn't noticed the man who'd slipped into the shadows of a doorway when he heard voices—but not quickly enough to avoid her catching his dim reflection in the window's edge.

The owner finally got the gate in place and locked while she leaned on her cane and watched. He crossed the road and got in his car, driving off with a nonchalant wave. The pipsqueak could have offered to drive her home. Not that she wanted that, but still. How did one hurry and hobble at the same time? She must make it to her chosen spot before her stalker caught up. The street felt dystopian now, thick with despair and abandonment. A stiff breeze pushed candy wrappers and other torn scraps around the gutters with faint crackles and scrapes, as if trying to breathe life into the place. Something dripped from a building behind her, and a gate across the road slammed shut and squeaked open in a haunting complaint.

She felt him closing in—a whispery soft footfall, the swish of nylon-clad arms—just as the dark alley gaped to her right. He clapped his hand over her mouth, dragged her halfway down the garbage-strewn strip, and pushed her against a cinderblock wall.

"Good evening, my dear. Let's have a little fun. I'm sure it's been years since you've been pleasured. You'll love it. Be a good girl and stay quiet so I don't have to hurt you." He fumbled at his zipper as he spoke. Raspy, well-spoken, and not that big. Big enough to overpower a real old lady.

"What do you want? I have money in my pocket."

"Let's see it, sweetie. A little icing on the cake can't hurt."

She reached deep and drew out the knife, thrusting it under his ribs and up. He staggered back before he sank to his knees.

"Fuck," he gasped.

She moved behind him and crashed her stick across his head, but it slipped in her cotton gloves and didn't knock him out like she'd planned. She should have worn leather, but she hated waste.

"Oh, fuck," he whimpered.

"Not this time, my dear!"

She couldn't allow blood to get on her clothes. She picked up one of the lighter trash bags and held it in front of herself as she pulled out the knife with a hard twist and gently set it down beside her. That should do it. She got out her halogen flashlight, shielding its beam with her hand as she watched his face from a safe distance. His eyes fluttered closed as his breath became sluggish and ragged. He opened his eyes and looked into hers in a puzzled sort of way. He tried to say something, only managing to puff out, "F…" before his eyes glazed over.

She left the alley and continued along the road, hobbling until she came to the next street. A bus should come along soon. The knife went over a wire-topped wall. Good, a quiet rustling landing, perhaps in long grass. She edged into the next doorway and opened her large purse. In went the gray wig and out came the red one and a pair of large tinted glasses—it had taken her over an hour to find everything in the storage unit. Her gloves went into a plastic bag. They'd go in someone's trash closer to home. The heavy cane was too conspicuous, though. She'd kept it for sentimental reasons. She almost laughed. Her, sentimental. Who would have thought it? She had time to get to the next alley and toss it in a dumpster before her bus arrived. Such a shame.

Part I

1

Iris drove slowly down Andrew's—Simon's—street. It looked like all the others in this neighborhood: gracious homes cocooned in huge trees and low split-rail fences. She liked Charlotte and even most of downtown was pleasant. Out here, near a small university campus, it was easy to get lost on streets that looped back on themselves and took unexpected jaunts into dead-ends. She thought it lovelier than even the best parts of Salton. This place had an old, settled feel.

It should be the third house down. There, number 34. She pulled to a stop. A young woman was planting a border with lavender. Pretty, petite, with short, fair hair. She'd be mousy but for her exultant face as she sang and almost skipped on her knees along the row. Iris rolled down her window. *"I feel pretty..."* An old song for this generation. The woman noticed Iris and stopped singing. A sudden protesting cry caused her to turn toward a stroller Iris hadn't noticed under the bay window. Her heart missed a couple of beats. The baby. She'd almost forgotten about him in her longing to see her son.

"Can I help you?" Not a Southern voice.

Iris got out and went to the gate. "Good morning. My name is Iris Hall. I'm house-hunting and particularly like this neighborhood. May I ask if you are happy here?"

"I'm Mandy Hale." She took off her gloves and extended her hand. A firm grip. "Yes, we love it here. Nice neighbors, a good school for when Victor here gets to that point." She gestured to the pram. "And it's not a bad drive into the city where my husband works."

Victor! After his late grandfather. Andrew had been fond of his father, even after he got sick and curmudgeonly, but it shocked her, nevertheless. She hadn't had one of those nightmares for several years. She hoped they wouldn't come back.

Victor started whimpering, clearly unhappy that his mother's attention lay elsewhere. "Excuse me just a moment." Mandy picked him up and brought him over. The baby inspected Iris and crammed his fist into his mouth. She grinned at this chubby replica of his father at that age, and the corners of Victor's mouth curled up. She wanted to take him and give him a good squeeze, but she was a stranger, and strangers mustn't do that.

"He likes you! You know, some friends of ours are moving out of state. They live across and to the right at number 29. Why don't you walk down there and say I sent you? See if you like it. It's quite a small house. Is it just for you?"

"Yes, just me. I don't need much space, just peace and quiet."

CHAPTER 1

"Her name is Sylvia. I'd better put Victor down for his nap. I'll give her a quick call and tell her to expect you."

Iris reached out and touched Victor's cheek, a gentle caress. He giggled. "That's so kind. Thank you, Mandy. Perhaps we will be neighbors soon." Absolutely, if she could pull it off.

Iris found the house exquisite. A large front parlor with wide picture windows on two sides that looked out onto a felt-like lawn, briefly interrupted by two large magnolia trees ringed by daffodils.

She felt as if she were on the set of one of those romance movies set in the Deep South. It looked so much like the house she'd dreamed up after poring through magazines in Manhattan all those years ago, even more than the one she'd eventually gotten in Salton and had to abandon. The Toronto house had been a good home, and she'd loved it. But this one was it. Her place. That tired cliché when people swore a house "spoke to them" suddenly made sense.

"Sylvia, I won't beat about the bush. I like the house and I like the neighborhood. Do you have a realtor?"

"We haven't signed yet, although we've more or less settled on one. A friend recommended her and the pricing seemed about right."

The price wasn't bad—Iris had done her homework. She negotiated a little, pointing out that they would bypass the agency fees and she would be paying cash. She didn't mind using their lawyer. They sat at the kitchen table in a nook that looked out onto a backyard surrounded by a high wooden fence, sipping iced tea while waiting for Sylvia's husband to rush home.

By five o'clock, the deal was agreed upon. As is, no agent, cash, and Iris had spoken to their lawyer to arrange for the bank transfer and the papers to be drawn up. She thanked her lucky stars for her "financial planner's" expertise in dealing with getting her money into the U.S. without raising questions in the wrong places. The couple looked somewhat shell-shocked as they shook her hand. She walked down to number 34 and rang the bell.

"It's all settled," she told Mandy. "We close on May 15th."

"So fast? That's unbelievable! Sylvia and Mark must be thrilled. I'm so glad we're going to have another nice neighbor."

If only she could have had a last glance at Victor. But there would be plenty of time for that.

2

Kate's B&B made a brave attempt at English gentility with its chintz upholstery, watercolors of flower arrangements, and cherry end tables. Iris had been there for a couple of weeks already. She hadn't rushed to find her son Andrew's house because she'd wanted to feel ready for the impact of seeing him again. She mustn't give herself away. The first day, she had an early lunch at a restaurant opposite his office and watched. After her second cup of coffee, she saw him come out with an older man. He looked relaxed and a little thinner than the last time she'd seen him. That was all she needed to know. Andrew was here, and he was fine.

Her time after that had been taken up with opening bank accounts (one for savings and one for checking, in different banks to be on the safe side), transferring funds, leasing a car, and making arrangements for some furniture to be shipped from Toronto and stored in Charlotte. She wanted to keep some of Hilda's and Magaly's pieces as they held precious memories of shared meals and good conversation in good times and hard. Those old ladies had been so dear to her, and she to them. She'd never felt so cherished. Well, to be fair, her late husband Victor had loved her well. That is, until he became so disagreeable that she'd had to let him go. It's not as though he'd enjoyed any quality of life, anyway. Poor Victor.

She often had tea or a pre-dinner sherry with Kate, and rather dreaded it today. Kate was 76 and Iris enjoyed the comfortable company of the older woman. Kate seemed to have become attached to Iris, too, and had no other guests at present.

Kate popped her head out of her sitting room as soon as she heard Iris open the front door. "Hello, Iris. A quick sherry?"

How lonely and cruel Kate's old age must seem sometimes. Her only son had moved to South Africa ten years before she'd been widowed. From tidbits dripped into the conversation here and there, Kate's husband had been "difficult." And there was that assault she had suffered before Iris had come on the scene, one of several attacks on elderly women in one run-down neighborhood over the past several months. Fortunately, someone had come along before he got too far with Kate and he'd run off. She was still very nervous and never went out alone after dark. The creep had wrenched her shoulder, too, and it still pained her. The friend she'd been visiting had her groceries delivered now. The police hadn't gotten anywhere, or so they said. They claimed they'd upped their patrols, but resources were limited.

Kate's mouth drooped when she heard Iris's news. She forced a grin as she congratulated her on her find. "That's a lovely street," she said. "We used to have some friends there, but they moved away a few years ago. People move a lot these days, don't they?"

"Kate, I want you to come and see me often. We'll have lunch, or tea, or go shopping. I value our time together. I won't just go away and forget you."

Iris, even now, was surprised at herself for uttering such sentiments. Only ten years ago, it would have been unthinkable for her to consider saying anything like that, let alone meaning it. Thinking for a few hours that Andrew might be dead a while back had woken deep feelings that, for once, had nothing to do with angry self-preservation and violence. After that, two elderly widows in Canada, Hilda and Magaly, had helped breathe warmth into her arid mind.

"Would you like to go out for a nice dinner to celebrate? My treat." That's how it had started with Hilda and Magaly in Toronto when she'd moved into Hilda's home as a lodger.

"Oh, yes, I would!" Kate didn't have money to spare for such things and couldn't drive at night anymore. Iris would choose a good place, one that Kate had probably never been to. She felt tearful suddenly.

"I have to go upstairs and freshen up. I need to make a reservation, too. I'll come down at seven?"

Iris escaped upstairs and had a good cry. She missed those old ladies, both dead now, only a few months ago. How she'd loved them, she who'd never before loved anyone except Andrew and, to a lesser extent, her other two children. And they'd relied completely on her toward the end of their lives, never realizing how much she had depended on them.

Enough wallowing. Iris wiped her eyes and leafed through her guidebook. She found an Italian restaurant not far away that had a great write-up. She was really going for nostalgia. So convenient to have a room with a phone, unusual in a B&B, she would have thought. The reservations made for 7:30, she slipped off her shoes and lay down. What unexpected paths her life always took. Miraculous twists and turns. Andrew (so hard to think of him as Simon), a beautiful grandson, a delightful daughter-in-law, and a lovely little house nearly opposite. A middle-class dream. Another one. Tomorrow she'd buy a bed. She would wait to see how her furniture fit before buying anything else. She'd need some extra china and silverware. She'd hung onto Hilda's prized tea set, the Royal Albert, with blue cornflowers.

And there was another piece of business she needed to take care of. Her heart started to speed up. Time to start planning.

3

Iris woke early, excited and nervous. Would this really happen without something going wrong? She took her shower, finished packing, and went downstairs for breakfast. Kate was already sitting at the big center table, moping over a pot of tea.

"Good morning, Kate!"

"Good morning. Ready for your big day?" Kate stretched her lips into a semblance of a smile. "Good timing. I've got a family coming in to look at Queens University with their twins. They've got two younger ones, too."

"Oh, Kate, I'm so glad. And graduation isn't far off. You usually get busy then, I'm sure."

"Yes. This might be my last year, though. I'm getting too old for all this work. If I can get a good price, I might sell before Christmas. I think I can live on my savings and Social Security."

"Kate, this isn't the last you'll see of me. You must come over to see me. We'll go out to lunch, go to a movie, have a little fun! I consider you a friend, you know."

Kate smiled properly this time. "You mean it? I'd really like that. Let me get your toast."

It was nice to see Kate smile. She'd perked up a lot after the man who attacked her had been found in an alleyway near Kate's friend's house, still wearing his balaclava, pants halfway down, and dead. Murdered. DNA matched that found on his victims. Case closed.

She looked at her watch. "I'd better get a move on. Closing is at ten and the movers are scheduled for noon. I'd like to be at the house in good time."

Iris hauled her bags to the car and looked back at her friend. Kate's gray bun sat at the nape of her neck, tidy as usual, and a striped cotton dress that had undergone too many washes draped her ample proportions. Her face showed her unfailing good nature, although her lips trembled through her brave smile. Iris waved goodbye. Kate waved perfunctorily and turned quickly back into the house. She must call Kate very soon. The phone should be connected by now. She drove to number 29 and parked. She'd arranged to drive with Sylvia and Bruce so they'd all arrive together. She still tended to get lost downtown.

They greeted her warmly, but looked sad. Iris knew how hard it could be to leave a home where you've been happy. Even one where you haven't. The house was empty, but for a couple of cases and the porch furniture they were leaving behind.

"Would you like to do a walk-through?" asked Bruce.

"Oh, no, I'm sure everything is fine. I know this is hard. Let me put my cases and bags of supplies inside and then we can go." She hoped everything was in good shape. It wasn't like her to be so trusting, but they seemed like decent people, and Mandy knew them quite well. No point in ruffling feathers.

The lawyer's office looked more like a parlor than a place of business. A very messy parlor, with stacks of papers and files covering most of the flat surfaces. The signatures were many and, as usual, the documents too long and numerous to be read, although she checked the address, names, and all the dates for accuracy.

Bruce and Sylvia drove her back to the house. Sylvia stayed in the car and nodded tearfully to Iris. Bruce went inside, shook her hand, and picked up their cases. "Be happy here," he said. "We have been." He turned abruptly, went back to the car, and drove off without looking back. Sylvia craned her neck until they'd rounded the bend, a handkerchief pressed to her mouth.

Wailing air brakes announced the arrival of the moving truck. Iris felt a little flutter of excitement in her stomach. She'd thought through where she wanted to put things and hoped it would work out. She also hoped the bed would arrive as promised.

The two men worked remarkably fast. By lunchtime, everything was set in its place and she had a home again. They even unpacked the crates. Two pictures stood against a wall, china and kitchen utensils sat on the kitchen table waiting to be washed, and the few photos of Hilda and Magaly posed on the sideboard. Happy memories of the years living with them in Toronto.

Hilda's favorite chintz armchair looked faded in this sunny room. She might have it recovered, but she would have to find a similar fabric so she could picture Hilda sitting in it. And Magaly's sofa, same thing. The old lady had always sat at the end next to the oak table where she kept her glasses and book. Iris sat at the other end. Magaly's cushion certainly looked more compressed than the others, even after being unused for a year. It felt strange to see them here. A fond remembrance, but out of context. Hilda's pride and joy, a lamp with its rose silk shade would stand next to her new bed. In her last weeks, Hilda had slept with that light on next to her, its soft glow making her ashen skin look almost healthy again. She'd outlasted Magaly by only a few minutes, worn out from watching her friend's suffering, then the shock of her sudden death from an overdose of painkillers. Iris had told the police that Magaly sometimes woke confused after taking her pills and had most certainly taken the overdose in error. The death had been ruled accidental, and the insurance had to pay out. Only Iris knew how she'd cut back for a few weeks to have enough to do the job. No one did the math. Magaly chose to suffer a few weeks' pain to end what was becoming an unbearable indignity.

Iris had first seen that lampshade when she answered Hilda's ad for a lodger, or "paying guest," as she liked to call it. Hilda had taken pains to point it out, but Iris, or Lily as she was known then, had not appreciated the old lady's pride, or the coziness of the room, nor the value of an emotional haven as opposed to mere physical safety. She had been a different person then. She loved her son Andrew—*no, Simon, must remember that*—very much. She loved her other two children, too, although that felt more like primal protectiveness than anything else. But she'd never loved anyone in the same way as those two old ladies, who had mostly healed her with their unconditional affection and friendship. She suspected they knew there was something wrong about her—at least, Magaly did—but they never asked. Thanks to them, she could open her heart wider now.

CHAPTER 3

The doorbell rang. The bed was soon placed in the master bedroom. She'd have to think about furnishing the other two bedrooms eventually, although she wasn't planning to have any overnight guests. One of the rooms had a nice view of the garden. Maybe she should turn it into a study. She'd had some success with her romance novel and a small Toronto publisher had published it under the pen name of Maggie Hilder. The trouble was, they'd paid her under her old name, Lily Porter. She'd left a small account open in Toronto to bank the royalties, but if she kept sending the money off to another name, would that seem suspicious? She'd like to write another, though. The press had a very good editor who'd helped her with the first book and taught her a great deal about the craft, in fact. Perhaps she should just try to publish here on her own. She'd think about it later.

Iris felt hungry. She had no idea how to order pizza around here. She'd better do some grocery shopping soon. The bell rang again.

"Mandy! How nice to see you!"

"Hello, Iris, how's it going? I left Victor asleep in the front and thought I'd drop by quickly to ask you over for a sandwich. I don't suppose you've got any groceries yet."

"That's so nice of you. I am feeling a bit hungry, actually. I was about to look in the phonebook for a pizza place. I'd rather have a sandwich, though."

"Come on over, then. I must get back in case he wakes up."

"Okay, I'll grab my keys. And that reminds me, I didn't check if the phone is connected."

Sylvia and Bruce had left three telephones behind, which was kind. No dial tone. Oh, well, she couldn't expect everything to go right. She grabbed her keys and left.

Simon and Mandy's house was very different from hers. A large living room had French doors at the end that led straight out onto a patio lined with white planters. The furniture was light and modern, the upholstery gray—which probably worked well with a baby who would soon become a toddler in the house. Even the paintings were modern, not quite abstract, but getting there. She could make out a black horse in one, part of a naked woman in another.

Mandy led her through to the kitchen, where she'd set out lemonade and a plate of sandwiches. They munched and talked about Charlotte, Victor, grocery stores, and all kinds of other trivia Iris had trouble focusing on. All she could think about was when Victor was going to wake up. She wanted to hold him, kiss that special place at the nape of his neck, feel those surges of love that had sometimes crept up on her with her own children, especially Andrew. *Simon.* Mandy mentioned a public lecture she would be going to at the end of the week at the nearby university.

"Where is the campus? Someone told me it was close to here. It seems so strange to have a university in a residential area like this."

"It was a Presbyterian college for girls when it started out," said Mandy. "Then a nursing school was added, and now it's a small private coed university with a few graduate programs. Quite well respected."

"Well, that's nice. Another amenity I hadn't expected!"

"Why don't you come with me? It's actually a reading and a talk with one of their poetry professors from the writing program. Do you like poetry?"

"I haven't read much, to be honest. But it's one of those things I've always been meaning to get to. Yes, I'd love to come."

A wail lifted Iris's heart.

"I'll just go and get him. He'll need changing, I'm sure, so don't mind me if it takes a few minutes. There are some magazines on the coffee table."

"Thank you. Don't worry about me. I'm really looking forward to seeing him again. It takes you back, being close to a baby again."

"Do you have children?"

"One, but he's abroad." She turned away quickly, walked into the living room, over to the coffee table, and picked up a magazine to steady her hands. She looked up at the black horse again and squinted. Now she could make out a child on its back.

Iris flipped magazine pages until Mandy came back down with Victor. He was still a little flushed and sleepy, and stared at Iris for a minute, not sure what to make of her. She got up and moved closer, stopping a few feet away so as not to frighten him. "Hello, little boy," she said softly. She felt ridiculously close to tears. His eyes almost disappeared as a gummy smile cracked open and he stuck out his arms.

"Wow, you are honored. He almost never does that," said Iris.

"Do you mind if I hold him?"

"Of course not."

Iris held him and turned so he could keep an eye on his mother. She couldn't resist holding her cheek against his for a few seconds. She sat down with him and started to play "This little piggy."

She was only dimly aware of the front door opening.

"Simon, what's the matter? Simon!" Mandy sounded panicked.

She turned to see her beautiful boy standing in the doorway, his face pale and sweaty. She held Victor tightly as she stood and took a step toward him. She didn't know how to act. *Get a grip, don't give yourself away, breathe in, deeply.*

"Simon, this is Iris Hall, the new neighbor I was telling you about. Are you all right?"

Iris could hardly breathe. He knew? The plastic surgery had completely fooled Toby when he showed up in Toronto.

"Sorry, darling. Iris, welcome to the neighborhood. It's a pleasure to meet you. I see you've made friends with young Victor." Victor started to squeal in excitement and reached for his father, who gathered him close and kissed him. "It's just that I thought I'd seen a ghost for a minute. I remember my mother playing that piggy game with my sister. And the profile... even the voice..." He sounded shaky again.

"Why don't you sit down, darling? I'll make us all some tea." Mandy was clearly puzzled. Iris wondered about the conversation they were sure to have later. How much would Andrew tell his wife about his killer mother?

"That would be nice, thanks. But first I think I'll just go and change out of my suit." Turning to Iris he said, "Victor always manages to spit up on my ties, so I've finally learned my lesson." He handed Victor over to Mandy and disappeared upstairs.

"Poor Simon. His mother died, you know. He never talks about her."

"I'm very sorry to hear that." And she was. Devastated, in fact.

"I wonder why he's home so early?"

"Mandy, I think I'd better go home. I need to call the phone company."

"How can you? Your phone's dead!"

"Oh, good heavens, how stupid of me!"

"Use our phone. I'll find the number."

Iris protested that she didn't want to outstay her welcome, but Mandy insisted, made a note of the number from a card on the fridge, and brought Iris the phone. She was put on hold three times before being assured that her phone would be connected in the morning.

"Thanks so much. I should get one of those cellular phones, I suppose. It can be convenient." She'd had one in Canada, but the battery ran down too fast to be that reliable, although she'd heard they'd improved.

"Simon has one he's pleased with. Oh, here he is."

Simon looked better now. Iris would love to hug him, like she used to. Not often enough. God, she was getting mushy. That had to stop.

"I was just telling Iris you are quite happy with your cell phone. She was talking about getting one."

"Well, just a maybe," Iris said quickly. "I really must be getting back. There are still quite a few boxes to unpack and clothes to wash. Some of them smell rather musty after being in storage." She was babbling. *Calm down.*

"It was lovely to see you, Iris," said Mandy. "We'll get together for dinner very soon."

She thanked them and they saw her to the door. Before she got to the bend, she turned around. They still stood there, Victor in his mother's arms, Simon's arm resting on Mandy's shoulder. She waved, and they all waved back, even Victor. She thought her heart might split.

4

Iris yanked out more weeds, sweat dripping from her forehead. Gardening in North Carolina was more than she'd bargained for, worse than Virginia. Maybe some local boy would do it once a week. No, he'd probably pull out the good stuff along with the weeds. Well, sweaty work was what showers were for, and what did she have to complain about? It was June already, three weeks in her new home. She'd seen Mandy two or three times a week, had dinner with them twice, and on Saturday night she was even going to babysit. She hoped she'd manage the diapers. They weren't what she was used to. It had been over thirty years since Lucy was a baby; nothing was the same. At all.

She sat back on her heels suddenly. Kate! She'd forgotten all about Kate. How could she? Kate didn't even have her phone number.

CHAPTER 4

She got up with some difficulty. Her knees ached. She left her trowel on the patio and went inside, not waiting to take a shower before looking up Kate's number and calling.

"Kate! You must have thought I'd forgotten you. I'm so sorry I left it this long, but you know how moving is."

Kate sounded almost tearful. Iris said she would pick her up tomorrow and bring her back to the house for lunch. She'd better make herself presentable and buy some food.

"You know, Iris, I know it's wrong to be glad someone is dead, but I feel so much better knowing that wicked man is out of the way."

"Yes, it was all very unpleasant, and frightening, too." Iris patted Kate's hand. "But it's over now."

"They say he was from a good family, whatever that means."

"Yes, he sounded like it." Kate looked at her, flabbergasted. "Iris, whatever do you mean?"

Oh God, I must be getting old, making a slip like that. "Oh, I meant I read that in some newspaper." She sprang up to get the dessert out of the fridge. "Here, I got us a lovely raspberry mousse cake."

"Maybe we should finish our crab cakes first." Iris set her elbows on the table, resting her chin in her hands. "You are hiding something, Iris."

"No, no, not at all. Well, not really. It's just that I have a neighbor who is a D.A., and the police had questioned the man once before. They didn't make that public, and I should never have mentioned it. Please, Kate, promise not to tell anyone." Iris hoped she looked innocent and earnest enough to lay the subject to rest. She could still lie like a pro. And she hadn't actually met any of the neighbors.

"Of course, I won't. I can keep a secret!"

"I'm sure you can."

"But I often feel there is something about yourself you keep locked away, Iris. As though you carry great sorrow in your heart. And how come you know a D.A. here already?"

She's more perceptive than I gave her credit for. "There is a great deal of sorrow, Kate. Family deaths, an unhappy and lonely marriage, but that's true of many people, isn't it.? Anyway, I don't like to talk about it. I'd rather focus on positive things. Oh, and the D.A. is the son of an old friend." *Too glib?*

Iris felt cold. How could she make such a silly mistake? She had become careless, too complacent in her newfound normalcy. She wasn't normal, never had been, and never would *Never forget it.*

"I'm so happy to know you, Iris, and whatever happened, I feel you are a good person and I will always be your friend. Now, our crab cakes are getting cold and the mousse cake is getting warm."

Iris laughed and put the cake back in the fridge.

"That's a lovely thing to say, Kate, and I feel the same way about you. Shall we have coffee on the patio afterwards?"

Iris finally gave up trying to sleep and turned on her bedside lamp, its familiar rosy glow as comforting as ever. She picked up her book and found her place. Perhaps reading about a small English village and its ever-vigilant spinster Miss Marple would ease her mind, even if a dead body or two were bound to crop up. Here, at least, murder felt genteel. Noises offstage and all that. Was England ever like that? Everyone in his proper place, tea at the vicarage, policemen without guns. She'd like to live in that kind of haven. No more killing. She clearly wasn't as sharp as she used to be, and she must watch herself. She'd rid the town of a monster, though, and her dear friend Kate felt safe again. No more funny business for her whatsoever. Unless absolutely necessary.

5

Iris pulled up her shades and looked over her garden. Her predecessors had left some good old favorites, and her own plantings were finally blooming after her late start. The early sun slanted over them all as if spotlighting star turns. And some of them were indeed stars—gerberas flaunting myriad saturated colors, chalk-white daises with cheeky yellow faces, and deep gold stella d'oros, which seemed to take care of themselves. And then there was the rose garden, the elegant plants sweet-scented and perfect, but always ready to fall prey to heat, aphids, and god knows what other pestilence.

A perfect summer day for a barbecue. Another Independence Day. Victor's first. She felt excitement begin to build in anticipation of the family party with Victor, nearly one, and the opportunity for a good cuddle. They'd kindly invited Kate today, too. He was used to her now as she'd babysat for them three times, and he gurgled happily when he caught sight of her, instantly pushing her into doting grandmother mode, an almost unrecognizable version of herself. She often had coffee with Mandy and had invited them over for dinner once, together with Kate, which had made the old lady very happy. Victor slept upstairs in her bed, surrounded by a barricade of pillows. Simon had taken him up there and she'd watched for a minute as he settled his boy down, much as his own father would have done. "Lie down with him if it helps," she'd said. "It's quite all right." She wanted to rest her cheek on a pillow her son had used. She watched with satisfaction as he did as she'd suggested. That night, she'd laid her head in the exact same place as he had and slept peacefully and dream-free.

She'd better get on with the dishes she'd promised to bring—potatoes and onions braised in broth with paprika, a Caesar salad, and a lemon chiffon pie. The first two were easy enough, but she'd never made the pie before and could only hope for the best. She'd bought ready-made pastry dough to give herself a head start. Coffee on the patio first. Maybe she should call Kate to see if she had made lemon chiffon pie before. She should have done it yesterday.

It was great to see Kate so happy, cheeks pink, as a couple of Simon's friends teased her gently and laughed at her jokes. Iris noticed Mandy starting to clear away the food and got up to help. Victor sat on Simon's lap, gurgling happily as his father played with him and nuzzled his fluffy hair. She was getting dangerously used to being happy. Even achieving a handsome lemon chiffon pie had lifted her heart.

The dishes were easy—only a large trash bag required—and the food was soon packed into containers and stashed in the fridge. It was nearly dark and almost time to walk down to the park to see the fireworks. Iris loved fireworks. Independence Day had been one of the few bright spots in her miserable childhood. Her father was usually still sober enough to get them down to Central Park to see the magical eruptions of color, sparkle, and bang. She'd felt removed from her everyday turmoil into a chaos with infinite possibilities careening across the universe.

They all ambled through tree-lined avenues to the already crowded park. She pushed Victor's stroller with the proprietary air only a grandmother could muster. She hadn't missed the amused glance Mandy and Simon exchanged. They found a good spot, not too far from the show setup and not too close, either. They spread a couple of blankets and settled down. Darkness was falling fast, and bursts of illegal fireworks sporadically pierced the hum of the crowd around them. Iris noticed that Victor had stuck both his fists as far into his mouth as they would go, and his face had taken on an anxious set.

"Do you think we should take him out of the stroller?" she said to Mandy. "Maybe he'll be frightened by the noise."

"Why not?" Mandy got up and unstrapped him, promptly plopping him on the blanket between her and Iris. Iris put her arm around him, and he seemed all too ready to snuggle in.

The show began shortly thereafter with some of the more decorative displays. Victor seemed a little startled by each bang, but soon got used to it. He squealed happily as Mandy and Iris pointed out the showers of sparkly color painting the sky. Iris reveled in his joy.

CHAPTER 5

It didn't last long. The last big explosions the older children loved terrified the baby, and he shrieked after the first one until he turned an alarming shade of crimson.

"I'd better take him home, Mandy. If you give me a key, I'll settle him down and put him to bed," Iris said. His fear was unbearable.

"I hate to put you out, Iris. Will you be all right on your own?" Mandy said, vainly trying to comfort her son.

"We'll be fine."

Iris pushed the stroller rapidly through the streets, alternately talking and singing to Victor to calm him as the terrifying bangs receded into the distance.

"See, my darling, they're going away, nearly all gone, nearly all gone!"

He settled somewhat, with only the occasional whimper interrupting the rhythm of his breathing. She let herself into the house and picked him up. She went through to the kitchen and rocked him, singing, "Hush-a-bye baby on the tree top..." What an appalling song. An ancient political in-joke, no doubt.

Victor yawned astonishingly widely. Fear could be exhausting. She warmed up his evening bottle and took him upstairs. The rocking chair in his blue room was one of her favorite places. But she knew without a doubt there was some diaper unpleasantness to deal with first.

"Let's get you cleaned up first, little man!"

He squealed his protest, but not too vigorously. He knew she would prevail.

Soon enough they settled down and he had latched on to his bottle. No budging him now, even when she heard the others come in. She looked down at the babe, eyes tearing as she thought of all she had lost, especially the love and respect of her children. How her ability to love them as she loved Victor had been quashed almost beyond redemption by her traumatic beginnings. She was able to allow herself to open up to those feelings now. Too late for Andrew (no, Simon, and that was her fault, too), but not too late for this little boy. A sudden intake of breath at the doorway. Simon stood there with a strange expression contorting his face, one she couldn't read.

"What's the matter?" she whispered.

"Nothing," he said. "You are really good with him."

"He's a most precious little thing. I love him to bits."

"I can tell. And so can he. He's very lucky that you found us. We all are."

Iris looked at him again, but his expression was bland now. Victor had fallen asleep. She got up and laid him gently in his crib. He fussed a little, and she rubbed his back, talking to him gently until he slid back into deep sleep.

"I remember my mother talking and singing to my sister like that." Iris froze. By the time she looked around, Simon had left.

6

Iris wanted a new skirt, and maybe a couple of sweaters. Autumn chill would soon arrive, although the early September weather was only marginally cooler than August's. The shops would be full of fall bargains, though, since a cold snap was more conducive to warm clothing sales than sunny skies and balmy temperatures. The leaves had barely begun to turn. She wondered if Kate was up to wandering around the mall. There were usually seats in the better stores—presumably intended to anchor restless husbands. She could only ask.

"Hi, Kate. How are you? I'm going to the mall this afternoon to look for a few fall clothes. Would you like to come? There are plenty of seats around if you get tired."

"Iris, how kind of you. I'd be delighted. My last guests just left this morning. There's no hurry to tidy up after them. They really were my last guests."

"Oh, Kate. Are you sad about that?"

"I thought I might be. But what I'm actually feeling is relief. It's all been a bit too much. A lot too much. I'll call a real estate agent next week."

"Where will you live?"

"I'd like a small condo. There's a lovely retirement complex nearby, but it's too expensive for me, I'm afraid. I really need to be on one level, though."

"I'll help you look. Anyway, does two o'clock suit?"

"Yes, I'll be ready."

"Okay, I'll honk my horn once."

The mall parking lot wasn't full, but Kate had brought her handicapped parking sticker, so they parked near the entrance to the upscale department store Iris favored. Unlike most of the others, this store's buyer understood that older women didn't necessarily want sleeveless and short outfits, nor did they want cute. They wanted quality and good tailoring. Class.

Almost right away, Iris found a gray woolen suit comprising pants, a skirt, and a jacket. It fitted her perfectly as her size was a reliable ten. It amused her to reflect that there was at least one thing normal about her. She came out of the dressing room to model it for Kate twice, once with the pants, and once with the skirt. Kate was content to sit in a comfortable armchair, watching the other customers.

"You look very smart in that, Iris. You could wear it anywhere. Liven it up with different accessories, or keep it plain."

With Kate's stamp of approval, Iris paid for the suit and they moved farther into the department. Now for some tops. A table in the women's department was stacked with piles of cashmere sweaters. A royal blue crewneck caught her eye. She had lapis earrings that would match it. A black turtleneck fitted a more sober look. She already owned a lighter silk and wool top in pearl gray that would do for fall and spring.

The sweaters hung over Iris's arm as she turned to find Kate fingering a pink cashmere sweater as if it were something wondrous. She couldn't afford cashmere, particularly now she'd given up the business.

"Is that your favorite color, Kate?"

"Yes, I love pink. And this one is so soft and pretty."

Iris looked at the tag. Medium. Perfect. She picked it up, gleeful when she heard Kate's sigh.

"I'll pay for these now. That's all I need right now. I'm all right for shoes and bags."

At the counter, she told the cashier to put the pink sweater in a separate bag, which she handed to Kate.

"This is for you," she said.

"Goodness, Iris. I couldn't possibly..."

"It's just a little thank you for being a good friend."

Kate's face was so joyful, and her eyes so near to spilling over, that Iris had to turn abruptly back to her purchases to control her own emotions, looking into the distance over the cashier's shoulder.

No, it can't be.

"Is anything the matter, madam?"

"No, no, of course not. I just had an idea, that's all."

The cashier looked at her and frowned. Iris abruptly turned to Kate.

"Come on, Kate. There's a nice little café upstairs that does English teas. I know you'll love it. The elevator's just over there by the coats."

Iris could feel Kate's eyes on her as they waited in vain for the elevator. She must control her expression. *Daisy.* Could it possibly be her in that ridiculous curly, blonde wig? Her sister always seemed to track her down, god knows how. And would she rat her out? She was right there when Iris tried to poison her friends—as well as Daisy. She must turn the tables and track her sister down, assuming it really was her. She'd been staring straight at Iris. And she smiled. Yes, it was her. *Damn the cow to hell.* After that wolfish smile, she'd walked toward the beauty salon. Could she be working there?

Kete pulled on her sleeve. "Iris, whatever's the matter? Are you unwell? We don't have to go for tea if you don't feel up to it." Kate was holding open the elevator door.

Pull yourself together. "No, I'm fine, Kate. I thought I saw someone I knew a long time ago. Then I remembered she was dead. It gave me quite a turn. I really need that tea." *And I need her well and truly dead this time. Third time's a charm.*

The café was delicately decorated in pale green and cream—even the china matched. Iris ordered Earl Grey tea, while Kate opted for oolong, to Iris's surprise.

"I didn't know you liked oolong," she said.

"A friend brought some back from Hong Kong a couple of years ago. Her husband did a lot of business there and took her with him on that trip. She loved everything about it, but especially the tea. I found it strange at first, but after a few cups, I grew to appreciate it. He retired, and they moved to Florida." Kate sighed.

Soon, small sandwiches and colorful little cakes adorned a three-tier cake stand, and they each had their own small teapot. A plate of scones lay beside a pot of strawberry jam and another of clotted cream.

The savory sandwiches took no more than a couple of bites, although there were plenty of them. After Iris showed Kate how to dress the scones, they cleared the plate. They just about managed to finish the cakes. Sated, they slowly sipped their last cup of tea.

CHAPTER 6

"Iris, I don't know when I've had such a lovely afternoon."

"I've had a lovely time, too. It's more fun when you have someone to share things with."

"That's exactly right. I don't have many friends left around here anymore. I'm tired of doing everything on my own."

"Well, we must do things more often. Do you like movies?"

"Very much. I haven't been to see a film for a couple of years."

"All right, that's next on the list."

An idea began to take root in Iris's mind.

7

Iris returned to the mall the next day. She found it strange that Daisy would taunt her like that. Wasn't she scared of her? She ought to be. What did Daisy want to happen? Perhaps she just wanted to torture Iris until she turned her in. Well, that wasn't going to happen.

She was wearing her own wig this time, a brunette affair that she rather liked. Her own hair was only a little lighter, but strands of gray had made their unwelcome appearance over the last couple of years. Gray hair would be a good disguise, but Iris preferred a more palatable approach. Her glasses were brown-rimmed and large—more of a bookish look than a fashion statement. A tan raincoat completed the nondescript outfit.

She strolled slowly in front of the salon. She sat on a bench to one side, but near enough to be able to see in. There she was, brushing out a customer's hair. A really old lady hairdo: short, a side parting, waves, and curls. The woman wasn't bad-looking. A more fashionable hairdo would have done wonders. Daisy never did have any sense of style.

What was she doing now? She opened a drawer and withdrew her purse. Another woman joined her and they made for the exit. Going on a break. Perfect. Iris stood and walked on a little, stopping to gaze at some lingerie in a nearby boutique. They walked past her. There was a café a little farther along, so that must be where they were headed.

Now what? She'd follow and try to sit close. Maybe she'd learn something from their conversation. She couldn't deal with it right now, in a lighted, busy mall with a companion. Iris fingered the knife in her pocket. A nice, dim parking garage was what she needed. She wondered if Daisy had a car. She should have come later and waited until closing. It's not as though she could make a styling appointment while wearing a wig.

They entered the café, a chic place with pretty pastries and coffee prepared in all kinds of trendy ways. Thankfully, it wasn't crowded. Iris found a table right behind Daisy. She sat facing Daisy's back and kept her eyes down—she didn't want her sister's companion to become aware of her vigilance.

The waitress came to take their order. Daisy ordered a large coffee with all kinds of flavored crap in it, plus a raspberry doughnut. The woman had grown heavier than ever. She'd never had any self-discipline. But why was Daisy talking so funny?

Her companion said, "Fiona, Pete's going to be really mad you're leaving. It'll be hard to find a good stylist before the Christmas rush."

"I really miss my family. And I can't bear to miss another Christmas. Granny isn't getting any younger. I've a mind to celebrate Hogmanay in Glasgow this year."

Iris leaned back and almost laughed.

"Fiona, you sure come out with some funny things. What in hell is Hogmanay?"

"Och, it's our celebration of New Year's. In Scotland, it's more of a big deal than Christmas. If we're up to it, New Year's Day is party time, too. I'll miss my friends here, but only a wee bit compared with how I miss my family and friends in the auld sod."

"That's a rude word."

"No, not always. Sod means turf. The auld sod means the old country."

"And just when I was getting used to your funny accent."

Iris didn't finish her coffee. She felt strangely ebullient. It wasn't Daisy, although this Fiona greatly resembled her. She was safe. And she didn't have to kill again. She'd not been keen on trying to kill her own sister, but there would have been no choice. She wanted to be done with all that. Unless Simon ever needed a little help along those lines. She'd hold on to the knife, just in case.

8

Iris invited Simon, Mandy, and Victor for lunch one Sunday. It was still warm enough to eat on the terrace. Iris had bought a second-hand high chair as well as a crib that converted into a youth bed for Victor, which she'd installed in the smallest bedroom. She felt it was a good idea for him to have a safe place to sleep and eat now that she sometimes babysat him at her place. Simon had been highly amused when she'd shown them off the previous week. He said nothing beyond, "How nice of you," but she knew that pursed mouth with its upward curve and the sparkling eyes. She was happy to see him smile more often than he had back in Salton. He was less pompous, too. Obviously Mandy's doing, and Iris loved her for that. They loved each other, and it lifted them both. Today, though, Simon seemed tense. He contributed little to the conversation, crossing and recrossing his legs and jiggling the suspended foot. He occasionally forced a smile when it seemed called for.

Victor banged his new Jemima Puddleduck spoon on the high chair's tray as he gurgled happily at his plate that showed Benjamin Bunny devouring a huge carrot. Iris put a few boiled baby carrots in front of him.

"Look, Victor, just like Benjamin Bunny. I hope that's all right, Mandy. I boiled them until they softened a little so he wouldn't choke."

"That's a great idea, Iris. Thank you."

They enjoyed a filet mignon, roast potatoes, and green beans. Victor tried a little of each, except the beef. Although the beef was very tender, he wasn't quite up to it yet. That would require a few more teeth. Instead, Mandy fed him meat out of a baby food jar for toddlers.

They finished the first course, and Simon helped Iris clear the plates. Mandy stayed with Victor. While he rinsed the plates, Iris brought in the last dish and said, "Okay, what's going on?"

"Nothing, Iris. I'm fine."

"No, you are not."

Simon sighed. "Just a work problem. I don't really want Mandy to know."

"Tell me. You know I can keep a confidence."

"God, you sound just like my mother." A brief bitter smile was replaced by a scowl. Iris kept her face blank, but Simon didn't meet her eyes. Simon turned to face her before sinking into a chair. He splayed his fingers on the kitchen table and took a deep breath.

"Okay, the partner I answer to has taken on this client. I didn't like him—his manner seemed too slick. He glossed over too many details. So, I did a little digging. The guy's a crook. It's apparently common knowledge around here. The partner, Harold Cane, must know this about him. And he wants me to work for him."

"Why has he hired the firm?"

"The first job is to think up ways to evict tenants from an apartment building he just bought. Full of old timers who are a waste of space and air, according to this Marvin Buck. He said to frighten them out, if necessary. I asked how he would suggest I do that. 'Any old way. Hire someone if you must,' was his answer. 'But do it. Just get it done.'

"After he left, my boss said he didn't like my tone talking with Mr. Buck. If I valued my position, I'd treat him with more respect. But I can't just evict old people from their homes, homes some of them have lived in for over thirty years. Not unless they have somewhere to go that they can afford. But this Buck fellow just wants to turn them out into the street without it costing him anything. He wants me to act in an unethical and no doubt illegal manner. I can't. But I need my job."

"I do see your problem. You are a good man, Simon. You'll find a way."

"I don't know about that."

"You may have to resort to some underhand tactics. Like recording the conversation next time he visits. Or bugging this partner's office."

"I think that's illegal, too."

"If it's to expose an illegal conspiracy? You don't have to use it in court. Just send it anonymously to the press."

"I'll have to think about that."

Mandy came in, carrying Victor, who reached out to Iris. She folded the chubby little boy into her arms, inhaling his scent, fragrant for the moment.

"Is something the matter, Simon?"

"Just a bit of a headache, that's all."

"I'll make some coffee and bring it out with dessert," Iris said. "Just as soon as I've finished cuddling this little prince. The temperature has dropped a little, so why don't you both go and relax in the living room? Turn on the TV if you like." She kissed the nape of Victor's neck. "I'll bring him to you in a few minutes."

Iris sang "Twinkle, twinkle, little star" a couple of times while Victor lay his head on her shoulder. She'd never loved anyone so much, even Simon, and she loved him a lot. But she was more open to loving people these days, thanks to Hilda and Magaly, those two lovely old ladies in Toronto. They'd opened her heart. She wished she could find the opportunity to love the other two more. Justin would be fine, but Lucy could be tricky. She might just see through her. Lucy would be unforgiving. Iris couldn't lose Victor and Simon.

She took the baby through to his parents. "He fell asleep," she whispered. "Simon, why don't you take him up to bed?"

She had the coffee maker prepared, so only had to switch it on. The dessert, a sherry trifle, was already plated and in the fridge. After a few minutes, the tray was set, and she carried it in to Mandy and Simon. They'd started to watch a British show on PBS set in the Scottish highlands. The hapless laird tried to blow up a pike in his lake because it was devouring all the other fish. Instead, he blew himself up. Death with laughs. Just up her alley.

9

Victor was to spend a Saturday night with Iris. She could have stayed at his house, but they decided to see how it went. Simon gave her a key in case Victor became too restless and she needed to take him to his own home.

"Thank you so much, Iris," Mandy said on Friday afternoon. "Simon has been so tense with worry over this situation at work. We really needed to get away for a couple of days."

"You know it's my absolute pleasure," Iris said. *So, he told her.*

"He loves the sea. It's too cold to do anything on the beach except walk, but the sound of it soothes him."

"I know how he feels. Would it surprise you to know I've only been to the beach once? And it wasn't the sea, but Lake Ontario in Toronto. There's a beach, and people go swimming in the summer. We never went when I was a child, and my husband hated the water. I think you've inspired me. I'll spend a week at the beach next summer."

"Maybe you should come with us. We usually rent a house in Nag's Head."

"That would be lovely. I could help with Victor. What fun it will be to see him play in the sand."

Iris stood on the steps, holding Victor while they all waved goodbye. He didn't make so much as a whimper. He'd turned one a few weeks ago. Poor kid, too close to Christmas. Well, there were worse fates.

She hoped her little misinformation campaign would be remembered and repeated to Simon. His father, Victor Senior, had actually loved the sea. They went to the beach for a couple of weeks every summer.

Simon had told Iris that when he protested to his boss about the eviction campaign, the man had threatened to fire him. He wondered if he should confide in one of the other partners. But what if they were in on it? Marvin Buck had visited the office after most of them had gone home, but maybe that was the crook's ploy to avoid notice.

Iris picked up Kate on Saturday morning to go for a picnic in the park. The weather was surprisingly warm for that time of year. They still had to dress warmly, but they could enjoy being out. Victor gurgled happily when Kate clambered into the front seat. She blew him a kiss. To her delight, he pursed his lips and made a big smooching sound.

CHAPTER 9

Iris hung a tote with sandwiches, cake, and mineral water on the back of the stroller, and carried a light folding chair for Kate, who wouldn't want to get down on the ground, let alone get up again. She gave the vinyl-backed rug to Kate to carry.

They walked for a bit until Kate needed to rest, then sat fairly close to the small lake. Iris kept an eagle eye on Victor, who eyed the ducks with cautious fascination. She'd take him over later to feed them some scraps of bread she'd put in a plastic bag for that purpose. She had read it wasn't good for the ducks. But just this once.

They ate their food and Kate read Victor a story while she snuggled him on her lap. Iris felt her bottom getting cold. Victor had sat on the rug while they ate, but at least he was wearing a diaper—which probably needed attention by now.

Kate held Victor's hand while Iris showed him how to toss the bread to the ducks. He was toddling already, but had not yet mastered the art of moving backward. As the ducks came ashore and waddled toward the food source, he tried to back away, but sat down heavily. Iris picked him up when he started to cry. She tossed the scraps into the water so the ducks all went away.

Everyone was tired, so they packed up and left.

"Why don't you come home with me, Kate? You can have a nap in the spare room and try out the new bed I just bought. Victor will take a nap in his room. I might take one, too." Good thing she'd bought that bed.

Iris gave Victor a bottle before taking him upstairs to change his diaper and put him down. Kate followed and Iris showed her the room, which she planned to keep ready in case Kate needed to use it.

"Kate, I've been thinking. When you sell your house, why not come and live with me? We get on well and we like having company. I think it could work out beautifully."

Kate's eyes opened wide and her smile grew wider. "Really? But you like your privacy, I can tell. Are you sure? I'll help with expenses, of course. And the housework and cooking."

"Of course I'm sure. I know you like to read, and so do I. If I'm having quiet time or not feeling well, I know you will respect that. You're that kind of person. And I will respect your needs, too."

"Oh, Iris, I bless the day I met you."

Iris took Kate home after dinner. Victor fell asleep in the car on the way back, which meant she had to carry him in. He roused a little, but soon settled when she set him in his bed. She rubbed his back for a few minutes. She'd taken the precaution of getting him ready for bed before going out.

The next day, Iris gave Victor a new toy she'd bought. When you pressed the cow, it mooed. When you pressed the horse, it neighed, the pig oinked, and so on. He loved it. At first delighted, she began to love it less as the day progressed.

Mandy and Simon arrived mid-afternoon, looking relaxed and happy. She wondered how long that would last. She was sad to see Victor leave, but at the same time was happy to have some time to herself. She'd forgotten how it was having to watch little children constantly to protect them from themselves. Exhausting.

The next day, she was just sitting down for lunch when the doorbell rang. It was Simon, looking disheveled and distraught.

"Something terrible has happened," he gasped, as she led him to the kitchen.

"What is it, my dear boy?"

"There's been a fire in that apartment building I told you about. My boss told me about it. Said I should have done my job and now the firm won't get paid. I went over there after he reamed me out. The fire chief was still there and said it was arson. He said some of the tenants had complained about being threatened. An old lady died."

"All right, Simon. You have to take action now. Perhaps hire a private detective. Let him set the bugs while you are somewhere in private. Let him follow your boss and this developer, see where it leads. And when you have proof, send it to the press. Stiffen up and take action."

Simon calmed down a little and accepted some lunch and a cup of coffee.

Iris said, "Now I come to think of it, it's better that I hire the P.I. Don't worry, it will be solved. You'd better get back to work. You don't want them to get suspicious."

10

Iris phoned a friend. An old friend in New York who knew anyone and everyone in the truly murky underworld. She'd bought a disposable cell phone for the occasion.

"Hi, Mort. It's Pansy."

"Pansy! It's been too long. How are you? Where are you?"

"I'm a lot better since last time you saw me. I've been abroad. And now I'm down south. Charlotte, North Carolina. I need a private eye. No wet work. But a good sleuth." She knew he'd keep his mouth shut. His business success depended on discretion.

"That was a fab escape, kid. I knew you'd make it. Okay, Charlotte, North Carolina. Can I call you back?"

"Sure, you picked up this number?"

"Yup. Later."

Mort called her a couple of hours later with a name and address. "The nephew of an old friend. Decided he didn't like Trenton. Actually, Trenton didn't like him so much, either." Mort's chesty cough melded with a belly laugh that bounced down the line at deafening volume. "Let me know how it went. Don't be a stranger."

"Sure, Mort. Thanks a lot. I owe you."

"Just returning the favor. I was well rid of that little skunk you took care of."

"My pleasure, Mort. Bye."

She'd forgotten about that little skunk Mort asked her to help him with. It hadn't actually been her who stabbed him, but Mort didn't need to know that. Just some addict who owed him money. She'd seen it go down, hidden in a store doorway while she stalked her target. The argument that became a blazing row, the quick thrust, the rifling of pockets, and the sprint back down the road. She melted away once the wretched boy was out of sight and walked three blocks before catching a bus. That was in her old New York life when she'd been Pansy. Being called by her given name again had given her chills.

Since the private investigator was obviously some New Jersey punk, she expected his office to be some dive in the more decrepit part of town. But this was an area of elite boutiques with attractive storefronts. When she entered the door next to one of them, she was even faced with an elevator, which opened right into an attractive office. A corridor on each side indicated a larger establishment. A young woman with her hair pulled into a ponytail and wearing black-rimmed glasses looked up.

"Can I help you, madam?"

"Yes, I'm here to see Mr. Robinson."

"I'll let him know you're here. Please take a seat."

A clean-shaven young man soon emerged from the left corridor. "Mrs. Hall?"

"Yes, Mort Sagan recommended you."

"Ah, good old Uncle Mort." He laughed. "Please call me Cort. Come this way."

He showed her to an office with a window overlooking the street. He indicated the chair in front of his desk.

"This seems to be a large enterprise," Iris said. "You must have a lot of clients."

"This is one of those shared office arrangements. You rent the office and share the receptionist. She takes on a little typing sometimes, too. It means small businesses can afford nice premises."

"I've never heard of that. It makes a lot of sense." More surprises. This young man was well-spoken and well-mannered.

"So, you have a problem you need help with."

"It's for a young friend of mine." Iris explained the issues and what they planned to do with the information. "Lots of photos and tapes for the press," she said.

"I know about that Buck guy. He's bad news. We might need to protect ourselves."

"Whatever it takes," Iris said. "Your retainer?"

"Five thousand to start. Fifty an hour, since you're Uncle Mort's friend, and expenses."

"Deal." Iris dug in her bag and counted out the cash she'd drawn from two different banks that morning.

They shook hands and Cort showed her out.

When she got home, she texted Simon.

[Talk soon?]

He called in on his way home from work. His shoulders up near his ears, he looked more tense than ever. "The old guy's not even talking to me. Not assigning me any cases. A friend who works for one of the other partners told me he overheard him telling another partner I was not up to par. I'll never get another job if they give me that kind of reference."

Iris told him about her meeting with Cort Robinson. "He came highly recommended. Your troubles may soon be over. Now, you'd better get home and cuddle that baby of yours."

Iris almost forgot about Cort and his mission in the flurry of getting Kate settled. He only called once to let her know he'd planted the bugs and taken some good photos. The real estate agent told Kate that it was better if the house was empty and freshly painted when it went on the market. Too much clutter.

"It's not really cluttered," Kate complained. "I can't help it if I've had a long life and collected some stuff along the way. She said she could organize an estate sale for my leftovers."

"Well, what do you need to keep for your bedroom?" asked Iris. "I'm afraid there isn't room for much else in my house."

"Oh, your bed is much more comfortable than my old thing. My chest is nice and big, so I'd like to keep that. And I love my Tiffany lamp. Well, it's not real Tiffany, but it looks just like one. And I think there's room for that cabinet in my living room that's got a few knick-knacks in it."

"That sounds good. Why don't we get you and your stuff moved and then your agent can do her thing?"

Iris found a firm that would handle small moves, so that part went smoothly. There were a few more trips for clothing and a couple of things Kate decided she couldn't let go. And there were papers Kate's bookkeeper said she should keep for a few years. A couple of filing boxes under the bed took care of that.

Iris suggested Kate not get involved in the estate sale, saying it might be too emotional. What really concerned her was some of the comments buyers might make. In the end, Kate netted just under seven thousand dollars from the proceeds, so she went to bed happy. The house sold a couple of weeks later. The painting, floor refinishing, and cleaning halved her take on the estate sale, but she ended up feeling secure for once with money in the bank.

Some habits die hard, and Kate insisted from the start on preparing breakfast. She was in the habit of getting up early, anyway. Iris certainly didn't mind. In November, eating outside was out of the question, but Iris looked forward to having their nice breakfasts on the terrace when spring made its appearance once more. Kate did a little cleaning up in the garden, too, which was one of those things Iris always meant to do, but never quite got around to. And Kate loved the British programs on TV, as did Iris. Victor loved coming over to see both aunties, and Kate soon fitted in seamlessly. She'd been making lists and getting increasingly excited after Iris told her she'd invited Simon, Mandy, and Vic for Thanksgiving.

It was almost Thanksgiving when Simon almost reeled through the front door. "I've been fired," he said. "What shall I do?"

"Oh, poor, dear boy," said Kate. "I'll put the kettle on."

Iris would have been amused at her take—gleaned from all the British shows she watched—on dealing with a tricky situation, had she not been so worried about Simon.

"Let me call Cort," she said. "I haven't heard much, except that he's getting there."

"Please let there be some good news," Simon said, clearly not hopeful.

Iris went into the living room. The less Kate knew, the better. Cort answered after a couple of rings.

"Cort, it's Iris Hall."

"Hi, how are you? I was going to call you this evening. I'm just about done. Can I come over this evening?"

"It's better if we meet somewhere else. I have a houseguest."

"Understood." He named a café within walking distance.

Iris went back into the kitchen, where Simon sat sipping tea. He never drank tea. Kate must have gone up to her room.

"He's just about wrapped it up. I'm meeting him tonight."

"Can I come?"

"Best not. Take the family away early tomorrow and stay through the weekend."

"But I can't spend money on that now."

"Yes, you can. Get out of town. I'll help if necessary."

After Simon left, Iris sat in the living room thinking about the situation. Marvin Buck might suspect Simon of having a hand in his downfall. Simon's boss certainly would. What would they do to hurt him? The old lawyer, probably not much. Although, did the firm know about the story of his mother, the so-called serial killer? Supposing he blabbed about that? Buck would probably have all kinds of low-lifes at his beck and call to do his dirty work. He might have to go.

She called up to Kate, "Is pizza all right for tonight? I have to go out for a little while later."

"It's fine. I'll be down in a minute or two."

Kate didn't ask, and Iris didn't volunteer any information. After they'd finished and cleaned up, she put on her coat.

"Do be careful, Iris," Kate said.

"I'm not about to do anything dangerous, you know," Iris replied, surprised.

"I'm not so sure," Kate said.

Halfway down the empty street, Iris pulled on a blonde wig. No need to take any chances. She wore jeans, a gray sweater, and an old, black jacket. She added glasses closer to her destination.

She pushed open the café door and looked around. Cort sat with his back to the door in the far right corner. She slid into a chair opposite.

"What…? Oh, it's you. Not bad."

"Thank you, kind sir! What have you got for me?"

He had it all. Copies of recordings she could listen to later, and photos. Lots of photos of men harassing the apartment dwellers, meetings in out-of-the-way places with Simon's boss, who would surely be disbarred.

"I have my ways of getting this to the paper without being traced. I might also try a national. With your permission, it will go out tonight."

"Tomorrow. The young person in question will leave town early tomorrow morning."

"Very well. Here is my invoice. Only just under a thousand more."

"I'll pay in cash. I'll drop it off at your office."

"Suits me. It's been nice."

He stuck out his hand. They shook, and he left, as did she shortly thereafter, hugging the precious materials to her chest. Once she'd absorbed it all, she'd stow it in her safe deposit box.

A couple of days later, the scandal hit the front pages of the papers. Simon called her to report that he'd been called into a meeting with the partners on Monday morning to discuss the matter, so he'd be returning on Sunday evening. He'd told the managing partner his side of the story over the phone. His former boss had left a threatening message accusing Simon of engineering the exposé. He'd reported the threat to the police. Marvin Buck was nowhere to be found.

Marvin Buck worried Iris. She called Cort. "I need to know where he is."

"He's got a place in Greenville—the North Carolina one. A modest Cape Cod an old aunt lives in. I bet he's there." He gave her the address.

11

"I have to visit a friend for a couple of days," she told Kate that afternoon. "I'll be gone overnight."

"Oh, yes?" Kate looked skeptical.

"Don't worry, I'll be fine."

Iris threw her bag onto the backseat and climbed in. She drove away, watching in the rear window as Kate waved goodbye with both arms.

After four dreary hours, Iris pulled into a side street not far from her target. She went through her usual transformation, which included a long raincoat and gloves. She decided against a hat as she needed her red wig to show. It was getting dark.

The drapes were closed in the little house, but the lights in the front room were on. Iris crept around the back. The kitchen door was locked. Maybe she should try a little diversion and not enter the house. She smashed a couple of the window panes and drew back behind the chimney nook.

A short, overweight man charged out, weapon drawn, circling around the small backyard, keeping his gaze outward. She sidled around behind him, hoping to stab him in the back. Suddenly, he wheeled around and she found herself with the pistol in his left hand practically touching her chest. She had to act fast or he could just pull the trigger and claim self-defense. She flung up her arm to force his weapon away from her and drove the knife under his ribs and up, immediately throwing herself down and to her left side. The gun went off as he fell. She felt a searing pain in her right arm.

She ran, scrambling into her car as if drunk, and started it. She had to get away before the cops swarmed the place. She drove at the speed limit, driving with her injured right arm, while clutching the wound with her left. Once she got clear, she would assess the damage and bind it up.

After half an hour, she pulled over. She got into the back seat and retrieved her first aid kit from her bag. She peeled off the raincoat, then the sweater. A long gash and a bloody mess, but only a flesh wound. She just hoped she hadn't left blood behind. The raincoat had probably held most of it until she got well away. It wasn't even bleeding much anymore. She applied anti-bacterial ointment and bound her arm. The raincoat would have to go. She had another jacket, one of the padded kind that packs flat. She put it on, threading it up her right arm, and took a deep breath. *Damn*! If they found that bullet, it would have her blood on it. *Damn*. She lay her forehead on the front seat and clenched her fists. *Control yourself and get away*.

Iris took a deep breath and sat up. She had a flask of coffee under the passenger seat. She felt cold now. Her teeth chattered. She hoped it wasn't shock. No, she didn't feel too bad. She'd get back into the driver's seat, drink a cup, and drive home. Oops, the wig. That definitely had to go. Maybe she shouldn't start discarding these things so close. Maybe another hour away.

The drive was an ordeal. She'd planned to spend the night in a motel somewhere along the highway, but now only wanted to get home to her own bed. She badly wanted to speed, but must not draw attention to herself. Her arm throbbed. She still felt cold. As she turned into her garage, she noticed a police car in front of Simon's house. Good. Buck might have already given orders to harm Simon. She hoped his demise had resolved any question of danger for her boy. She left everything in the car and went inside.

She called upstairs. "Kate. It's me. I wasn't feeling good, so I came home instead of staying with my friend."

Kate appeared on the top landing as Iris toiled upstairs. "Iris, you look pale. Whatever's the matter?"

"I hurt my arm, that's all. Nothing a good night's sleep won't heal. I bandaged it and put on ointment. I'll be all right. I'm just feeling cold and need to get into bed. "

"I knew you were up to something. I'm going to help you into bed, then get you a nice cup of cocoa."

That did sound good. Kate exclaimed at her bloody sweater, but pronounced herself satisfied with the bandage, which she declared must be changed in the morning. She took the sweater to put it in a cold water wash before making the cocoa. How divine it was to be mothered again. Iris thought fondly of Hilda and Magaly. They'd mothered her when she needed it, too. And then she'd mothered them.

Iris woke several times during the night after a succession of nightmares concerning guns and fat men chasing her down a never-ending street. But she finally fell into a deeper sleep and didn't wake until nearly ten. She put on her slippers and robe and went downstairs. Her arm ached, but not too badly. The important thing was to keep it clean. The breakfast things were still laid out. Kate was nowhere to be seen, but something in the oven smelled like fresh bread. Iris poured herself some coffee and sat at the counter, where Kate had set the paper. Iris read the headline: Crime boss in arson scandal murdered. She hadn't been absolutely sure she'd killed him. Spirits lifted, she got up to get more coffee, turning as Kate walked in.

"You've seen the paper?" Kate asked, settling herself on a stool.

"Yes, the creep who set fire to that apartment building got killed. Serves him right."

"Quite. Was that the business Simon's firm was caught up in? The crooked boss who fired him?"

"Yes, it was."

"He told you everything, did he?"

"Yes, he did."

"You love him very much, don't you?"

"I do."

"I see. I made some fresh bread. It'll be ready now. I'm having some with butter and jam. How about you?"

"Sounds like just what the doctor ordered."

"Except, no doctors, I think. I'll look at it later."

Kate was too perceptive sometimes.

The national papers soon dropped the story, but the local papers fed on it for weeks—it was quite the windfall. The law firm had fired the errant partner without delay and reinstated Simon. With Marvin Buck dead, Simon felt safe again, although frustrated by the frequent calls and visits from the press. Iris was thankful she'd thought of giving her boy an alibi, both for the revelations to the press and the murder.

Her arm gave her trouble, as a slight infection made it ache and itch. But Kate soon brought it under control with an ointment from a local natural products shop that she "swore by." She also persuaded Iris to wear a sling. She didn't do much for a week, telling Simon she'd fallen and cut her arm on one of the rocks that lined her path. He said, "I'm sorry. Anything I can do?" She assured him that Kate had everything under control and that she just needed to rest it. He looked at her hard and long, and said, "Thank you for everything," before leaving.

Mandy called the next day.

"Simon told me you hurt your arm. Are you all right? What did the doctor say?"

"Oh, I'm fine, thank you. Just a small cut and some bruising. Kate's been doctoring me. It's nearly healed."

"That's good. Simon seemed worried."

"The dear boy worries too much."

"Yes, he does tend to."

"Mandy, I hope you will join Kate and me for Thanksgiving. Kate is all excited about it. So am I, come to that."

"Why, that's so nice of you. Are you sure it's not too much trouble?"

"Of course not. We'd love to have you."

"Why don't you come on over and we can have a drink before dinner?"

"Sounds perfect."

12

It poured with rain on Thanksgiving morning. Iris hated the rain and the grayness it brought with it. So depressing. But she'd invited her family, and they were going to enjoy a real celebration. She'd wanted to pick up a pumpkin pie from a bakery in town, but no, Kate wouldn't have it.

"It's not real Thanksgiving to me if everything isn't homemade. This is my first good Thanksgiving in years. Guests almost never came around this time, so I was mostly on my own."

"I understand, Kate, but that's so much work for you. I feel guilty not to be doing more."

"Don't feel guilty. I'm enjoying myself! It was a blessing for a while to be alone after my husband died, although I missed my son. But I don't think my son missed me. He only writes Christmas cards now. I don't know if he's married. I

could be a grandmother for all I know. Now I've had enough alone time."

Kate looked so sad suddenly, it made Iris sad, too.

"Well, you have family now, Kate. Victor loves you. We all love you."

Kate cheered up. "Well, I must get on with things. The pies won't bake themselves. I'm making an apple one, too."

That had been three days ago. Iris had done what seemed like a massive amount of grocery shopping to fulfill Kate's very long list.

The house had smelled lovely from the baking, though. And now a hint of roast turkey was beginning to perfume the air. Iris went into the dining room to set the table. This was a job she enjoyed. She stood back for a minute to admire the flower arrangement she'd set there the day before: copper-colored chrysanthemums she'd bought at a nearby florist and thin branches she'd cut from a maple tree in the garden that had turned a spectacular shade of red. It was the first time she'd actively arranged flowers, as opposed to just plonking them into a vase of water.

"A killer arrangement," she murmured before taking platters through to the kitchen table.

After a few hours, the house was redolent with turkey and other less definable, but delicious, cooking smells. Kate's cheeks were rosy by this time, and a few tendrils had come loose from her bun. She hummed as she worked though, clearly happy. She allowed Iris to whip the cream and put the cranberry sauce that had been in the fridge overnight in a porcelain bowl. Iris felt happy and carefree as she set out the drinks. Even the rain had stopped and the sun had made a few sorties from behind the cloud cover. This was the life.

A clatter at the back door announced the arrival of their guests. Iris went to greet them.

"It smells wonderful," Simon exclaimed, his face happily tilted back to inhale the aromas.

Vic made them all laugh by making little sniffing sounds and saying, "Umm!"

"It certainly does," Mandy said. "Kate, you've been working so hard. What can I do?"

"Nothing for now," Kate replied. "In a while, I'll need some help taking the platters through."

"Absolutely," Simon said.

They all went to sit around the kitchen table until Kate shooed them away. "I need the space," she said. "Go and make yourselves comfortable in the living room." This unusually bossy Kate kissed Vic on the top of his head and turned to check the oven. Amused, they all did as they were told.

"She hardly let me do anything," Iris told them as they took their seats. "I think she's really enjoying herself. She said she hasn't had a proper Thanksgiving in years."

"She feels needed," Mandy said.

"And wanted," Simon added.

"Yes, well, she certainly is," Iris said.

Iris poured everyone a drink. "I got some apple juice for Victor," she said.

"Maybe later this afternoon," Mandy said. "I brought some toddler food in jars."

"We could mash up some potatoes and carrots. I guess turkey is a bit too much."

"Yes, let's do that. I've got meat in one of the jars, and he can enjoy fresh vegetables."

Finally, the call came to carry the food through. Kate preened at the compliments everyone showered on her for the beautifully arranged dishes. Iris received compliments for her centerpiece. She lit the candles in silver holders on each side of the arrangement.

“Those candle holders are so pretty, Iris.”

“Thank you. I inherited them from the English lady I lived with in Toronto. They are a treasured memory.”

“I’m sure.”

They had a merry time, Kate getting a little tipsy from the white wine she favored, but obviously feeling happy and fulfilled. They had just finished dessert when Vic’s eyes began to droop. Iris carried him into the living room and cuddled him.

She heard everyone clear the table and take everything into the kitchen. She didn’t feel guilty as she nuzzled her grandson. Her precious little boy.

13

A few days later, Mandy called. “Iris, I’m calling first to thank you for a wonderful Thanksgiving celebration. We can’t remember when we’ve had such a marvelous meal. Secondly, to invite you and Kate for Christmas dinner. Well, a late lunch, really. We usually eat at around four. Simon’s brother and sister are coming to stay for a long weekend since Christmas is on a Saturday this year.”

It was a good thing Iris was sitting on a sofa because she felt the blood run out of her head. She clutched the armrest and tried to breathe normally.

“Iris, are you all right? Are you still there?”

“Oh, yes, sorry. I dropped my phone and it fell between the cushions. I had trouble fishing it out. Christmas Day sounds lovely. It’s so kind of you to include us.”

“Victor woke up from his nap. I’d better go up.”

“See you soon!”

God almighty, what should she do? What could she do? Justin would be fine, but Lucy was more on the ball. She might see through her, at least after a couple of hours. Then what? Simon would be in a terrible spot as a lawyer. Justin would let it go, but would Lucy? Would Kate still be her friend if she found out? Would Mandy let her anywhere near Victor ever again?

Kate called out, "Just walking up to the store for some milk and butter."

"Okay, I've got a slight headache. I'm going to lie down for a bit." She had to think.

Kate rushed in. "Is your arm hurting? Let me feel your forehead. I don't think you have a fever. But you are very pale."

"I'm fine. I don't think I need the sling anymore. It's almost completely healed. Maybe I'm coming down with something."

"Can I get you anything? I'll check on you when I get back."

"No, don't worry. I hope I'll be asleep."

Kate left at last. Iris dragged herself upstairs. She'd have to get into bed now so she could feign sleep if Kate peeked in, as she most certainly would.

Iris removed her pants and sweater and climbed under the duvet. She stared at the ceiling. Her past was attached to her like some sort of ectoplasmic strand that expanded and shrank at will. Was she never to feel safe? Does the past ever truly remain in the past? The line between past and present is only a day, after all. What happened even a short time ago can have consequences far in the future, not all of them bad. Putting off a visit to the doctor when you shouldn't, meeting someone who becomes important in your life, loving a little boy who became a father and loving his little boy, committing crimes and getting away with them—for now.

She couldn't lose Victor and Simon. She didn't want to lose Kate. She loved her house. But how could she avoid meeting her other children without arousing suspicion? She'd have to brazen it out. Her hair was completely different. She'd lost it after the fire and it had regrown gray and curly. The plastic surgery had altered her appearance a good deal. It didn't take more than a nip here and a tuck there to make a person look completely different. She'd mostly worn classically tailored clothing in Virginia, and still did, only adding a little flair here and there. Maybe she'd buy an outrageous Christmas sweater. And dangly earrings. She never wore dangly earrings. That should put them off the scent. She'd go shopping tomorrow. Or maybe look online. There were only ten days left. She hadn't even shopped for gifts.

Having made up her mind, she relaxed. She'd always taken risks, she'd always come through. She heard Kate coming upstairs and closed her eyes. The door opened gently, then closed. She drifted off to sleep.

14

The big day arrived. Iris and Kate had spent the day before wrapping gifts and trimming their small tree. The kids were going out to dinner, but Iris had declined the invitation to join them, saying she had left shopping too late and was behind with wrapping. No need to be with them any longer than necessary.

Iris went down to the kitchen in her robe.

"Merry Christmas, Kate," she said, trying to be chirpy. "This is for you."

"And to you, Iris. I put a little something by your plate."

They poured coffee and sat down.

"I put some frozen almond croissants in the oven. They'll be ready in ten minutes." Kate said.

They opened their gifts. Kate was thrilled with a new tweed skirt and a cashmere jacket. The skirt was a blue and green tartan, and the jacket a dark green. Iris had also bought a cream silk shirt.

"I don't know what to say, Iris. They're so beautiful. I've never had such fine clothes in my life. How did you get the size right?"

"I'm afraid I got into your closet while you were out. I looked at the size on that gray skirt that fits so well, and the matching shirt."

Kate's cheeks were pink with excitement. "I'll wear them today. It's a special occasion, after all, and these are special occasion clothes. But I only got you something small."

"It's not the size that counts, Kate, you know that. It's the love and friendship behind the gift." *Well, listen to you. Unthinkable ten years ago.*

Iris unwrapped the little parcel. She opened a jewelry box to find a gold ring with a sort of knot in front that looked like the infinity symbol. She slipped it on.

"It's a friendship ring," Kate said shyly. "You are my best friend. My only friend, really. It looked as if you and I have hands and fingers around the same size, so I bought it as if to fit myself. Is it all right?"

"It's perfect. I'll always treasure it." And she would.

The oven timer dinged. Kate got out the croissants, and they devoured two each.

"Those are so good," Iris said. "It's a good thing dinner is five hours away." That thought sobered her. She'd soon be running the gauntlet of estranged children.

"Let's have some more coffee and watch TV. There should be a carol service on one of the channels."

Kate looked so happy, Iris didn't have the heart to say she really wasn't into carol services, or any other church service, come to that. She trailed after her into the living room. As it happened, the first channel Kate turned to was one featuring Christmas songs with dance routines and so on, rather than a churchy affair. It was quite pleasant and festive, especially with the Christmas tree lights twinkling.

They'd both had their showers and got dressed. Kate looked pretty in her new clothes. She couldn't quite hide her surprise when Iris appeared in black velvet pants with a bulky and very loud Christmas sweater, topped by dangly Christmas elf earrings.

"My, you do look festive," she said.

"I know. Outside my comfort zone, but I think it will amuse Victor."

"I don't think he has any idea about Christmas. And watch out for those earrings. He'll yank them off if you're not careful."

"I hadn't thought of that. Ouch!"

They tried to gather armfuls of gifts, but there were too many. Iris had bought gifts for Justin and Lucy. Godiva chocolates, which she knew they liked, but were impersonal enough not to be suspicious. And, of course, they'd both indulged Victor.

"We'll use that roll cart I take shopping," Kate said.

It was practical, but Iris felt elderly dragging the thing down the road.

A man loitered outside Simon's house. He looked agitated, but was clean-shaven and wore a cashmere coat, so was no beggar.

He looked Iris in the eye. "Do you know the man who lives here?"

"Why do you ask? Who are you?" she said.

"I'm his former boss. I want to talk to him. He doesn't want to talk to me."

"Ah, you must be the notorious Harold Cane."

"How the hell do you know that?"

"The whole town knows that. Now, get lost, or I'll call the cops."

"Fucking bitch," he growled before striding away.

"Goodness, Iris, you certainly told him."

"Nasty corrupt fellow. No respectable law firm will hire him now. I hope that cashmere coat lasts. He won't be getting another."

"It's Christmas, Iris. Let's stay nice."

Iris snorted. "He tried to destroy Simon's life."

They moved up the path and rang the bell. Simon opened the door and hugged both of them.

"Good God!" he said, holding Iris at arm's length while inspecting her sweater. "I love it!"

She knew she beamed wider than called for because the old Simon—her rather stuffy son Andrew—would not have approved.

"Come and meet everyone," he said, leading the way to the family room. Iris knew it would be beautifully decorated, but could only concentrate on keeping her expression in check while her stomach danced an Irish jig.

"This is my sister, Lucy, and her husband Dirk." *Husband!*

"How do you do?" Iris said, shaking their hands. They returned the greeting. Lucy looked softer than she used to. She had always been so feisty and opinionated, but she had mellowed, perhaps because she was in love. Her husband was tall and spoke with an accent that sounded Germanic. Justin hadn't changed—hair too long and messy, sweatshirt and jeans, and dirty sneakers. He was carrying Victor, who seemed quite content in his arms. Well, Justin was a gentle soul and babies sense that.

"Hello, Victor," she said, holding out her arms. Victor looked at her and grinned, before laying his head down on Justin's shoulder. "Awoo."

Mandy laughed. "He's really taken a shine to Justin."

"Should I be jealous?" she asked, laughing to soften the question. She was certainly jealous. "Let's put these things under the tree."

"Is it all right with you if we open presents after lunch?" Simon asked. "We opened a lot this morning, and I think it was a little overwhelming for Victor."

"Of course," she said. "Mandy, is there anything I can do to help?"

"No, I think we're all set. I'll take out the turkey soon, and carving is Simon's job. Lucy helped with the sides. She's a terrific cook." *Another surprise.*

By two, the table was laden, and they all sat down. Iris sat beside Victor's high chair, with Justin on the other side and Mandy at the end next to him. Lucy sat at the other end next to Simon, to her relief. Sitting right opposite for a couple of hours was more exposure than she cared for. She ate better than expected. The meeting had gone so smoothly that her nerves stopped zinging. Dirk sat opposite.

"Have you been over here long?" she asked.

"Two years. I am doing a PhD in marine biology at Stanford. I have finished my coursework and soon I will leave to do my internship in Sweden. That is where I am from."

"Interesting. I suppose you will have to write a dissertation after that?"

"Yes, back to California to do that, although I will begin it in Sweden."

They went on to talk about other things. Mandy had been to a lecture at Queens University on something or other in the business school. Iris lost track because Victor suddenly decided that only she was allowed to cut up his turkey. He'd started by holding up the slice and chewing on it, but got bored with it in favor of soft foods that didn't ask for much effort. Iris felt puffed up until he handed Justin his spoon. Apparently, all that spooning was too much work. She sipped on her wine, which she'd been consuming very slowly lest she get careless.

They all helped clear away the dishes. Mandy apologized, saying it would take a little while to finish preparing the desserts. Everyone agreed that would not be a problem, as they needed a break before dessert. They all sat around the table again, chatting while Mandy and Lucy did whatever was needed in the kitchen. Finally, Lucy emerged, holding a platter loaded with mince pies and one with an apple pie and whipped cream. Mandy followed with a trifle.

"You've worked so hard. It's all so wonderful!" Kate exclaimed. "I think this is my best Christmas ever."

Everyone looked at her happy, pink face and sparkling eyes, hands clasped as if in prayer, happy for her happiness.

"You are most welcome," Simon said.

"Absolutely," Mandy added. "You are like family."

Kate's eyes welled, and she had to dab at them with her napkin a couple of times.

"I'd like to make a toast," Simon said, rising. "To friends and family, without whom this Christmas would not have been as joyful."

They drank. He rose again.

"And this time, to absent friends and family."

Simon's face looked stern. Lucy's had hardened as she stood. Iris couldn't look at Justin without being obvious, but she heard him push back his chair.

"It's just a family tragedy," Simon explained to the other guests. "We remember who and what we lost."

Iris tried to still her breath. She must not pant. She must not cry. She must show nothing. She raised her glass to her lips and emptied it. Justin reached across and filled it. He looked her in the face and smiled, his sweet nature shining through. It broke her heart. How could she have been content to ignore her feelings for him? Would Lucy have a child soon? A child who would be lost to her grandmother? She'd always favored Andrew—Simon—but these other two were also special.

The siblings sat down and the chatter soon started up again. Victor started to whine, rubbing his eyes.

"I think you're ready for your nap," Mandy said, coming around to lift him out of the chair.

"I'll be happy to put him down," Iris said, getting to her feet. "Come on, sweetheart." He came to her willingly, wrapping his little arms around her neck and laying his head on her shoulder. She climbed the stairs slowly, savoring every moment. She changed his diaper and kissed him before laying him down and gently rubbing his tummy. His drooping eyes soon closed in peaceful slumber. "Merry Christmas," she murmured.

"Hello, Mother."

She froze, feeling the blood draining from her head. She clutched the crib's post and slowly turned.

"Justin. I'm so sorry about everything. I love you very much, but I know you can't love me anymore. Can you begin to forgive me?"

CHAPTER 14

"Simon finally sent us a copy of your journal. He kept it to himself for a few years, but decided we had a right to read it. I understand. I forgive you, and I still love you."

"How did you recognize me? Lucy didn't, and I don't think Simon has."

"Your voice. When I heard your voice, I could look past the surgery."

"I was living in Canada. I was very badly burned in a house fire."

"What brought you back?"

"I was in an airport and saw Andrew. I listened to his conversation with the people he was traveling with and found out he was with a firm down here. So I moved. I missed my children. And now there is Victor, too."

"Yes, Victor is precious. I'm moving to Boston soon. I got a job with the ballet orchestra. I like Boston, although I don't know about the winters. I hope you'll come and visit me. No one needs to know anything. You don't know anyone there, do you?"

"I do not. And I would love to see you. Just the two of us and not having to hide and pretend."

"I'm glad you're close to Simon and Mandy, not to mention Victor. And Kate seems pretty special."

"She is a very special friend. There were two old ladies in Toronto, too. I was very close to them until they passed away."

"Did you like Toronto?"

"I did. Except for the winters. Worse than Boston."

"We'd better go back to the others, or they'll wonder what's going on," Justin said. He closed in and gave his mother a big hug.

Iris felt giddy with joy as they sat around opening gifts. Simon opened champagne, and the gathering became even merrier. After an hour or so, Victor let his demands be known, and was brought down to open his. He looked around at all the delights—including a purple teddy bear from Iris—not knowing where to start. Still a little groggy, he lay down next to the bear and sucked his thumb. He was done for the day.

At around nine o'clock, Kate suggested they should leave. "Let the kids catch up," she whispered. Justin walked them home, embracing each with a furtive kiss for Iris.

"See you soon, I hope," he said.

Iris almost floated up to bed. It had been the best Christmas.

Part II

15

Fickle spring darted in and out, pushing green tips through the soil and showing off a blaze of yellow in the forsythia bush outside the kitchen window. The afternoon's temperature was warm enough to venture out without a jacket over her sweatshirt. Iris glanced at the clock. Three-fifteen, nearly time to go wait outside Simon's house for the school bus. Mandy had a doctor's appointment, and Iris was more than happy to oblige.

"He can eat dinner with us, too."

"In that case, maybe I'll meet a couple of girlfriends for a drink afterwards."

"Why not? You deserve a break."

Mandy had been having trouble with one of her knees. She'd hurt herself playing tennis, and might need surgery.

CHAPTER 15

Time to go. "I'm going to meet Vic's bus. Do you want to come with me?" she called to Kate, who sat knitting in the living room.

"No, not this time, dear. I'm feeling a little tired this afternoon."

Kate was always feeling tired these days. It was high time she had a thorough check-up. Iris had mentioned it before, but Kate blew it off. She wouldn't take no for an answer next time.

Iris went out the front door, peering at the beds lining the path. Good, lots of daffs pushing up almost to full height. She'd soon have some cheerfully yellow vases of them sitting around the house. As she crossed the road, she noticed that Mandy's pride and joy, her tulip magnolia, had many buds ready to burst open. Only another day or two. She had to stifle a laugh. This urchin from Hell's Kitchen reveling over spring flowers—who'd have thought?

She waited less than five minutes. Vic waved and leaped off the bus, so happy to see her. How had she deserved such joy? Just dumb luck. He hugged her and they crossed the road to Iris's house.

"Mom told me you'd be meeting me today. I love going to your house. What's for snack?"

"Chocolate chip cookies Auntie Kate made this morning for you. What would you like to drink? I've got lemonade."

"I love your lemonade."

"By the way, it's shepherd's pie for dinner. I know you like that."

His smile broadened. When she agreed to look after Vic for the afternoon, she'd thought for a long time about what to give him for dinner. It was always such a treat to have him.

He took off his blazer and threw it on a kitchen stool.

"Now, now," said Iris. "Those uniforms are expensive. I see your tie has another stain on it. Take it off."

Vic sighed and took his jacket to the hall closet. When he returned, he pulled off his tie. Kate appeared as he came back into the kitchen.

"I'll take care of that stain," she said.

"Thank you, Auntie Kate. For the cookies, especially."

"Anything for you, poppet," she said.

"Poppet? What's that mean?"

"Just that you are very dear."

He blushed and pulled himself onto a tall stool without too much effort. He was tall for a nine-year-old. Iris put a small plate of cookies and a glass of lemonade in front of him, watching indulgently as he gorged himself.

"Do you have homework?" she asked him.

"Only some spelling words to memorize. And a couple of math problems."

"Do you want to do anything in particular this afternoon?"

"Can we go to the park and feed the ducks?"

"Yes, I thought you might say that. I've got some old bread. You can do your homework when we get home while I get dinner ready. I'll hear your spelling while I'm working."

They enjoyed a peaceful hour under a clouding sky, welcoming the ducks that paddled frantically toward the bank where Iris and Vic waited. Vic always got a kick out of this activity. He was an innocent, happy with simple pleasures. She'd never felt such surges of love as she felt for this child. She'd never allowed herself to.

Back at home, Kate was making a salad. Iris had made the shepherd's pie ahead of time, so she got it out of the fridge and turned on the oven. She set three places at the small table. Not much to do, except pay attention to Vic's homework.

CHAPTER 15

"Okay, Vic. Get out your homework now."

"Can I have some lemonade?"

"Not now, with your dinner. Let's just get it done."

"Okaaay. The math is so annoying."

"Why? Is it hard?"

"No, it's so easy. It's a waste of time writing all those stupid problems. We have to write it all out."

"You're lucky. I bet some of the kids are struggling with it."

"Huh."

"Start with that, since it's so easy, even if it's boring."

He got through it, then they recited the spelling words until Vic had them down pat, and by that time, dinner was ready.

Vic ate with the gusto typical of most young boys, adding cringe-worthy lashings of ketchup. Iris had always loved shepherd's pie and ate well, but noticed that Kate ate tiny mouthfuls at a time and could hardly finish her helping, which had been small to start with.

Vic thanked Iris and Kate for dinner nicely, before rushing off to watch TV. Iris started to clear away, telling Kate to go and rest. She heard her climbing the stairs. Too early for that. She hoped Vic was watching something suitable. Should she check? Maybe just trust him? On the other hand, Mandy would be back soon, and she wouldn't want to be thought careless. She wandered into the living room. It was a program about space. She would have thought it a little advanced for a nine-year-old, but he seemed entranced. She'd just finished putting away the leftovers and loading the dishwasher when Mandy arrived.

"I had such fun with my friends," she said, her eyes bright. "Thank you so much."

"It was my pleasure. You know I love to have him. He's done his homework, and he's watching a space program on TV."

"He's obsessed with space. Claims he's going to be an astronaut."

"My nerves wouldn't stand it," Iris said, shuddering.

"Nor mine. Where's Kate?

"She went up to her room. I'm worried about her. She's resisting it, but I'm going to insist on a full check-up."

"She has been looking tired lately."

"Yes, she's always tired these days."

Mandy went into the living room to retrieve Vic.

Iris heard the expected negotiation—five more minutes, and so on.

They didn't reappear, so Vic had clearly won a concession. Maybe he'd be a lawyer.

16

Easter was early that year, at the beginning of April. Simon and Mandy had bought a retriever puppy for Vic, so the Easter egg hunt posed a problem. Iris said she'd do it at her place, which was easier with Vic out of the way, anyhow.

Even Kate perked up while they hid the eggs on Easter morning. Such fun. Iris bought a big cardboard egg and filled it with tiny figures of astronauts and planets, and another full of miniature dinosaurs. She'd picked up a large chocolate bunny, too. They did it close to the time of their guests' arrival, as the weather had turned warm.

Vic was so excited with his finds and sat on the floor in the living room playing with his little toys. He'd reluctantly agreed to leave the chocolate until after lunch. They all sat down to a traditional lunch of roast lamb. Simon laid down his silver.

"Iris, we have something to tell you."

"Oh dear, that sounds grim."

"No, it's nice. We plan on a trip to Switzerland this June, after school's out. We'd love you to come with us. Kate, too."

"Please say yes," Vic pleaded.

"I'm just not up to it these days," Kate said. "A few years ago I would have loved to. I'm 82 now, you know."

"Iris? You're practically like Vic's grandmother, after all." Simon watched her intently.

"Thank you, I'd love to. But I hate to leave Kate on her own."

"No, you go, Iris. I'll be fine, really I will."

She'd find someone to keep an eye on Kate. But she'd go. Like his grandmother? You bet.

"Then thank you. I would love to go. If you make the arrangements, I'll pay you what I owe."

"No, my treat," Simon said, looking pleased. "I've done well over the past few years. Got a nice Christmas bonus, too."

"Oh, no, I couldn't possibly..."

"I insist."

"I must renew my passport." *And that's a whole other issue.*

Vic was bouncing in his seat. "I'm so glad you're coming. You can tell me things. And another thing. Dad said you're practically like my grandmother. You are. Can I call you Gran?"

Iris felt the prick of tears, the rising blush.

"It depends on what Mom and Dad think."

"I think it's a great idea," Simon said. He winked at her. *Holy crap, he knows.*

"I do, too," Mandy said.

"I'd be honored," Iris told Vic. "Very honored."

I don't deserve this. It can't last.

Renewing her passport would be tough. Her forger in New York had died. Did someone take his place? If it didn't work out, she'd have to make up some story about why she couldn't go. But she wanted to go. Switzerland!

She called the old number after Kate had gone through to watch TV. There was quite a bit of clearing away to do, but she needed to do it while Kate was out of the room. To her relief, someone answered. She'd hoped someone had taken over the business after she'd had to do away with his predecessor.

"Is Mr. Oliver there?"

"No. He's dead."

"Oh, I'm so sorry. It's been a while. He used to do some work for me."

"I took over the business. Who are you?"

"Pansy."

"Ah, he told me about you. Said you turned up on the regular, like a bad penny. What do you want?"

"Passport. U.S."

"Okay. Bring the usual."

"How much?"

"Three grand."

"What? That's gone up."

"Everything's gone up, lady. And they're much more complicated now. When are you coming?"

"Wednesday okay? Same place?"

"Wednesday's good. Different place. I do better on my own. Got a pen?"

"Yes." He rattled off an address, not that far from the old place.

"I'm flying up. Not sure of the times, but I'll try to be there before lunch."

"I'll be here. I'm always here."

"What's your name?"

"Haven't got one." He hung up.

So, the old man had talked about her. Not a good thing.

She'd have to think up an excuse to tell Kate. She would also call Kate's doctor when she got back. She wasn't sure if they'd take the appointment from her since she wasn't a relative, but she could try. She was spending a lot of money these days. She'd better watch it.

She took a cab from La Guardia downtown and had it drop her a couple of blocks away and a street over from her destination. She walked at a normal pace so as not to attract attention to herself in this grungy district. She'd taken the precaution of wearing an old raincoat and donned a wig in her car on the way to the airport in Charlotte. She had all the necessary passport photos and descriptions in her large purse, as well as three thousand dollars in cash. She climbed carefully down some crumbling concrete steps and rapped on a new oak door. A spy hole opened.

"Who is it?"

"Pansy."

She eased in sideways, because the man didn't open the door wide enough to make it easy. The hallway was still dim, although she could tell there was a fresh coat of paint on the walls. The man led her through to his workroom. To her surprise, the windows weren't covered and she could see people walking past, albeit only from the knees down.

"It's one-way glass," the man said with an old man's cackle.

She turned around to face him. He didn't look much different from Ned, her old forger, before the awful Mr. Oliver. Maybe a bit younger. Short, thin, stooped, bald. They even had the same straggly beard and mustache. They both looked like crooks, although she wasn't sure how one would describe a crook, exactly. Some would say she was a crook.

"You and Ned could be brothers," she said.

"We were. When he died, a new chap muscled me out. Then he died. A fire in some art store he used as a cover. Fire chief said it was set."

Iris shuddered. "That's terrible. Who would do such a thing? Did he have enemies?"

"Plenty." The old man cackled again before doubling over coughing.

"Can I get you some water?"

"Nah. Emphysema. My punishment for smoking too much. Gave it up, but too late. Yeah, Oliver had enemies. Ned, too. They both cheated everyone. Even me. I guess Oliver had it coming. He was a real nasty piece of work. And a witness saw a woman leaving the scene with a suitcase." He leered at her. Fear crawled up her spine.

A witness. "I'm very sorry to hear it." Iris handed over the envelope. "Photos, name, and other details. And, of course, your fee."

"Come back at four."

Iris walked for four blocks before she could hail a cab. Good thing she was wearing sensible shoes. Now for some lunch. She couldn't go where she'd like to in this getup. Museums. They had restaurants. "MOMA," she told the driver.

"You don't look the arty type," the driver drawled.

Cheeky sod. "Takes all sorts," she replied.

She chose the chef's tasting menu and tried to enjoy it. She hated this new old man and hoped he wouldn't mess up her passport deliberately. He suspected her, she was sure of that. Would it never end? Would her past never leave her be? This long strand stretched way behind her all the way to Hell's Kitchen, and she couldn't seem to break it.

She wandered around the impressionists and took in a few of the other halls. With half an hour to spare, she went outside to hail a cab, taking the same precautions.

"It's ready," he said. "One of my best."

"I bet you say that to all the girls."

No cackle this time. "I wouldn't want to upset a nice lady like you," he said, looking at her square in the eyes.

"No, never wise," she said, boring her eyes into his.

She scanned the passport without another word and left. She'd planned to spend the night because she hadn't expected him to finish so quickly. She'd wanted to do some clothes shopping for the Swiss trip, but now only yearned to go home. Her Charlotte home was her real haven. She trudged along for only a couple of blocks before she spotted a cab dropping off a man in front of a ramshackle movie theater.

There was a plane leaving in two hours with a few open seats. She sat back in the waiting area with a large latte, trying to relax. The flight was as turbulent as Iris's thoughts. That old man knew her address. Well, just let him try something. But she didn't want to have to do those things anymore. Unless she had to.

17

Iris's fears were confirmed after Kate's first visit to a doctor Iris had consulted when she'd suffered flu symptoms that lingered and found she had mild asthma. Dr. Gibbons was a woman of fifty or so with hair and demeanor that both resembled slate. Iris didn't mind her, but she realized that Kate might find her manner off-putting.

"Your symptoms are concerning. I am going to refer you to Dr. Barnes, who is an oncologist. You need a full workup."

"Oncologist!" Kate gasped. "You think I have cancer?"

"Vaginal bleeding at your age? It's more than likely. And with that cough and your breathlessness, it has probably spread."

Kate sat rigid as the sphynx, her hands gripping the chair arms as if trying to anchor herself to earth. She looked at Iris with eyes full of pleading. Did she expect Iris to tell her it wasn't so?

Iris felt numb. "Surely, there could be other outcomes, Dr. Gibbons. You have frightened my friend."

"Possible, but unlikely. Always best to face facts."

Iris determined not to go to Dr. Gibbons-again. How could she scare Kate that way?

Kate wept all the way home. "Dying of cancer is terrible, terrible. It's really painful, and it can go on for a long time. Why me?"

Iris was thinking the same thing. Why this hardworking, sweet woman? "Now, we don't know anything for sure, Kate. It might be something simple. And they have ways of keeping patients very comfortable these days. Dr. Gibbons was really mean, talking like that. I won't see her again."

"She was only telling the truth."

"She was giving an opinion. Not the same thing at all."

Iris took the referral slip from Kate's bag and made the appointment as soon as they got home. Kate was still weeping and went up to her room. Iris felt like having a good weep herself. She loved Kate. She needed her.

There were many appointments for scans and tests. And Dr. Gibbons was right. The ugly C word. Stage 4 uterine cancer that had spread to other areas, including her lungs. Surgery and chemotherapy would prolong Kate's life for maybe a year. Dr. Barnes was a kindly soul who spoke gently to Kate, outlining her options. The surgery to control bleeding would be difficult, and the chemo even more so, with no guarantees. At this late stage, Iris couldn't expect much reprieve. They could keep her pain at bay, though.

"All that surgery and chemo for maybe a year? A year of pain and misery? No. I don't want that. I want peace in my last days and months. I want to be at home."

Kate had mostly stopped crying by this time and seemed resigned to her fate. Iris wondered if she believed in God. They had never discussed it.

Kate came down to breakfast the next morning and seemed calm. "Good morning, Iris. Did you sleep well?"

Iris was surprised by this rather formal greeting. "Er, yes, very well, thank you." She hadn't. "Were you able to sleep?"

"Yes, on and off. I'm going to call Dr. Barnes and ask for some pills to help me sleep through the night. I may as well be well rested, in spite of everything."

Iris just smiled. She didn't know what else to say.

Kate went to clear away the breakfast dishes, but Iris took the plates from her hands. "No, you don't need to do this. Just relax and do whatever you like."

"Thank you. I think I'll call Dr. Barnes now."

"Here, use my cell phone. I have his number programmed in." Iris set it on speaker and dialed before handing it over. The receptionist put her on hold for a few minutes.

"Good morning, Dr. Barnes. Thank you for taking my call. I need to have a good night's sleep for a change. I wonder if perhaps you could prescribe a little something to help me sleep through? I know you have to be very careful with such things, but I'd like to have the option of taking one from time to time."

"Of course, Kate. We have called in several prescriptions for you and I will add some sleeping aids to the list. What is the name of your pharmacy?"

Once that was dispensed with, Kate went to watch TV. Iris did the dishes and went to sit with her. There was some morning program on with yuppie hosts sharing the "issues of the day" with their audience. Iris could tell Kate wasn't paying attention. She stared at the screen intensely without any change of expression, still as a statue.

"I would like to have a lovely dinner out," Kate said, turning suddenly to Iris. "Just you and me."

"Whatever you like, Kate. Where would you like to go?"

"Let's go to that Italian place you took me to that evening you moved in. That was so special."

Iris picked up Kate's prescriptions before going home to make a reservation. Kate had turned off the TV and was napping on the sofa. Iris decided to go up to bed and read before making an omelet for lunch. Try as she might, she couldn't concentrate. She'd read a paragraph, but had no recollection of the content. She put the book down, frustrated. She woke up when Kate knocked on the door.

"I've made some ham sandwiches for lunch," she said.

"Oh, Kate, I didn't mean to fall asleep. I meant to make you an omelet."

"That's fine. We mustn't eat too much before our dinner tonight."

"True, I made reservations for six-thirty."

"Perfect."

She was like the old Kate again. Except tired.

Iris weeded the front garden for a couple of hours after lunch. Warmer weather welcomed the invaders along with the daffodils and other spring beauties.

After a cool drink on the terrace, Iris went upstairs to take a shower and put on a bright pink dress she hadn't worn before. She liked to put on something a little surprising sometimes, and if any occasion called for bright, cheerful colors, it was this one. Sleeping pills. She'd have to keep an eye on Kate. It wasn't time. Not yet. She remembered Magaly's suffering and how she'd wanted to go with dignity. She wouldn't deny the same reprieve to Kate when the time came.

She went to wake up Kate so she would have time to freshen up, and was surprised to see her writing at her desk.

"Just writing a note to my son," she said. "Let's post it on the way to dinner."

Kate seemed unnaturally cheerful all through dinner. She ordered the most expensive dish and a bottle of champagne. "My treat, my celebration of a good life."

They clinked glasses. Iris smiled and went along, an uneasy suspicion nagging. Would she? This soon?

Immediately after they got home, they hugged tearily before Kate went to bed. Iris slept fitfully, waking every couple of hours. Finally, she entered Kate's room at dawn. There she lay under the covers, her face bearing a slight smile. Iris looked at the papers on her desk. A large white envelope with WILL written on it, accompanied by a note.

Dear Iris,

When you entered my life, everything changed for the better. You have made my final years happier than I could have imagined. And thank you for dealing with that horrible man.

You have been the best friend I have ever had. Thank you. Please give my love to Simon, Mandy, and Victor, and thank them for always welcoming me into their family. I am sorry to leave everyone like this, but it is the best way. Better than getting frailer and sicker, better than wearing you to a frazzle taking care of me, as

I know you would. Better than you having to watch me die.

All my love,
Kate

Iris wept as she had never wept before.

18

Iris wandered through the rest of spring with a heavy heart. Vic had cried, heartbroken, after Kate died, and, in a way, that had been the hardest part. By the time the June vacation rolled around, Iris needed a change of scenery. She'd finally cleared out Kate's things, saving a few keepsakes, including her chunky dresser. She had not entered the room again after the final clearing, but instructed her cleaning lady to dust and vacuum once a month.

They took a cab to the airport. Iris began to feel almost cheerful. They checked in, made the annoying serpentine trek through security, and were soon on their way to the gate. Now that she was older, the few forehead creases and graying hair, not to mention her plastic surgery, ensured that no one would recognize her. She'd been tempted many times to color her hair but decided it was too much of a nuisance. After all, gray hairs comprised cheap and easy camouflage.

Vic was anxious because Wanda had cried when they'd left her at the boarding kennel. He loved his dog almost as much as she loved him.

Charlotte's airport was up to date and fairly manageable, but Washington Dulles was a tiresome relic involving a train to the gates and weird buses to get out to the aircraft. They traveled business class, which was lovely, although it must have cost Simon a fortune. It was an overnight flight. Simon and Vic fell asleep right after dinner. Mandy watched a movie, as did Iris. She needed help from the flight attendant to get it started. She felt pretty silly when it turned out to be relatively simple, but the young woman seemed to be used to dealing with first-timers. She enjoyed the story of two old English ladies who robbed a bank. *Don't get any idea*s.

London was quite a long way by cab from Heathrow, although it probably felt longer than it truly was because of rush hour. They checked into a chic hotel that Simon told her was just around the corner from the British Museum. They could walk to the theater district, too. Vic had been uncharacteristically quiet from the time he woke up. He seemed bewildered. Of course, at nine years old, he probably didn't fully understand the time difference. Here it was, sunny and cool, whereas his body told him it was about three o'clock in the morning. Iris didn't feel too chipper, either.

Their rooms weren't ready. The desk clerk assured them they'd try to get them ready early, perhaps by ten.

"That's the trouble with these overnight flights," Simon said. "We could have taken a later flight, but that would have been difficult with the connection from Charlotte. We would have waited in Dulles for many hours. Let's have breakfast."

CHAPTER 18

They left the bags in a small room behind the reception desk and went into the dining room to find a long buffet table. The hostess informed them they could either choose the buffet option or select something from the menu. Iris didn't have much of an appetite, so opted to find them a table and look over the menu. Earl Grey tea for a start.

"What is this porridge?" she asked the waiter.

"I believe you Americans refer to it as oatmeal," came the starchy reply.

"Good, I'll take that."

"Very well, madam."

Madam. She liked that. And now she came to think of it, her mother had called the slop she sometimes gave them for breakfast porridge. Ugh, maybe that hadn't been the best choice.

The others soon came back with full plates.

"What did you order?" asked Mandy.

"Tea and porridge," Iris replied.

"What in the hell is that?" Simon asked.

"Oatmeal."

"Oh. Well, it's in the Bible, isn't it? A mess of porridge."

"I think you mean a mess of pottage," Mandy said, laughing.

Iris wouldn't know. The Bible had not featured in her desperate childhood. Or Simon's happier one.

She was just finishing her tea when a couple was shown to the next table. Her heart missed a beat when she heard a familiar voice. She turned slightly. Silly little Sally. And with a man who wasn't the husband Iris remembered. There were children with them, too. Twins, it looked like. Maybe seven years old, a bit younger than Vic. Her jerk of a husband, Jack, must have finally died from his injuries. Iris hoped she hadn't chosen another jerk. She'd always been a pushover.

"Robert, I'm so looking forward to the museum. You know the Rosetta Stone is there?"

"I do, darling. And the Elgin marbles. And a funny chess set that was found in Scotland after a storm."

He had a slightly English accent and sounded nice.

"Dad, do we really have to go to a stupid museum?" the boy whined.

"We'll go for a little bit this morning and have lunch there," Sally said. "Then we'll go to the London Eye. I showed you both a picture, remember? It's really high."

"Yay, Mom, that sounds exciting." The little girl had a halo of fluffy blonde hair like her mother used to. Now Sally's hair was well cut and styled. Chic in fact. Silly little Sally was happy and chic. With a family. She'd finally come into her own.

Iris suddenly felt in need of a nap. Seeing Sally had dredged up memories she'd rather stay buried. Of all places to run into one of her Salton circle, it had to be one three thousand miles away in a hotel in London, England. The long arm of the past. She'd better keep her mouth shut in case Sally recognized her voice. She concentrated on her porridge, which turned out to be quite satisfying and nothing like what her mother had thrown together. No surprise there.

She looked at Simon. He was sitting at the side of the table with his back to Sally's family. He was clearly listening to the couple, too. This could be awkward.

He leaned forward. "A person from my old town I'd rather not talk to," he whispered to Mandy. "I'll go check on our rooms. Meet me outside. We can take a little walk if they're not ready."

Mandy looked bewildered as he got up and walked out quickly, keeping his face to the front. If she recognized

Simon as Andrew Hale, she might well connect the dots to Iris—or Rose, as she called herself in those days. Rose was a fugitive from justice. *We can't have that.*

She tuned into Sally's family again as she finished her porridge. Yes, it was oatmeal, but very creamy and delicious.

"You know that by lunchtime tomorrow you'll be at Grandma's and Grandpa's house?" Sally was saying. "You remember the beach? And the New Forest ponies?"

"Yeah," they chorused.

"I can't wait," the little girl said, bouncing up and down. "Do you think Grandma will have baked a cake for tea?"

"For the day after. We won't get there until dinnertime," her father said. "But I bet she made mince for dinner."

"Ooh, with all that lovely gravy and mash," the boy said. "And we'll go on a train. I love going on the train."

They were all excited about getting to their grandparents' house tomorrow. Iris was all excited about them getting the hell out of London tomorrow. Mince? What in God's name was that? A memory nagged Iris again. It was what her mother had called ground beef. But there wasn't any yummy gravy. Just plain meat. Awful, but better than nothing, and in her childhood nothing had been on the table more often than not. Mandy signed the check, and they went out to find Simon.

"Our rooms are ready," Simon told them.

"They're going to the museum this morning. The London Eye this afternoon. Leaving to go to the grandparents' tomorrow," Iris reported.

"What's going on?" Mandy said.

Simon looked at Vic. "She was someone my mother knew long ago. It was not a good relationship. I'd rather not get involved. Let's have a little rest and go to the museum this afternoon. We can go to the London Eye late tomorrow. We have the whole day before we fly to Lucerne the day after."

"Do you know them, Iris? It seems like you do."

"No, no. I saw Simon's reaction to them, so listened in for him."

"Oh." Mandy didn't seem convinced.

They rode up to the fifth floor in the glass-enclosed elevator, which Iris found unnerving. She looked straight ahead after a stomach-churning glance down at the busy lobby. As her heart regained its usual steady rhythm, she fiddled with her card key.

"Let me help with that." Simon let Mandy and Vic into their room and came to help her figure out the right way to position the key under the sensor. "See you in the lobby in a couple of hours."

Iris loved her room and its marbled bathroom—with a phone! She only unpacked the essentials, as they weren't staying long. She took a shower and lay down. She tried not to think about the last time she saw Sally. She hadn't attended Rose's trial. Her husband was in a nursing home by that time. It had nothing to do with Rose's activities—he'd brought himself down with his vicious temper.

It was true she tried to do away with her friends with poisoned iced tea. But they confronted her and forced her hand—and in the end, it was they who outwitted her. She, in turn, outwitted the court and ended up in a facility for the criminally insane rather than on death row. She wrote a journal while incarcerated and left it for the police to find when she escaped. Apparently, they passed it on to Andrew—Simon. So at least he knew everything wasn't really her fault. What else could she have done? No one looks out for a kid from a rough home in a rough neighborhood in a tough city.

19

Two hours later, they stopped at the reception desk, where Simon inquired about theater tickets. There were good seats available tomorrow for a matinee performance of *Oliver*. They walked around the area for a while and wandered in and out of shops until Vic got bored, and they opted for an early lunch across the street from the hotel. Vic insisted on toad-in-the-hole because the name sounded delightfully disgusting. Iris decided to try it, too. It turned out to be English bangers baked in Yorkshire pudding served with a rich onion gravy, new potatoes, and minted peas. The sausages were outstanding.

"You don't know what you're missing," she told Mandy and Simon. "These sausages are fantastic."

"I love it," Vic added. "Can you learn to make it, Gran?"

"I'll try. It's not too complicated, although I doubt I can get British sausages in the U.S. I like the mint in the peas. Do you?"

"Yes, it's different. I wasn't sure at first, but I like it."

Iris had a dim memory of her mother shaking dried mint into a saucepan of canned peas. It wasn't quite the same thing.

"You haven't eaten so well for months," Simon told Iris, looking pleased.

"No, I guess I haven't had much of an appetite. This vacation is a new start."

"I hope so," Mandy said, patting Iris on her hand.

"Are you still sad, Gran?" Vic asked.

"A little. But I'm beginning to feel better."

Vic nodded. "I can tell. I am, too."

"All right, time for the museum." Andrew motioned the waitress over to pay the bill.

The façade of the British Museum was a picture of stone grandeur. They mounted the outside steps, then a flight of inside steps, and soon found themselves facing a cabinet full of ivory chessmen.

"They are so funny looking," Vic said. "See, the knights are sitting on horses, but their feet are almost touching the ground. The king looks so sad."

"I expect he's had some bad news. His knights lost a battle," Mandy said, laughing.

"The queen doesn't look much better," said Iris. "She looks downright depressed."

"Looks more like a toothache to me," Vic answered. "And look at that soldier biting his shield."

Simon read the legend and told them about how they were found on the island of Lewes in the Hebrides after a storm. They were very old and had been carved from walrus tusks in either Norway or Iceland.

"The person who carved them had a sense of humor," he said. "They are quite comical. See how funny they all look, not like traditional chess sets at all, and certainly not the way royalty was usually presented, especially then. And the infantrymen are biting their shields like berserkers. Berserkers were very fierce fighters in Norse mythology. Quite mad, in fact." He peered some more. "They gave us a map when we came in, so let's look at what we'd like to see the most. It would take weeks to see everything in this museum."

They chose the Rosetta Stone, the Egyptian collection, and the famous Elgin marbles. If they still had the energy, they could choose another collection later.

Iris loved the Egyptian artifacts. The Rosetta Stone was interesting and, she knew, very important in that it allowed the translation of ancient hieroglyphics, which taught archeologists a great deal about life in ancient Egypt. But you couldn't maintain much interest in staring at a big stone for more than a few minutes. Same with the Elgin marbles. Beautiful, but not particularly arresting. She was relieved when Vic said he was tired. They took the elevator to the tearoom.

Iris was surprised she could manage a full English tea after such a robust lunch. The porcelain was all of the same pale green and white pattern, and made for a lovely setting.

The three-tier cake stand held little crustless sandwiches and dainty cakes. A separate plate held scones, which they ate halved, with good dollops of clotted cream and strawberry jam on each half. The Earl Grey tea was of top quality, too.

"I'll be the size of a house by the time we get home," Mandy exclaimed. "I think jetlag is catching up. Maybe it's time to head back. Vic needs a nap."

"I don't take naps anymore," Vic protested.

"It's not a baby thing, Vic," Iris said gently. "We are all tired because of the seven-hour time difference. It will take us a while to get used to it."

"I s'pose."

They walked back to the hotel.

"I'm really looking forward to the show tomorrow," Mandy said, her face bright with pleasure. "London is famous for theater."

"What about the London Eye?" Vic whined.

"We can do that after the theater. I read that it's a lovely view when it's getting dark and all the buildings along the Thames light up. Especially Parliament."

"Evening sounds best," Iris said. "The sight must be spectacular."

They were almost at the hotel when Iris felt a sudden tug at her bag as a motorized bicycle slowed beside her. She whipped around and kicked the rider's leg as hard as she could. He screamed as he was thrown in front of a taxi, which tossed him into the air like an enraged bull. He lay very still, leaking red. People shouted and gathered, craning their necks to get a good view. Iris assumed someone would have called the police, so stayed where she was.

"Go back to the hotel," she told Simon, who stood motionless as if in shock. "I'll deal with this. He tried to steal my purse. Take Vic away from here."

"I think I should stay with you," Simon said. "Mandy already left with Vic."

"Good. Did you see what he did?"

"I saw him holding the strap of your purse just before you kicked him."

"Good. That will help. A purse-snatcher. I just reacted." *I sure as hell wasn't going to lose that passport.*

CHAPTER 19

Within minutes, an ambulance arrived and bore the man away after a policewoman had a good look at him. She took Iris and Simon's statement, as well as that of an elderly gentleman who saw the thief grab the purse strap, and the taxi driver who had had a front-row seat. She was pleasant and polite, examined Iris's and Simon's passports, wrote down their contact information, and asked when they were leaving. Simon told her, and she left, seemingly satisfied. She said the local police were familiar with this character.

Simon and Iris walked into the lobby and sat in a corner. He went to the counter to ask if tea could be brought as the lady had suffered a shock. Not five minutes later, a cheerful, roly-poly young woman placed a tray of tea and biscuits in front of them.

"You saw that accident outside, did you love?" she asked solicitously. "Here, a nice cuppa will soon put you to rights."

"Thank you," Iris said faintly. She couldn't help finding it amusing.

"Did you do that on purpose?" Simon asked quietly.

"Push him in front of a taxi? No, of course not. It was a knee-jerk reaction. He was trying to steal my purse, so I kicked him."

"Okay. That's good. Yes, good." He sounded shaky. Did he think she was up to her old tricks? Assuming he really did know who she was. "Are you all right? I'd better see how upset Vic is."

"Did he see the man on the ground?"

"No, I pulled him back and told Mandy to take him to our room."

"Good. What will you tell him?"

"Just that a thief tried to steal your bag, so you kicked his bike and he fell and hurt himself. That you didn't mean to hurt him."

"That sounds appropriate."

Simon gave her a long, hard look and walked over to the elevator. He didn't look back as he got in and disappeared skyward. Iris spent the evening in her room watching TV and reading. Did he think she meant to kill him? She hadn't. Not really. She just reacted, that white anger flaring at the threat of losing her passport. There would be no record of it and trying to renew it while abroad and the questions that would arise—no, couldn't be allowed to happen.

The next morning Simon called her room and said they would have room service deliver breakfast and suggested she do the same. They'd see her downstairs at ten. Mandy would like to do some shopping. Iris had developed a cough, too, so she would find some medicine to ease it. It seemed to have started on the plane. The dry air, maybe. Although she'd coughed a lot in the spring, so she'd probably developed allergies.

The three of them behaved like their usual selves when they met up, although Mandy kept glancing at Iris in a worried sort of way. She probably expected Iris's nerves to be in shreds. They took a taxi to Regent Street, where a friend had told Mandy she'd find all the best shops. She was right. Iris hankered after Harrod's and Fortnum & Mason, though. They were so famous that even she had heard of them. Next time. Next time, she'd try to find Pinner, too. That's where Ma and Pa lived before coming to the United States, and where everything was so much better than where they found themselves. Iris believed that just about anywhere had to be better than Hell's Kitchen in New York City. At least in those days.

They soon came to a large drugstore with the strange name of Boots. It had an enticing array of goods, both health-related and cosmetic. A young sales assistant showed

Iris to the shelves with cough medicines and lozenges. Iris chose a bottle recommended by the young lady and bought some lozenges, too. Simon and Vic began to get impatient as Mandy reveled in the wide range of cosmetics. Next, they trailed around all the big stores, and each got something to remind them of London. Iris bought a silk shirt, and an illustrated book about London. Simon got a silk tie. Mandy found a chic silk pantsuit. Just as Vic was getting whiny, they found themselves outside Hamleys, a world-famous toy store. The range of items was extraordinary. Iris worried that Vic wouldn't find anything he wanted that was both affordable and portable. To her relief, he fell in love with a set that featured a colony on the moon. With the aid of more than a few batteries, vehicles and animals moved by means of a remote control and there were plenty of figures in space suits that could be manipulated to adopt various poses. Of course, it was rather a large box, but Mandy had provided Vic with a much larger suitcase than he needed as she assumed they'd be buying souvenirs.

They ate lunch across from the hotel again. Everyone ordered toad-in-the-hole this time. Soon, their purchases were back in their rooms and they were on their way to the theater in a taxi, where they enjoyed a rambunctious production of *Oliver*. Iris read in the program that it was first staged over fifty years before, and was glad they brought it back because the songs and production numbers were fabulous.

The walk back to the hotel afterward took about twenty minutes. They passed bars with plenty of outside seating and found their way easily. The traffic crawled past unceasingly. Iris wondered if the thief was alive or dead. He had certainly been badly hurt. In the brief glance she had of his panicked face, she'd gotten the impression of a clean-cut young man with short blond hair, a white shirt, and a red bow tie. She hadn't really registered the bow tie and white shirt until now. How odd. Maybe that get-up allowed him to blend in with a respectable crowd?

They had dinner in the city, not too far from Big Ben. They could walk to the Eye from there. It was one of those places with starched tablecloths and waiters who gave the impression of schoolmasters standing ready to whack their charges' knuckles with a ruler for any minor infraction. The service was impeccable, however, and the food delectable. Iris had never eaten lobster thermidor before, and she relished its creamy succulence. It was seven-thirty by the time they finished. It stayed light late in London in the summer.

"Do you think it will be dark enough for the lights to come on?" Mandy asked Simon. "They close at eight-thirty so we don't have much choice."

"I think some will come on, but I wish they'd operate later. We'll see. It'll be fun either way."

They waited in line for some time before getting on. The wheel never actually stopped, but continued to roll slowly and they had to jump into one of the cabins, which Iris didn't appreciate. But the view was magnificent and once they got to the top, lights blinked on in Parliament, sending shining ripples over the River Thames. Iris drank it all in, awed, as she and Vic stood hand in hand. They jumped off the moving wheel, Simon getting off first to assist Iris, for which she was grateful. She hadn't realized her balance was not as steady as it used to be. They didn't talk much as they walked in search of a taxi, which took a good while. It was a perfect end to their London adventure.

20

The next day, their flight left in mid-afternoon, which meant getting to the airport by one. They regretted deciding to eat lunch near their gate. The place was packed. They decided on sandwiches and bottled water, but even so, they stood in line for twenty minutes. They ate in the waiting area, unable to get seats together. Finally, their flight was called.

The Swiss Air flight was uneventful, and they soon found themselves in Lucerne, where immigration and customs were handled with military precision, so proceeded without undue delay. Their bags were on the carousel when they got through, customs officers just waved them past, and they easily found the hotel's courtesy bus.

The hotel sat across the road from Lake Lucerne. Iris turned at the entrance to gaze across at the panorama of ice blue water with its slash of a dark green distant shore.

Beyond lay slate blue mountains with other mountains stacked behind, ranging from deep purple to the palest lilac. She breathed in the fresh mountain air. How magnificent, how utterly different from anything she had ever known.

They checked in and were told that the dinner hour began at seven, only just over an hour away. If they wished, they might enjoy an apéritif on the hotel's boat, moored across the road. One could also swim from there. Simon and Mandy decided to unpack and relax in their room before dinner. Vic and Iris said they'd freshen up in their rooms and meet in the lobby. Iris felt pulled to the view, and Vic was just plain restless.

The traffic was light, so they got across the road easily and walked across the gangway to the boat. It was more like a barge, with plenty of seating, steps down to the water, and a bar at the end. They sat at a small pull-up table near the bar and ordered their drinks. Iris chose a Swiss white wine, and Vic a ginger beer. He'd had one in London and liked it. Pale in color, it was a little like ginger ale, but with more of a gingery kick.

It was nowhere close to sunset, but the light was not as bright as before, deepening the hues of the hulking mountains and their rugged furrows and planes. Their snowcaps grayed slightly, tipped with yellow by the sun anticipating the end to its working day.

"So much beauty, Vic. I never imagined such a sight."

"I looked at lots of pictures on the internet, Gran, but it's not the same as seeing it for real."

"It makes me want to learn how to paint."

"Why don't you?"

"I've never tried it. I can't imagine I have what it takes."

"Well, you don't know until you've tried. I'm pretty sure there are classes you can take."

"I'll think about it." Maybe she should. And maybe she should go back to writing her romances. It might be fun to set one in a place like this.

The low menacing rumble of a man's voice coming from a table at the other end of the boat drew Iris's attention to a couple farther along the deck. The man had his back to her and Vic, but the tear-stained face of the young woman across from him piqued her curiosity. The girl looked barely out of her teens. Even from the back, her companion was clearly much older—at least forty. She made a few weak protests: "I didn't mean to," and "I would never," and "No, of course I didn't." Suddenly, he stood up and said, "Let's go." He gripped her upper arm—forcefully, judging by her wince—and marched her off the boat and back to the hotel.

"Wow, he wasn't very nice to her," Vic said.

"No, he wasn't."

A gong sounded, signaling that the dining room was open. Iris and Vic finished their drinks and walked back to the lobby to meet up with Mandy and Simon.

The next morning, they decided to walk across the covered bridge over the River Ruess. Simon read from the guidebook how it used to be the oldest bridge in Switzerland, built between 1290 and 1300, but burned down in the nineties. Each gable in the crossbeams had contained a painting depicting a Bible scene, but nearly all were lost and the survivors badly damaged. The bridge was rebuilt in record time, but was not the same without the paintings. It was still a pleasant stroll, however, and the old water tower adjacent to the bridge still stood. Boxes of flowers hung all along the side walls, the view of the town was beautiful and the tourists were mostly quiet and orderly.

About halfway across, about level with the water tower, a couple overtook Iris, who had fallen behind the others. It was the people who'd been arguing on the boat the night before. As the young woman passed, Iris noticed that her sunglasses couldn't quite hide her black eye. She was wearing long sleeves and a scarf around her neck—strange on a warm summer's day. Iris had no doubt there were other bruises under her clothing. Poor kid. Was she in Switzerland against her will? Should Iris do something? It wouldn't be wise to draw attention to herself, though. It would make Simon mad, perhaps spoil the wonderful holiday he was giving them all. *Stay out of it. Mind your own business.* Iris told herself that several times as she trailed the couple across the river.

Lunch on the other side was a succulent pork schnitzel and a cold, crisp white wine. Iris reveled in these lovely moments—looking out at the lake on one side of her and the mountains on the other. It was hard to believe that little urchin Pansy would one day sit in such splendid surroundings, enjoying a glass of good wine. *Forget Pansy.* Pansy was dead. Hardly a shred of her remained. But she'd like to do something about that brute who now sat a couple of tables away with his downcast victim. Were they married? Iris tried to see if she wore a ring, but her hands remained in her lap, except when she forked a minute portion of food into her mouth with her right hand.

When Simon suggested they should go back over the bridge and walk around the town for a while, she reluctantly rose. As she passed the table, she stopped and greeted them.

"How do you do? I am Iris Hall. I noticed you on the hotel boat yesterday while I was having a drink with my grandson. Since we are staying in the hotel, I just wanted to introduce myself."

The woman started to speak, but the man spoke over her. "We are Barbara and Larry Wentworth. We won't be staying long. Off to Bulgaria in a couple of days." He didn't stand or take Iris's extended hand.

"Bulgaria, goodness. I've never met anyone who has been there. Have you been before?"

"Yes, my parents are from there."

Iris could just make out that English was not his first language, although his accent was British and the anomalies hardly noticeable.

"I hope you have a pleasant trip."

A couple of tears rolled down under the sunglasses.

"My wife is not feeling well. Please excuse us."

"Of course."

Iris patted Barbara on the shoulder before hurrying to catch up with the others.

"What did you say to them, Gran?"

"Just introduced myself. There's something not right there. The woman has a black eye. They're going to Bulgaria in a couple of days."

"I bet he hit her and gave her the black eye. He was so mean to her last night."

"What's this all about?" Mandy asked.

Iris explained.

"I don't think there's anything we can do about it," Simon said, rather more forcefully than called for, in Iris's opinion. A warning?

Iris could see why a man would take a young woman out of Bulgaria, but why would he take one there? She knew next to nothing about the place. Were there millionaires who would pay for girls there? But surely there were enough poor girls in the country to be taken advantage of without importing one. And what Bulgarian would have a name like Wentworth? Fishy. Stinking to high heaven fishy.

The rest of the day was spent wandering in and out of small boutiques, up and down narrow streets until they came to a large square. To their amazement, there was a huge chessboard laid out on the ground in black and white stone. Close to life-sized chessmen were being manhandled across the squares by the players as the game progressed.

"Wow, they're as big as me!" Vic gasped. "You know, I can learn chess next year at school. There's a club. I think I'll join."

"I never learned, I'm afraid," Iris said. "What about you, Simon?"

"I used to love chess," he replied.

Iris knew full well that he did, and was quite a good player. But she felt pressed to keep up the charade.

"Well, that's nice. You can play together," Mandy said.

"Dad, can I have a picture next to the board?"

The players were in stasis at the time, as white pondered his next move, so Vic didn't bother them when he stood beside a black chessman close to the edge. He smiled broadly for the camera.

They found a café just off the square and sank down gratefully into comfortable chairs at an outside table. Iris felt worn out. It must be her age.

"I think I'm going to have hot chocolate," Mandy said. "I know it's not the weather for it, but I read that the Swiss are famous for it."

"Me, too," Vic and Iris said together.

Simon opted for coffee and ordered a plate of pastries to share. The hot chocolate was creamy and just sweet enough, the quality of chocolate, superb. Iris and Vic sighed with pleasure at the same time, which made Simon and Mandy laugh.

"I have never tasted anything as good," Iris said.

"Me neither," Vic agreed. Mandy wiped off his frothy mustache.

"It's quite hot. Can we go for a swim?"

"I warn you, the water will be very cold," Simon told him.

"That's okay. Will you come in, Gran?"

"No, I don't like cold water." Iris shuddered. "I'll come and watch you, though."

"So, can we go back now?"

They finally got back to the hotel after a good half-hour's walk. They went up to their rooms.

"I'll just wash my hands and meet Vic in the lobby. Don't worry, I'll keep an eye on him," Iris told Mandy.

"Thanks, I could do with a nap."

To Iris's annoyance, the Wentworths sat at the table she and Vic enjoyed the night before. She liked the privacy of the table near the bar, with only one other on the other side. She sat at the other table, which didn't have such a good view. The reception clerk had told her they kept towels on the boat. They could leave them in their bathrooms later if they wanted to bring them back to the hotel.

Vic slipped off his pants and shirt and ventured down one of the ladders. He gasped when his feet went under.

"Oh, oh! It really is cold."

"Of course," Iris said. "The water is melted snow running down from the mountain tops." She'd read that in Simon's guidebook.

Vic continued down, inch by painful inch. Iris ordered a beer and sipped while keeping watch. She wondered if such cold water could cause cramps. They should have come earlier in the afternoon, when the sun was warmer. He started to swim, first breaststroke, then freestyle. She rushed to the side of the boat when she felt he had gone too far out. He stopped and trod water, waving to her. She took a photo.

"Hi, Gran, it's lovely. You should have come in!"

"Not bloody likely," she muttered.

Larry Wentworth laughed.

Larry Wentworth. *What are you up to? Who are you?*

21

There wasn't much to do after dinner. Victor's swim had tired him out, and he wanted to read in bed. A group of Swiss folk dancers would entertain the hotel guests in the ballroom at eight-thirty. Simon wasn't so keen and insisted on staying upstairs with Vic, claiming there would be plenty to entertain him on the TV.

"That's very nice of you, darling," Mandy said, laughing.

"Yes, much appreciated," Iris added.

"No problem, I need a rest. Anyway, you know, folk dancing, not my thing really."

"We know," Mandy said, pecking him on the cheek.

Mandy and Iris enjoyed an after-dinner drink in the bar, finding a table at the window that looked out over the terrace, with the lake and mountains beyond, now only visible as a vast gray patch guarded by black monsters. It had turned too cool to sit outside without a jacket or a shawl, which neither had thought to bring down from their rooms.

They got to the ballroom with twenty minutes to spare so they could get good seats, which they found in the front row.

"Perfect," Mandy said, sinking into her seat.

"Just about everything on this trip is perfect," Iris answered. "Except for that little problem with the bag-snatcher."

"Yes, most unfortunate. I can't get over how cool you acted. It didn't seem to upset you at all."

"Well, he had it coming. He couldn't have expected to get away with it forever."

Mandy looked uncomfortable. "Well, no, I suppose not. I wonder if he's alive?"

"I wondered the same thing. But I doubt it would have been in the papers. I could do an internet search, I guess. I don't even know his name."

"Let's look now," Mandy said, getting her phone out of her bag. "I just put a SIM card in my phone, so I should be able to manage a search."

She fiddled around, tapping away for a full five minutes before handing it over to Iris. "There."

Iris read aloud. "Reginald Hughes, 34, was run over by a taxi on Kensington High Street yesterday. A petty thief known to the police, he was riding a motorized bike and trying to snatch the handbag of an American tourist, who inadvertently pushed his bike into the path of a taxi. He passed away at hospital four hours later without regaining consciousness."

"Oh, dear," said Mandy.

"Oh dear, indeed," Iris replied. She liked "inadvertently."

They sat silently as the seats filled, and the musicians took their seats. The female dancers swirled in wearing blouses with white puffy sleeves, beautifully embroidered vests, and bright skirts. The male dancers entered shortly after in black pants, white shirts, and black or red vests, also exquisitely embroidered. The women wore bands of flowers on their heads, while the men wore black pork-pie hats.

The music was lively, as were the dances at first. After a while, the performance became quieter and more lyrical, suggesting a romantic or pensive mood. Iris enjoyed every moment. This was a culture with a flavor. Traditional food, dance, music, costume, and probably other traditions she was unaware of. Home seemed so banal in comparison.

They joined in the applause with great enthusiasm as the dancers curtsied and bowed before disappearing through doors at the end of the hall. Iris and Mandy sat for a few minutes to allow the people behind them to clear the doorways.

"Lovely," Iris said with a sigh.

"Yes, it was. But I can see how it wouldn't be Simon's cup of tea," Mandy said. "It was kind of him to stay upstairs, though. Vic really isn't any trouble, but it's nice to be free of responsibility sometimes."

"I can imagine," Iris said.

They made their way up to their rooms. Iris quickly got ready for bed and climbed under the covers. She turned on the TV and searched for something entertaining. An American quiz show kept her amused for a while until her eyelids drooped so often she turned it off.

Iris dreamed of her parents fighting, her father throwing small tables and chairs around their flat and pounding his fists into the wall while her mother yelled obscenities and hurled plates at his head. She woke with a start to the sound of someone pounding on the door. She got up and opened it the fraction possible with the chain still fixed.

"Who is it? It's very late."

"Please, it's Barbara Wentworth. Please let me in. Please!"

Iris slipped the chain and Barbara ran past her, sobbing. Iris locked up again.

The girl collapsed into an armchair and leaned back, hugging her ribs. One eye was closing, her face swollen and red. She still had the black eye on the other side. She took a deep breath and gasped, sitting up slowly.

"I think one of my ribs is broken."

"He did this?"

"Yes. I get on his nerves. When he's been drinking, he punishes me. He's really drunk tonight. Says it's my fault."

"But it's not, you know. Are you married?"

"No. But he tells everyone we are. Wentworth is my name. I can't even pronounce his."

"I thought it was a funny name for a Bulgarian. You're short of breath. We need to get you to a hospital."

"No, it'll make him mad. He'd kill me if I mess up his plan."

"What plan is that?"

"He brings homeless girls to Bulgaria and sells them. He's only got me this time, but there are usually more. He tells everyone they're his daughters. This time he says he won't make as much money, so he's using me. But they pay more for virgins, so it doesn't make sense."

"Who does he sell the girls to?"

"'Rich people abroad,' is all he'll say. He's part of a ring. He won't think of looking for me here. Can I stay for a bit?"

"You can stay until I've solved the problem and I can get you to a hospital."

Barbara looked at Iris, her one open eye wild. "What can you do?"

"I'll see. How did you know which was my room, by the way?"

"I overheard them telling you when you checked in."

CHAPTER 21

"I'm going out. If anyone asks, I never left you." Iris looked at her watch. "It's twelve-thirty now. If anyone asks, I'm going to tell them you came down at eleven-thirty. You pleaded with me not to call anyone in case it made him mad. Got it?" Barbara nodded. "Room number?"

"611. Top floor."

"Give me your key card."

Iris pulled on a pair of slacks, sneakers, and a hoodie and filled her tote with ice before sliding out the door. Ice wouldn't do more than slow him down, but it might give her time to make one hell of a scene if he threatened her. She quietly opened the door to the stairway. Iris had never seen anything like the snail-shaped cascade of steps. *Could be useful.* She only had to climb two levels and arrived at 611 at the end of the hall to find the door ajar. Good, her entry wouldn't be registered. She leaned against the wall for a few minutes, surprised by how breathless she was. As soon as her breathing calmed, she pushed it gently and edged in. Larry—or whatever his real name was—sat in a corner of the room, staring morosely at his drink.

He raised his head slowly. "What do you want? You're the nosy bitch who spoke to us over the bridge there."

"Yes, I'm the nosy bitch. Do you want to know where your wife is?"

His face twisted into a scowl. "I'll kill that ungrateful little cow. Pulled her in off the streets, I did."

"I understand. She told me that."

"Where is she? I'll drag her back here if she wakes the whole fucking hotel. See if I care."

He rose unsteadily.

"Come with me. I'll take you to her."

He followed her out. Iris told him, "We'll take the stairs. No need to draw attention to ourselves."

He grunted. Iris led him to the stairway and opened the door. "Oh, go ahead. I think I dropped my key card."

Larry clutched the rail at the top of the stairs. "Hurry up."

"Sure."

She swung the tote at the back of his knees. He teetered back and forth, so she helped with a gentle push between the shoulders. He gasped and started to scream as he bounced from step to step, too drunk to help himself. Iris closed the door on him. She went back to his room, poured the ice into the bathroom sink, and waited a few minutes before venturing back down the stairs. She strained her ears, but heard nothing. Peering over the rails, in the dim lighting she could just make out his inert figure on a landing several floors down. She got back to her room. She reckoned the whole thing hadn't taken her much more than fifteen minutes.

Barbara lifted her head groggily when she entered. Her breath was labored, and she gave out little moans of pain.

"He won't trouble you anymore. I'm going to call security."

"Are you sure? What will become of me?"

"I think you will be treated in the hospital and they will probably call on the British Embassy to arrange for you to get back to England. Do you have parents?"

"Yes, but they threw me out because I was pregnant."

"Where's the baby?"

"I had a miscarriage after I got raped while I was on the streets."

Poor girl. *Bastard parents.* "Well, your parents might help you if you apologize and promise to reform."

"Are you serious?"

"Yes. You cannot go back on the streets and they can give you a roof over your head. You have a goal. Do whatever schooling you need to get trained for something. After that, you can leave. Yes, your parents were cruel. So use them."

"Gosh, you're a really strange woman. I've never met anyone like you before."

"And you probably never will."

Iris called security. When the two poker-faced gentlemen arrived, she told them her version of events and Barbara agreed. They asked her about Larry, and she told them the whole story of trafficking and abuse. One of them called an ambulance. A couple of heads popped out of bedroom doors when the EMTs arrived trundling a gurney, but soon retreated. Iris was surprised that no one had reacted when Barbara banged on her door. Maybe they had, and she hadn't noticed. In that case, she hoped they hadn't noticed the time.

"Iris, what's going on?" She'd wondered when Simon would arrive.

"It's that lady who was being beaten by that man she was with. She banged on my door this evening to escape from him. He beat her badly this time. She's going to the hospital."

"Good god, poor girl."

"Who are you, sir?" asked one of the security guys. She could hardly tell one from the other.

"I am Simon Hale. Mrs. Hall here is a close family friend. We are traveling together with my wife and young son."

"I see. I am sorry your sleep has been disturbed." He turned back to Iris. "We will call the police and go to speak to Mr. Wentworth," one of the security officers informed them.

"Good," Iris replied. "I didn't dare approach him if he was that drunk and violent."

"You should have called us immediately when Mrs. Wentworth arrived," he told her reproachfully.

"Well, she pleaded with me not to because she was so scared of him. I just wanted her to calm down and rest. And I wanted to make sure he hadn't followed her."

"Very well."

Iris wondered how long it would be before they found him and whether he had survived.

"I think I'll try to get some sleep," Iris told Simon. "You should, too."

"You really do get involved in things, don't you?" he answered. "Good night, sweet dreams."

At breakfast the next morning, the hotel manager came to their table.

"Mrs. Hall?"

"Yes, I am Mrs. Hall."

"I wonder if you would be kind enough to step into my office. A policeman would like to speak to you."

"Of course."

"Shall I come with you?" Simon asked, his brow furrowed.

"No, no, it's quite all right. I'm sure it's just about last night."

Iris rose and followed the manager. A young man with almost white hair rose as she entered.

"Good morning, Mrs. Hall. I am Karl Peter. I need to ask you some questions about the visit of Barbara Wentworth to your room last night."

"Of course. Did you find the man?"

"Yes."

Iris told her story again, including what she had noticed on the hotel boat and while crossing the bridge.

"I'm afraid I don't know anything about them except what Barbara told me when she came to my room last night."

"And what time was that?"

"Eleven-thirty. I looked at my watch because I wondered how long I'd been asleep."

"Someone else who heard her knocking said it was more like twelve-thirty."

"They must have been mistaken. I looked at my watch again after Barbara had been in my room for a while and it was around quarter to twelve. I wanted to call for assistance, but the idea panicked her so much. I kept putting it off until I noticed she was getting short of breath and decided I should delay no longer."

"I see. A cleaner found the man near the bottom of the stairs very early this morning. He was dead."

Good. "From what Barbara told me, he was very drunk. I wonder if he thought she'd left the hotel, or was hiding in the lobby."

"We do not know. The autopsy and blood tests will show how drunk he was. And you say Barbara never left your room?"

"No. She was in no fit state. She certainly had at least one broken rib, and I couldn't help wondering if it had punctured a lung."

"It did not, but could have if she had she not gone to the hospital when she did. She had three broken ribs and her eye is being assessed for any serious damage."

"Poor girl. Have you any idea how old she is?"

"She is seventeen years old."

"So young. Did she tell you her parents threw her out?"

"Yes, we have contacted them. They will arrive tomorrow."

"Good. I asked her about family and she told me. I advised her to mend things with her parents and get some training for a good job."

"Yes, I think you are quite right, Mrs. Hall. Thank you for speaking with me."

"My pleasure. I'm glad Barbara will be all right."

Iris went back to the table.

"What happened? Did they find that awful man?" Mandy asked.

"Yes, a cleaner found him at the bottom of the stairs early this morning."

"Will they try to blame the girl?"

"I doubt it. She has three broken ribs and her eye might be permanently damaged. I'm sure the autopsy will show he was very drunk. He probably went out looking for her and lost his balance."

"Well, another drama," Simon said, a little too sourly for Iris's taste. "Paris tomorrow. Let's try to keep that part of the trip on an even keel."

"Simon!" Mandy said.

"I'm sorry. I guess I'm just tired."

Vic had been watching them talk, wide-eyed. "Gran, let's just go to the boat this morning. You're tired, I can tell. You can just sit and have a nice drink and read your book. I want to color in my new London book."

"That sounds good," Iris said. Vic behaved with a maturity beyond his years sometimes. "You two can do a little more sightseeing," she told Mandy and Simon.

"Yes, there are a couple more things I'd like to do. And we have to pack later. Our train leaves at three."

"I can't wait for a lovely long train ride," Vic said, his sweet face shining with enthusiasm.

"There should be some fantastic scenery, too," Simon added.

"Will you swim this morning?" Iris asked Vic.

"No, I don't feel like it. It was fun that one time, but boy, is it cold!"

22

They all got settled in their assigned seats on the train from Lucerne to Paris. Mandy and Iris had window seats facing each other across a table, and Simon and Vic sat across the aisle. Vic seemed fascinated by the busy crowd in the station, but Iris wondered how soon he'd get bored with the scenery, however splendid. She wondered how Barbara was doing. She'd thought about visiting her in the hospital, then decided against it. Some things are better left alone.

She got out her Kindle and opened it to the detective series she'd been bingeing. Set in England, the crimes seemed a little weirder than she'd read in American novels, but the characters more realistic. One becomes tired of detectives who are worn down, at odds with their bosses, divorced, and borderline alcoholics. She was waiting for the next book in a fantasy series to come out. She hadn't expected to appreciate it, even though it had rated well on the bestseller list, but she had been enthralled throughout. Fantasy took her to another world, one where anyone can be a hero and where the rules are different.

The train finally started, and the view wasn't particularly attractive as they wound their way through the less salubrious suburbs. After a while, the scenery became more rural, and they passed a couple of quaint villages filled with attractive wooden houses that seemed to be in competition for the best window box award. They all seemed too good to be true, as if constructed for postcards or even a movie set. Then things changed again. As they neared the mountains, they passed spectacular rocky crags, gorges, and even a slick of ice or two. Iris closed her Kindle and gazed at it all, knowing she must store it in her mind forever. After a couple of hours, an attendant came around with sandwiches and beverages and they all took their pick. Iris and Mandy both chose a sandwich of brie, tomato, and basil, and sparkling water. The sandwich tasted so upmarket, despite its simplicity. She glanced over at Vic and Simon. Simon looked back at her and nodded with a half-smile before turning back to his tablet. Vic was engrossed in some game on his device, nibbling on a sandwich grasped in his left hand. Well, he had plenty of time to come back.

After they crossed the border, the scenery calmed down and became rural once more. Iris leaned back, and to her surprise, started awake when a loud voice announced in French and English their imminent arrival to Gare de Lyons. They packed their hand baggage and got ready to leave.

Simon handed their cases down to a porter, who led them to a line of taxis. The taxi drove them through wide streets—those famous boulevards, Iris surmised—before pulling up in front of a small hotel with impressive columns supporting a covered walkway entrance.

CHAPTER 22

The mahogany reception desk had been polished within an inch of its tree rings and the young man in a blue uniform standing behind it looked as if he had, too. He welcomed them and checked them in in heavily accented, but mostly correct English. He spoke rapidly into a phone, and another young man appeared in minutes, ready to take them and their baggage to their adjacent rooms. Vic would share with his parents here. Iris was a little surprised, as she would have expected the young couple to want a little romance during a stay in Paris.

Her room was small but comfortable. They would only be there for three days, but she wanted her clothes to be in good shape, so unpacked completely. She would feel strange going out for dinner in Paris looking less than pristine.

Paris. London had been wonderful, Lucerne enchanting, but being in Paris was a dream she never expected to come true. Still, she reflected, her life from the time she found her son again, and especially her grandson, was a dream come true. Too good to be true? She shivered.

She had a shower and changed her clothes before going downstairs to join the others for dinner. To her surprise, Mandy was chatting in French with the concierge who had been absent when they arrived.

"The gentleman suggests a small restaurant just up the street for dinner. He says it has a small menu, but is very good. Favored by the locals, apparently. Always a good sign."

"How do you know?" asked Vic. "We haven't been in another country before. And how come you speak French so well?"

"I traveled to Europe several times with my family when I was younger and lived with a French family in Lyons for a semester in college, before I met your father. And don't forget, my college major was French, with a minor in Italian."

"Oh, I forgot. You mean you haven't always known Dad?"

"Well, no. People usually meet the one they're going to marry when they are older. In university, perhaps, or at a party."

"Let's go," Simon said. "It's six-thirty. I think the French tend to eat later, so we have a better chance of a good table if we're early."

Iris wondered why Simon had broken in like that. Mandy had looked relieved, too. She realized that they had never talked about how they met. She had to find some way of getting the story out of Mandy when Simon wasn't around.

They turned left and strolled down the street until they came to *Le Cochon*. Its milky old windows and canvas awning looked too quaint for tourists to pass up. The street at that point was too narrow for outside dining. Anyway, the air had a nip in it, even though it was June. They were shown to their table by a pretty young woman who turned out to be Scottish. Iris had to concentrate hard to catch everything she said. Her blue eyes were striking against her almost black hair, and her shapely mouth seemed fixed in a permanent smile.

The menu was short and mercifully had English translations under all the selections. They all decided on Blanquette of Pork. There was only one choice that was not pork and that was *Coq au Vin*, which Iris had eaten in New York. Their choice sounded suspiciously like an ordinary stew, but she'd heard that French chefs managed to add a special touch to their dishes that tended to make them memorable.

It was a stew with a difference—a big difference. The meat was tender and succulent, the sauce and vegetables deliciously savory, and the accompanying baby potatoes almost like a new kind of vegetable.

CHAPTER 22

"This is marvelous," Iris said. "I wonder why the potatoes taste so different?"

"I'd guess because they've just been picked," Mandy said. "My grandfather had a huge garden and grew potatoes. They taste like this when they're freshly picked. Goodness knows how old potatoes in the supermarket might be."

"Yes, it's really good," Simon said, his face a picture of ecstasy.

"Dad, you talked with your mouth full."

"Sorry, Vic, I shouldn't have. But it's just so good."

Vic giggled. "You did it again!"

The adults had crème brulé after dinner and Vic had ice cream.

"I think we'd better go for a walk after all this," Mandy said, inhaling deeply. "Although I feel as if I might fall over after eating so much."

"Well, we can take it slowly," her husband said as he signaled the waiter for the bill.

They walked around the neighborhood and came across a small square that was surrounded by trees that seemed to be scented. Iris gratefully sat on a bench, exhausted. She started to cough, and couldn't stop. Mandy joined her, concerned.

"Are you all right, Iris? Do you still have the medicine you got in London?"

"It's in my room. I've got a cough drop in my bag, though. I think I've developed allergies. You and Simon go on. I'm quite happy here."

"Are you sure? Simon, why don't you go on with Vic? I'll sit here with Iris. I'm pretty tired, anyhow."

"If you're sure, Iris."

Iris shooed them off and dug in her bag for the black currant-flavored lozenge.

"You'd better see the doctor when we get back, Iris. You've had a cough for months. Even before Kate died."

"Not that long? It's not so bad. Just allergies, that's all."

"We'll see when we get back."

"I wonder what these trees are?" Iris said. "Have you ever smelled this before?"

"Yes, they're silver lindens," Mandy said, hugging herself. "I find the scent delightful. It brings memories of my parents the last time I came here with them. My mother loved these trees. Did you know there's a herbal tea flavored with the blossoms? It's called *tilleul*."

"You sound sad, my dear."

"Yes, they both died in a car crash in San Francisco not long after that trip."

"I'm so sorry."

"It's all right. I'm as over it as one ever is. I'd just graduated high school and had been accepted into Stanford. I did my first year there, then transferred to the University of Virginia. I just wanted to get far away."

"Did it help?"

"Not really."

"No, it rarely does. Is that where you met Simon?"

"No. He was already practicing law in Washington, D. C. and I was visiting an old friend in Georgetown. I had a blind date my friend set up because she had theater tickets and had to leave me alone for the evening. Simon was with a girl I think he'd already proposed to. We met at a party my date took me to. We started talking because our dates were dancing and we didn't feel like it. We talked all evening." She opened her arms and leaned back, staring at the stars. "His girl got drunk and yelled at me, hit me, pulled my hair. It was a horrid scene. Then my date informed me loudly that he was going home alone. Simon took my arm and pulled me out of there, and we went to an all-night café. We exchanged addresses and phone numbers. He walked me home and was a perfect gentleman. Just pecked me on the cheek once I'd opened the door, and went home. He visited me the following weekend in Charlottesville, and things got pretty serious pretty fast."

"I can see him behaving like a gentleman," Iris said. Simon—Andrew—had always behaved correctly. He used to be a little stuffy in the old days. He'd loosened up a lot. "Well, it may have started with an ugly scene, but ended with the best possible outcome from what I can see."

"Yes, it has. He's always been wonderful to me, and now is a great dad to Vic. I'm very lucky."

"Me, too," Iris said.

"You don't talk about your family at all."

"I don't have any. They all died long ago in Pennsylvania. My parents were alcoholics. I had two sisters. One died as a baby, and I'm not sure what happened to the other."

"That's so sad. What about before Charlotte?"

"Ontario. I moved there years ago, then got sick of the winters."

Simon and Vic arrived just after Iris had spilled her sanitized version of her background.

They all wandered back to the hotel and went to their rooms. Iris wondered why she had been so forthcoming about her family. She thought back to what she'd said. She hadn't actually revealed that much, and certainly nothing that could be traced back to her real story. Satisfied, she got into bed and opened her Kindle. When she awoke in the small hours, the bedside light was still on and her Kindle lay on her chest. She tried to remember the fleeting remnants of a dream, something to do with her father, but it remained out of reach. Not a dream, but a nightmare—that much she knew.

The next day, they took a sightseeing bus trip around Paris. They sat on the top level because the view would be better and Vic would find it more fun. He seemed to enjoy the ride, but not because of history or stately buildings.

After a café lunch where they could sit outdoors, they went to the Louvre. Like the British Museum, they sat with the map of the place and picked exhibits that interested them.

"This is boring," Vic whined after they'd examined impressionist paintings.

They moved on to a display of medieval weaponry, which pleased him more, then to the Egyptian exhibits, which had some interesting depictions of life in ancient Egypt.

"Okay, let's find a snack," Simon said. "I think a couple of hours is enough for Vic."

It was enough for Iris, too. She must be getting old. She'd be seventy next birthday. Was that old in this day and age?

They spent the rest of their time in Paris on short visits to various historical sights, doing some shopping for souvenirs—mostly clothes for Iris and Mandy—and enjoying memorable meals before packing for home. Best of all, Iris met no one she knew and no one who wanted anything from her.

Iris slept on the plane, feeling worn out. She woke up for lunch and watched a movie before sleeping again. Customs was a real pain in Dulles. After waiting in a long line, Simon was interrogated as if he were a smuggler. They opened both his and Mandy's bags and rummaged through them without any care. Mandy had to repack them at another table. They didn't bother Iris. Maybe old ladies don't ever smuggle.

CHAPTER 22

They finally got home. They were all tired and jet-lagged, but Vic insisted on going to retrieve Wanda from the kennel. He told Iris later that his parents allowed her to sleep on his bed that night instead of beside it, as usual. He started to bring the dog to Iris's house from time to time. She'd never had much to do with pets, but started to grow fond of the goofy creature. She liked the feeling of a furry body draped over her feet while she watched TV.

23

Iris stared at Dr. Coren, unable to react in any way. She wanted to scream, pound his desk, pound him, in fact. She couldn't even cry. She'd seen death, caused death, but never imagined it for herself.

"I understand this is a terrible shock, Mrs. Hall, but there is still hope. Chemotherapy is never pleasant, but can be very effective. It all depends on your outlook."

"Outlook?" she managed to croak.

"Yes. And your religious views, naturally."

"I am not a believer."

"Pity. Faith brings great comfort to many. There is always the question of quality of life. First, there would be surgery, of course. A lobe of your right lung must be removed. We will check as best as we are able that it has not migrated anywhere else, especially to the left lung. There is no guarantee that chemo will destroy any remaining cells, but there is hope. The chemo will go on for some time and will make you feel very unwell, maybe for up to a year. And there are side effects, as you probably know."

"I'll lose my hair."

"Probably. But it usually comes back. I can refer you to an outfit that makes wigs from your own hair. I would recommend that you have your hair cut very short just before you start therapy so that they can make you a realistic wig to wear until it's all over. Nausea and weakness are usually the main problem."

"You sound as if I will opt for surgery and chemotherapy. Maybe I'll decide to do nothing."

"You strike me as a strong woman who will do whatever it takes to survive."

"I'll call the office in the morning to let you know my decision."

"Very well, Mrs. Hall. I'm sorry I didn't have better news for you."

She got into her car without knowing quite how she got there and rested her head on the steering wheel. She wasn't ready to go home yet. Mandy would be looking out for her return. She and Simon knew she was going to the doctor to get the results of scans and other tests. They had been so anxious when she told them about it. At Mandy's urging, she'd gone to her G.P. to complain about breathlessness and a cough that didn't clear up. He'd ordered an x-ray, and that had led to a referral to Dr. Coren and a slew of tests and scans.

She'd been very taken with the handsome Dr. Coren, who she'd looked up on the internet. He was only five years younger than her, handsome and with the nicest smile—a smile that could make her go weak at the knees. She'd thought about him a lot, but not enough to focus on why she was seeing him. It couldn't happen to her, she'd assumed. What a sap.

She couldn't face Simon and Mandy's anxiety and pressure regarding her decision. Water. She needed to be near water, to hear lapping waves, watch it rolling on timelessly, each drop its own world. She started the engine and made her way down to the boardwalk. It was a breezy March day. After a week of rain, the water should be running fast and loud.

She parked her car and walked to the benches along the railing. Even this short walk left her breathless. She'd managed fine on their summer adventures in Europe. Yes, she'd coughed a bit and got tired easily, but hadn't thought it serious. She'd ignored the symptoms, vowing to increase her exercise to improve her stamina. But she hadn't, because walking longer than usual made her feel worse. By winter's end, she realized that all was not well. She was so tired, for a start. She never felt tired unless deprived of sleep. She'd still resisted Mandy and Simon's entreaties to go to the doctor. Finally, Vic had persuaded her.

Simon and Mandy invited her to dinner. They all ate together, and a little later Vic was reminded that it was bedtime. Before he went upstairs, he kissed Iris and said, "Gran, you are not well. You're no fun anymore. You cough all the time and you're always tired." He looked teary. "Gran, you have to do something to get better. For me."

As soon as Vic went to bed, they urged her again to see her doctor. They'd worn her down, and dismantled her assertions that all she needed was this or that. She knew in her heart there was trouble, knew she was in denial. And she'd probably left it too late. But she still hadn't expected this bombshell. Death was something she watched happening to other people.

CHAPTER 23

She got out of the car and went to lean on the railing, inhaling the scent of the river and absorbing its relentless current. Was she ready to leave Simon and Vic without a fight? What might be waiting for her beyond? She had always thought that death was the end. A reunification with the soil. Decay and oblivion. Could there be an afterlife, a divine being? She hoped not, because she would likely be severely punished if the Christians had it right. She wasn't sure about other faiths, but she assumed they believed much the same things. Such hypocrites. They all killed each other without a qualm if they felt their god demanded it. What kind of god would demand such misery?

She could end it right now by clambering over the railing. How would that feel, cold to the bone and fighting to breathe with lungs full of water? No, of course not. She'd do it with pills like Kate. Just a nice deep sleep that started with dreams and went on forever. But how would that affect Simon and Vic? She was pretty sure that Simon had realized her true identity by now, but she would leave a letter to be read after her death just to make sure. She hoped he wouldn't think this was divine justice. She wanted him to love her, miss her, grieve for her.

And her sister Daisy? What about her? She felt nothing for Daisy, and Daisy must hate her. Surprisingly, she hadn't managed to track her down to Charlotte. She wondered if she and Simon had ever been in touch. Maybe after the trial, but he would have mentioned it if he'd heard from her recently. Or would he? And what if he'd told her about this neighbor who was like a grandmother to Vic? No, she would have put in an appearance by now. And why be concerned about Daisy at this point?

Because she didn't want to die in prison.

Their mother must be long dead. She'd never thought to check. Iris supposed there must be ways to search city records for death notices. It really wouldn't make any difference to anything, though. She'd despised that alcohol-ridden, foul-mouthed slag, old before her time.

Iris shook her head, as if to clear the memory banks. Never mind the past. The future was what mattered—if she had one. She felt a little weak at the knees and returned to the bench. Simon and Vic. Dear little Vic and darling Simon. She supposed she loved the other two, but she'd only seen them at Christmas for years. She did exchange emails with Justin, who had guessed her identity almost right away that Christmas years ago when Vic was still a baby. He'd let her know he understood and loved her, anyway. Why hadn't she made the effort to visit him more often? He'd have welcomed it. She'd been so wrapped up in her lovely little life, she'd thought of it as something she could put off. Well, now she couldn't. She'd visit Justin before she had surgery.

Back to the question at hand. Take extreme measures to overcome, or go gracefully? Fight or succumb? She thought of what Dr. Coren had said. She was a strong woman and a survivor. He'd read her well. He was a man about her age and very good looking, with a deep, soothing voice. Tall, he had the body of a man who still worked out regularly. That's what she would do after she got well. Work out. Get toned. Maybe some nice man would find her attractive again. Someone just like Dr. Coren.

She stood up suddenly. She would fight. Nothing to do with finding a man. All to do with her loved ones.

She sat in her kitchen drinking hot chocolate. She'd become a little chilled down at the river. She felt the cold more these days, too. Maybe that wasn't the cancer, but part of getting old. She'd put out a plate of cookies and had extra hot chocolate in the pan because she knew Mandy would come by very soon.

The knock on the door sounded just as she'd drained her cup.

"Come in."

"Hi, Mandy, how are you? Let me pour you a cup of hot chocolate. I'll warm it a little in the microwave."

"More to the point, how are you?"

Mandy looked at her sideways, clearly afraid to hear the worst.

"Well, it is lung cancer, stage 3."

"Oh, no, I'm so sorry." Tears welled in Mandy's eyes.

"Me, too. I've decided to fight it. Surgery, then chemo. It's going to be a bad year. But I hope it will be worth it in the end."

"You'll stay with us, of course," Mandy said. "You can't possibly go it alone. Stairs, meals, doctor's appointments, and so on."

"That's very kind. But that's going to be too much for you."

"Simon and I won't hear of anything else."

"You are such a blessing in my life. You and Simon and Vic. You know what? I can hire someone to come and help out in the early days. That should save you going up and downstairs to wait on an old woman."

"We shall see when the time comes. When will you have the surgery?"

"I don't know. I told Dr. Coren I'd let him know my decision in the morning. I'd prefer to do it after Easter, but I suspect he will want to do it as soon as possible. I already left it too long."

"Well, there'll be other Easters. Focus on looking forward to Christmas. You'll join us for dinner tonight?"

"No, Mandy dear. I need to be alone tonight."

"I understand. I just didn't know whether you'd prefer not to be alone. But that's you, isn't it? Independent and working things through on your own."

"You know me well! Don't tell Vic. We can just tell him I have to have an operation when I get a date."

Mandy finished her chocolate and left, pecking Iris on the cheek as she put on her jacket. She hesitated by the door, then returned to envelop Iris in a bear hug. Her tears looked as if they might spill over at any moment. Iris knew hers would and gently pushed Mandy away.

"I'll be okay."

24

Iris drove by Dr. Coren's house several times before she saw him exit the front door to go to his office. She knew his first appointment was usually at eight, because she'd usually been offered that slot when she made an appointment. She never went that early. She liked a calm, quiet morning with her tea and paper. She'd just had her last appointment before surgery. Tomorrow she'd be at the hospital for the necessary pre-op tests.

She'd waited by the office the afternoon of one of her appointments and followed his car home. She wanted to know everything about this attractive man: what kind of house he lived in, what he did in his spare time, what his wife looked like, and so on. He had a picture of his wife and three children on his desk, but it had obviously been taken years ago before his hair turned white and those cute creases at the corners of his eyes formed. At seven-thirty, she parked across the street from his front gate. She could always duck when he came out. Goodness knows her car was nondescript enough to avoid attention. Fortunately, a tall hedge to her right obscured anyone in the house opposite his from noticing her.

His home was one of several large white Georgian houses—almost a mansion. Cancer paid well, it seemed. She didn't begrudge it. He'd trained for years, and saved lives, comforting his patients in the most wonderful way.

The front door opened. She took off her seat belt and bent down so that only the top of her head showed above the window. What on earth was going on? He rushed out to the Mercedes parked in the driveway, closely followed by an overweight woman in a pink terry bathrobe, who shouted and gesticulated. She looked a lot younger than him. Iris opened the window so that she could listen.

"You promised me that vacation months ago! Your word is worthless, do you hear? Worthless!"

"I have patients who might die if I postpone their treatment. Why can you never think about anyone but yourself? Go to Bermuda on your own if you're so set on it." The good doctor slammed his car door and screeched out of the front gate, fortunately open.

"I will, and take my lover with me, you son of a bitch!" With that parting shot, Mrs. Coren slammed the front door behind her, causing the ivy around it to tremble like an aspen.

Iris's anger flamed. That would be her surgery the woman wanted postponed for a cruise in the Caribbean. Her recovery that she wanted her husband to get some junior doctor to supervise. Iris clenched her fists. The woman must be taught a lesson. Her pre-op appointment would be early tomorrow. Maybe she should come straight from the hospital. But would a serious incident affect the doctor's mood?

His dexterity? Probably not. He looked as if he'd had enough of this harridan.

Iris felt grumpy when she got up at six the following morning. It was too early to have to get herself together. She had her shower, got dressed, and had her tea and toast before getting her kit together. She'd rather have acted in the dark, but the woman had to be alone, and Dr. Coren had to be at the office with an impeccable alibi. She gathered the dark brown wig she had used a couple of times before, gloves, big black-rimmed glasses, and a good sharp knife. Kate had left a few good knives behind, but not a set that could be identified as missing one, so she had her pick. Her own knives would sit undisturbed in their holder. The old frisson she'd missed recently ran through her.

The hospital tests took most of the morning. There were questions about her post-surgery arrangements, and she received several recommendations for visiting aides. She'd call those tomorrow. The operation would take place in less than a week and she'd be in the hospital for at least three days, so that should be enough time to arrange something. She didn't want to cause Mandy too much work. She needed yet another x-ray, and the blood tests were done with only one draw. She was out by eleven-thirty.

She drove to a quiet spot near some woods and donned her wig and glasses. Gloves, too, as the weather was cool enough that they would not look out of place. She wore one of Kate's old jackets—one she always kept in the car for some reason. It was a little big, but that would make her description more muddled, so that was fine. An application of blue eyeshadow and bright red lipstick completed the disguise. Finally, she practiced her little speech with a generic Southern accent. Once satisfied with her appearance, she drove to a quiet street a few blocks away from the Coren house. She sucked a cough lozenge as she walked.

She strolled to the house as if she hadn't a care in the world, although there was no one around that she could see. She rang the doorbell. No response. Damn, was the woman out? She rang it again. Finally, she heard footsteps approach. Mrs. Coren flung open the door. Iris smelled the gin on her breath, not to mention sweat. She was still in her bathrobe—the same pink one Iris had seen the other day—and her hair was disheveled. Iris felt an overwhelming pity for Dr. Coren. He deserved better.

"Waddya want?"

"Why, good morning, Mrs. Coren? Your husband asked our firm to drop by to discuss some travel arrangements with you."

"Travel arrangements? What the hell yer talking about?"

"He mentioned a recent disappointment regarding a cruise? He wants us to arrange something nice for you."

"Oh! Well, I s'pose you'd better come in. Excuse the mess. I've been busy."

Iris followed the drunk as she wove her way into the kitchen, where the smell of old fried food and crusted plates in the sink nauseated her. She looked around. Plenty of knives in the holder here. Why use hers? How could she grab one without arousing suspicion, though?

Mrs. Coren settled herself on a bar stool at the counter, a half-empty glass in front of her.

"Mrs. Coren, can I make you some coffee?"

"No, why? Yer think I need it?" Her tone had turned back to aggressive.

"Of course not. It's just that time in the morning, is all."

"Just get on with it. No, hold on, I need to make a quick visit to the little room, know what I mean? Then we can get down to biznis. I got things to do."

What a stroke of luck. As soon as the horrid woman was behind the closed door of the hallway washroom, Iris darted to the knife holder and selected a small, sharp, paring knife.

After a long five minutes, the woman returned and tried to mount her perch again, only to succeed in knocking it over.

"Damned stools," she said, kicking it with a slippered foot that made her double up in pain.

Iris darted over as if to help her up and held her in a headlock. "This is for abusing your husband, you selfish bitch. You don't deserve such a fine man. And you certainly don't deserve any cruise. She cut the woman twice across each cheek as she screeched in pain and terror. I won't kill you this time. And your lover won't fancy you anymore. Live and learn."

Iris shoved the woman so hard that her head bounced on the tile floor. She curled into a fetal position, crying and screaming for mercy as blood flowed onto her pink robe and across the pale tiles. Iris picked up her official-looking black tote and got out, her heart racing as she forced herself to keep to a steady pace. She sighed in relief as she got into her car and started it. She drove to the other end of the city while pulling off her wig and glasses until she came to a fast food place. The parking lot was almost empty, and she found a spot around the side facing a blank wall. She pulled down the mirror and removed the eye shadow and lipstick with an oily pad, drying off with a tissue. She shrugged off the jacket. Her black tee wouldn't be warm enough, but it wouldn't be for long. The jacket would go out of the window on the road back home, as would the gloves. She got out of the car. The wig, tied securely in a plastic bag, went into the restaurant dumpster. On her way around to the front, she ground the glasses under her heel. She went in and got herself an iced tea and left again. She started to sing on the way home before coughing so badly she had to pull over. Funny how she hadn't coughed in the Coren home. That would have been a giveaway. When her cough had calmed enough so that she could drive on, she turned onto a road with woods and heavy undergrowth right up to the shoulder and hardly any traffic. She pulled over, opened the passenger side window, and tossed out the gloves. She drove a little farther and did the same thing with the jacket. She suddenly felt as if she'd thrown Kate out along with it. But still, it had to be. Mission accomplished.

She tuned into the local news at six-thirty, hoping to hear something. Sure enough, it was the first item. The wife of a distinguished local oncologist ... crazed woman ... somehow knew about a trip Mrs. Coren wanted to take ... deep cuts on her face that required the attention of a plastic surgeon ... a fake southern accent. Huh? Iris thought she'd done it rather well. What would that stupid woman know about accents, or anything else for that matter? The anchor finished with a description that was pretty close to accurate—that of a woman with dark brown hair who wore heavy make-up and glasses, about five-five, and stocky. Ah, the jacket worked. Hopefully, it was helping some homeless person keep warm right now.

Simon drove Iris to the hospital very early two days after the incident. Iris had been expecting a postponement, as Dr. Coren doubtless missed a day. But no, all was on schedule.

CHAPTER 24

She got shown into pre-op, undressed, and donned the dreaded gown, front open, although clutched closed for the moment. Simon was waiting by her gurney, hands clenched together. The dear boy was worried. Iris was a little worried, too. Dr. Coren had promised her good pain control, and she hoped it would be so.

"Don't worry, Simon, I'll be all right."

A nurse came in to take her vitals before leaving to attend the next patient.

Simon leaned close as soon as she was out of earshot. "I know, I know, I'm sure you will be. It's just that..." He seemed lost for words.

"Do you want to tell me something?"

"I know, you know. I saw the likeness early on, but told myself it was wishful thinking."

Iris sighed. "I rather thought you did. I didn't want to burden you with it."

"I couldn't let on to anyone that I know. I'm a lawyer. I have a duty to the court."

"I understand that. Justin picked it up at once from my voice. Would you believe? He's a musician, so he tuned into me, as it were."

Simon looked alarmed. "Justin knows? Will he keep quiet?"

"Yes, he will. He said he understands completely. He doesn't want me to go to prison."

"It's been a gift to have you back. And you're such a wonderful Gran. Vic loves you a lot. We all do. I can't bear to lose you again."

"Dr. Coren is a marvelous doctor. I'll get on fine. Just you see."

They both had tears in their eyes when Dr. Coren appeared.

"Good morning, Mrs. Hall. Just checking with you. Let me have a listen to that chest of yours. You can stay, sir."

"I'm sorry about your wife's assault. How is she doing?" Iris asked.

"She's healing well, although traumatized, as I am sure you can understand."

"Of course. Is she afraid to be at home alone now?"

"Yes. She's gone to Raleigh to stay with her sister for a while. Best thing for her."

And you.

The doctor was soon done with his exam.

"Has the anesthetist met with you yet?"

"No, she hasn't."

"I'm sure she'll be around soon. See you in a little bit!"

"Thank you, Dr. Coren." She gave him her widest smile.

"He seemed very nice," Simon said. "What was all that about his wife?"

"Didn't you see it on the news? Some woman attacked her at home and cut her face."

"Good god. Do they know who?"

"I don't think so. I didn't hear anything more."

"Where did you go after you escaped?"

"Toronto. But that is a very long story, and it needs a couple of hours. Another day, perhaps. Just know that I came to a happier place with good people who loved me."

"Don't they wonder where you are?"

"They passed away. Two old ladies who were very good to me and let me feel again. I took care of them until the end."

The anesthetist came by, a thin woman with slate gray hair pulled back into a short ponytail. She asked a couple of questions and listened to Iris's chest, before an abrupt "Goodbye" and departure.

"I doubt she's cracked a smile since puberty," Iris remarked.

"No. And why on earth are they listening to your chest? What else do they expect to hear?"

"Damned if I know. Probably one of those things they have to do to cover all the bases if they get sued."

"Anyway, I just didn't want to let this moment go by without telling you how I feel. You will always be my mother."

Iris had become more used to acknowledging her emotions since she moved in with Hilda in Toronto, and later moved to a condo with Hilda and her best friend Magaly when the old ladies became frail. They had loved her without probing her background, and she had finally been able to open up and love them back. After they died and she moved to Charlotte, she'd received the best gift possible in becoming close to Simon and his family.

She felt like breaking down and weeping for hours, as if the tears would wash away the tragedy and evil of her past and leave the present sparkling clean. But this was not the time. She had to be strong for her dear boy. She took a deep breath and composed herself. And she had the future to think of. A future that may be shorter than she would like. *Don't think about that.*

"Don't worry, Simon. I always come through, somehow. I guess you read the journal I left behind?"

"I did. I'm glad I read it. I understand everything. I let the others read it, too. Justin felt as I did, Lucy not so much."

"I don't blame her. She always stands by her principles."

Simon smiled. "Yes, no gray areas allowed in Lucy's world."

The porter came to take her to the ER. "Time to go, Mrs. Hall."

Simon kissed her cheek. "See you on the other side."

25

The other side sucked. When Iris came around, she was aware of a burning, prickling sensation in her chest. She raised her hand to scratch it, only to have it grabbed by someone stronger than she.

"No irritating your wound, Iris. I'll give you some morphine in your drip. It'll feel better soon."

Better was a relative concept. Over the next couple of days, Iris was always aware of the wound, even when it wasn't hurting. But it often did hurt. The dressing was changed daily, and it felt a little calmer for a while afterward, but she still knew it was there at all times, especially when she moved. Sleeping on her side was out of the question.

Dr. Coren visited every morning and inspected the incision before the nurse changed the dressing. He looked so much happier now that his wife had left and often chatted for a couple of minutes. The third morning, he assured Iris that while he was sure that everything of concern had been removed and she was set for a full recovery, chemo was still a necessity, just to make sure.

"I know what a strong woman you are, Iris. You must do whatever it takes to stay well."

"Yes, Dr. Coren, I will. And how is your poor wife?"

"Her face has healed without too much scarring. She's afraid of coming home, so is still at her sister's. Probably the best thing for her. The police are completely baffled."

"Yes, it's most probably her best option." *For sure.*

"Now, what about you when you get out of here?"

"I'm going to stay with my neighbors. I'm very close to them and their son. They have always been very kind to me. I've arranged for an aide to come help for the first week, though. I don't want Mandy running up and down stairs all the time. She has knee issues."

"That's wonderful. I can see why they're so fond of you."

"Nice of you to say so."

The morning Iris was discharged, she sat in a wheelchair by her bed, her packed bag next to her as she waited for Simon. When the door opened, not only Simon and Mandy entered, but Justin, too.

"Justin, what a surprise! I didn't expect to see you."

"I've actually left Boston, as of last Saturday. I'm going to be teaching part-time at Queens University in September and also playing for the Charlotte Symphony. I thought you might need a hand."

A nurse came in. "Let's get you down to the entrance."

Iris knew it was silly, but she felt self-conscious being coddled like that, even though her forays to the bathroom had shown that a long walk was not in the cards for her yet.

Simon went to retrieve his car, and the nurse insisted on staying until she was safely installed in the front seat.

Folding herself in order to slide in was very uncomfortable. She couldn't help letting a little moan escape.

"Take one of those painkillers as soon as you get home, Iris," the nurse said. "Eat a little something first, of course."

"Yes, I certainly will. Thank you for all you and your colleagues have done for me. You've all been very kind." They had, too.

When they got home, getting out of the car was equally painful. Justin took one arm and Mandy the other as they walked slowly into the house. Iris kept her elbows close to her sides to avoid any pulling. Her incision was still very tender.

"Would you like to go upstairs and take a nap?" Mandy asked.

"I'd rather sit and look out at the garden for a while. I'm sick of looking at white walls. Are the bird feeders active?"

"Yes, the birds are nesting, and we seem to top up the feeders nearly every day," Mandy said. "Justin, would you mind moving that recliner to the French doors?"

Justin rushed to pull it into place, which took him a while, as it was obviously heavy. "I hope I didn't scratch your floor," he said, panting.

"No, it's fine."

Iris sank into it and Mandy pulled the lever to raise the leg rest. "Do you need a cushion at your back?"

"No, it's very comfortable. Good lower back support. Thank you both."

"I'm going to get you a snack now. A slice of chocolate cake? And what to drink?"

"Chocolate cake sounds perfect. The only sweet thing I've had lately is artificially flavored Jello. Yuck! And I'd love a cup of coffee."

"Coming right up."

CHAPTER 25

Iris rested her head back. Her chest hurt and she felt out of breath. Only to be expected, they told her. It would take a while, but she had her life. And soon, all kinds of new life would come into the garden out there. Chicks and leaves, birds and bees. She watched a blue jay chase off a couple of sparrows before he tucked into the pile—probably scarfing all the sunflower seeds. A woodpecker hung on the suet cake, his red head glinting in the sunlight that had finally poked through the rain clouds.

A wet nose nudged her hand. She looked down at Wanda and stroked her head. "Hello, girl." Wanda grunted. Iris rested her hand on the noble head. Such a beautiful animal.

"Are you all right?" Simon asked.

"Yes, I'm fine. Just a little tired. It's the pills. But I'm enjoying the bird feeders. I must get a couple at home."

"Yes, Justin or I can see to that for you. And the spring bulbs will flower soon. Is Wanda bothering you?"

"Oh, no. I find her quite a comfort. I was sorry to miss Easter, but Dr. Coren didn't want to wait."

"I know. Just as well to get it over with. I have to go to the office, but I wanted to run something by you first. Justin is staying here while he gets himself settled. He'll be busier when the fall semester starts, but we wondered if you'd mind him moving in with you once you get back home. He would take you to chemo and doctor's appointments and generally help with things."

"That sounds wonderful," Iris said, excited. "Are you sure he doesn't mind? It won't be too tiresome and boring?"

Justin moved next to her. "It would be my absolute pleasure," he said, taking her hand.

"My two beautiful boys," Iris whispered, her eyes wet.

"Here we are," Mandy said. "Simon, can you grab that end table?"

Simon left, Mandy went upstairs, and Justin sat down next to her again.

"You're sure you don't mind?" he asked.

"Mind! I'm thrilled. It's you I'm worried about. Won't it be an awful drag?"

"Not at all. I'd treasure the time. We've lost a lot of time."

"Yes, we have. How I regret everything."

"Regret is a good thing, as long as you put it aside. Look forward. We were all devastated when everything blew up, but I've put it behind me and it's going to stay where it belongs—in the past."

"You have a very healthy attitude, Justin. I admire that."

He squeezed her hand. "Your coffee is getting cold. I'm going to practice upstairs for a little while. I'll be down to help you when you're ready to go up."

What had she done to deserve these boys? They had turned out to be well-balanced and happy, despite the disgrace she'd brought upon them. She sipped her coffee, reveling in its fragrance. Being deprived of the good things in life for a while made them all the finer when you got them back. Now for that cake. And the pill. The cello started its melody. "The Dying Swan."

The couple of weeks Iris spent at Simon and Mandy's were peaceful when she wasn't hurting. It was a good thing she had company, because her concentration was shot. She dozed off before she got through anything—a chapter of her book, the critical finale of TV shows, a paragraph of the romance novel she wanted to write now that she had all this time on her hands—and felt like a zombie most of the time. She couldn't help turning on her side in her sleep, only to wake up in pain. There were digestive issues, too, because of the opiates, necessitating more medication. It was rough, but could only get better. Although chemo would start in a few weeks. She wanted to be home for that. She missed home. She loved seeing Vic every day, though. He always cheered her up with his chatter about school and other things important to him. Wanda slept beside her bed instead of Vic's.

"I'm sorry. I'm sure you miss her," she told Vic the first morning.

"Oh, no, she knows you need her. She'll let us know if anything is wrong."

Justin did some food shopping the day before Iris moved home. As long as she had good coffee and something sweet to go with it, she didn't much care what he bought. He'd bragged a little about his culinary skills, so she hoped she wouldn't hurt his feelings with her lack of appetite. He'd made a set of keys for himself.

"Use my car whenever you need to," she told him. "And you must let me pay for the food."

He'd refused to take money from her, but she'd correct that situation later. With a little support from Mandy, she managed to walk home, which pleased her. Wanda followed close behind. Her daffodil shoots looked plump, and shimmering green halos of nascent leaves in the treetops promised another glorious spring. Her spirits rose.

When they got inside, Iris found an armchair and a side table by the French doors leading to the terrace, together with a new footstool. Mandy went over to the coffeemaker.

"Justin told me he'd gotten the coffeemaker ready to go. All I have to do is push the on switch. And there's a caramel apple cake right next to it."

"Everyone is so kind. I can't get over it."

"You deserve it."

"I start chemo in a couple of months. Dr. Coren said the surgery had gone so well that I could get a little more of a grace period. I'd better make the most of it."

"It won't be easy, but just so long as you beat this thing,"

"Yes. Let's dig into this cake."

Iris managed a few chapters of her romance novel, this time about a young woman married to a violent man who falls for her colleague at the office, during her respite. She didn't feel much enthusiasm for the project. Maybe that part of her life was best left in Canada. She still got some royalties from her previous publications via a post office box, but it didn't amount to much. She'd never taken up painting as Vic had suggested in Switzerland. Maybe she'd give up on writing. Make a fresh start with painting. She'd enjoyed doodling at school, and the art teacher had been the only teacher to take an interest in her. He was a weedy young man who always wore corduroys and plaid shirts and encouraged her to work on her paintings. She'd let it all go, though, as she left school as soon as she was old enough. She regretted that. So, when the chemo nightmare was over, she would find a class, buy the stuff she needed, and go for it. No matter if she turned out to be any good or not. She craved the joy of it.

The first day of chemo arrived. Justin drove her to the appointment after breakfast. The nurse told him to come back at four.

"Four! It takes that long?"

"There will be several infusions, and you'll get a short break in between."

"Will there be lunch?"

"If you feel like eating." *Sounds like fun.* "This is your chair." *Great, just like my dentist's chair.*

"Good luck," Justin said, kissing her cheek.

A nurse set up her portal, which was relatively painless, if you didn't count the numbing injections. A bucket stood on the table next to her. "If you should feel like vomiting," said the angel of mercy.

The first round wasn't too bad at first. When the nurse asked her if she'd like a cracker and some water, she said yes, and regretted it a few minutes later. The heaves went on relentlessly. Finally, Iris rested her head back and closed her eyes. She heard the nurse remove the bucket. And another being set down.

"I'm going to start the next infusion," Nurse Ratchet told her.

Iris didn't bother to open her eyes. Gradually, her head started to spin faster and faster. When she opened her eyes, the swirling fluorescent lights turned green, then dark gray, before lightening to glowing magenta. She reached for the bucket, which wasn't there anymore. She vaguely realized that the nurse was already holding it under her chin.

The day progressed from worse to worst. By the time she was aware that Justin stood beside her chair, she barely had the strength to hold up her head. It felt too heavy. The last time two nurses hustled her to the bathroom, her legs felt like noodles.

"She's very weak," the nurse said. "We will use a wheelchair. Why don't you bring the car to the entrance?"

Getting into the wheelchair took all Iris's willpower. The nurse put two paper bags on her lap. "Just in case," she said, prophetically.

Poor Justin, he turned pretty green himself before long. Iris felt too deathly ill to be sorry for more than a moment. "Justin, there's a dumpster by the side of that pizza place on Fairclough. Let's dump the bag there."

Big mistake. As soon as Iris caught a whiff of pizza, her stomach started to reject—what? Itself?—once more.

"Sorry, I'll close the windows, gotta go..." Justin rushed to some bushes behind the restaurant and emptied his own stomach.

He'll regret this. He won't be able to go through with it.

"I'm so sorry. I couldn't help it."

"I know. I'm so sorry to put you through this."

"Oh, no. We'll get through it. Together."

Iris started to cry. She had no reserves to call upon to pull herself together. Total depletion.

When they got home, Justin almost dragged her through the door and upstairs. Iris didn't have the energy to undress, let alone take a shower.

"There's a bottle of water on your bedside table. I'll get a bowl as well, just in case. Call if you need anything."

"Do you have anything for your dinner?"

"I'll find something if I get hungry. Right now, I think I'll take a nap. Don't worry about me."

Justin brought a bucket from the utility room. "It's all I could find. Sorry."

"That'll do fine. Thank you. I'm sorry."

"Nothing to feel sorry for. You're the one suffering."

She slept fitfully, her incision and portal both itching like crazy. She felt too drained to find the soothing ointment Dr. Coren prescribed. When she woke, it was to the sound of rain pounding at the window. She peered at her watch. Nine. She had been in bed for hours. She sat up slowly, feeling her head swim. But her stomach behaved itself. Her mouth was as dry as a desert. She grabbed the water, reminding herself to take it easy. No gulping.

The door opened slowly and Justin's head peeked in. "Oh, you're up. You slept a long time. I was getting worried."

"I guess I needed it. I'm a bit lightheaded, but I really must take a shower."

"Tell you what, why don't you eat first? The nurse suggested dry toast and jam. No butter. And no coffee for now, because the acids might upset your stomach."

"Yes, I think I could manage some toast. Believe it or not, I don't even fancy coffee. Water will do fine."

"Why don't you get back into bed? I'll be back soon."

The toast made her feel better. She drank more water, then made her way to the shower.

She gradually felt better as the week progressed, but all too soon, it was time for the second round.

After the second session, she found a few locks of hair on her pillow. They looked obscene, somehow. She threw them into her wastebasket, leaned over it, and plucked out a few more wads. Time to start using the caps she'd bought in preparation. Her spirits ebbed low. She felt naked and ugly with half her hair missing.

The misery went on for several weeks. Iris was back to feeling like a zombie again, but from fatigue and nausea that depleted her beyond recognition. She didn't even care about her bald head anymore. Simon, Mandy, and Vic visited, but she could barely keep up a conversation. It was just too tiring. Simon picked her up twice from her session when Justin had a rehearsal, and looked as appalled as Justin had been that first time. Justin seemed to have become used to it. Iris just let it all wash over her. What else could she do? She looked old now. On the rare occasions she faced herself in the mirror, deep despair gripped her as she searched the sunken eyes, the hollow cheeks, and the etched traces of dry skin that covered her face for signs of her former self. Her head looked like a plucked chicken. She not only looked old, she was old. Soon her body would be spent, only fit to be buried deep.

Wanda spent many nights sleeping by her bedside. The dog wouldn't know or care how she looked. Wanda just stayed, knowing that her presence was a comfort in itself. Iris loved the silky feel of fur and the soft brown eyes. Wanda was pure love. No complications.

Finally, she was two weeks past her last chemo. Her appetite started to improve. Mandy drove her to the park where she and Vic could feed the ducks. He seemed to enjoy it as much as he had as a very little boy. Ten now, he was still a child, but had grown up so much.

Her visits with Dr. Coren were enjoyable. It seemed his wife had not returned. She allowed herself the luxury of fantasizing about a relationship, even though she knew it could never be, partly because of professional standards, but mostly because she looked like a scarecrow. One with hideous scars.

26

The late August sun shimmered as hot as ever. Soon it would be fall and then the cold of winter. Too much of the year had passed her by. But she was alive. Justin was still with her. She hoped he would stay. What would she do with herself now? Painting. She had thought about trying that.

"Justin, can I ask you to do something for me?"

"Of course."

"Before all this chemo started, I thought about taking art classes. Could you go online and find somewhere nearby where I could take some?"

"That sounds like a great idea. Which medium do you have in mind?"

"Medium? I don't know."

"Well, there's watercolor, which is quite difficult, I'm told. Acrylic, which is easier, and doesn't smell and is much easier to clean up than oils. There are colored pencils, some of which can have water added to them to make them like watercolor. Then there's charcoal and pencil for drawing."

"How on earth do you know all that?"

"I went out with an art teacher for a while. It didn't work out."

"I'm sorry. Didn't you ever find Miss Right?"

"No. I'm afraid I can be a bit of a soft touch and give in too much. There's a violinist at the symphony I like, though. I might ask her out."

"Go for it! Anyway, make up my mind. Which medium?"

"I think acrylic would be a good place to start. As you take more lessons, you can decide to branch out into something different if you want to."

Iris started her art class a week later. It was an afternoon class within walking distance. She used her overnight bag with wheels to carry her supplies. She wasn't up to carrying much yet. Painting exhilarated her, although drawing proved to be a challenge. She briefly considered abstract painting, but then she'd be stuck with pictures she wouldn't want on her walls. She'd learn. A new start. And after a few weeks, her drawings seemed to look like the real thing. That barn was only lopsided in the way many old barns are, but the hay bales didn't look quite right. By the time Thanksgiving rolled around, a painting of Simon and Mandy's house really looked like their house. They were thrilled. Would she paint her house? Maybe wait for the spring flowers to come out. Was it possible she had some talent? Her instructor seemed pleased with her progress. Casey, a cheerful, plump young woman always festooned in paint and smiles, applauded her students' every effort. Maybe she was just being nice.

Iris's hair started to grow back, another uplifting event. White and curly, as long as she had a good cut, it would be easy to take care of. Spending time messing around with her hair no longer appealed. Once it grew another inch, it might even prove flattering. Her incision didn't itch so much anymore and the ointment soon soothed it. Her darling Victor, her sweet attentive sons, a loving daughter-in-law, a loving dog from time to time, art, a head of curly hair, a glass of Vouvray every now and then—life was worth living. Life was good. She hoped never to take another.

Time seemed to pass at breakneck speed. The weekend after Thanksgiving, she realized with a jolt that was almost time for Christmas. Mandy took her shopping for the boys. Simon and Justin were easy—beautiful matching shirts and cashmere sweaters were all next to each other in the first men's department they set foot in. Victor had made his wishes known early on, so that was easy, too. Some sort of electronic device that Iris didn't quite understand. What did it actually do? Well, it didn't much matter just so long as it made him happy.

They had lunch in the mall, then Mandy asked if Iris minded sitting on her own for a while as she had something personal to take care of. Iris didn't mind at all, since it was obvious that Mandy wanted to buy Iris a gift. In fact, as Iris wanted to buy Mandy a gift, it suited her very well. She'd spotted just the thing on the way out of the department store where they'd shopped in the men's department.

Iris loved the feel of cashmere and knew Mandy liked it, too. Most people did, reveling in its soft luxury. She'd seen a matching pale blue sweater and hip-length jacket that would suit Mandy's fair coloring and petite build perfectly. It cost a small fortune, but Mandy was worth it. She'd always been kind, and her help during Iris's surgery and treatments had been wonderful. Iris felt an uptick of excitement as she anticipated the joy of gift opening on Christmas morning.

Iris got back to the bench a couple of minutes before Mandy returned with an extra shopping bag.

"I hope I wasn't too long," Mandy said.

"Not at all. I've been people-watching," Iris replied.

"By the way, did Simon tell you that his aunt called out of the blue? He hasn't seen her in so long, he can't even remember what she looks like."

Iris felt dizzy. "What aunt?" she gasped.

"Iris, are you all right? Has this been too much for you?"

"No, no, I'm fine, don't worry. I get the occasional dizzy spell. It's nothing. Which aunt?"

"Daisy, I think it was. He said she lives in Ohio now. She mentioned paying him a visit."

"When?"

"He was a bit funny about her, actually. He told her we were thinking of moving and he'd let her know our new address when we were settled. Said he didn't like her—rather a rough type, he said."

"Well, I'm sure he knows best."

"It is rather odd, though."

So Daisy had tracked down Simon. At least he hadn't chatted much, so he wouldn't have mentioned this neighbor who was like Victor's grandmother.

Iris went upstairs to her room after they got home. She'd wrap the gifts tomorrow. Hopefully, her nap would be dreamless. It wasn't. Daisy appeared in her bedroom doorway, much larger than life—she had to duck to enter. She moved to the bedside as if on wheels and stared down at Iris. Her hands closed around her sister's throat and started to squeeze. This was how it would end, Iris thought, without fear or any attempt to defend herself. When she struggled for breath, she awoke, her eyes opening slowly. She felt calm.

Or was it numb? Damn Daisy if she showed up. She was almost bound to.

The door opened a crack. "Justin, you're home early."

"It's not early. It's six already. Are you all right?"

"Yes, I'm fine. I didn't realize I'd slept so long."

"I stopped by Simon and Mandy's because I needed some ideas for a gift for Vic. Mandy mentioned you'd been shopping and had a dizzy spell."

"Actually, I was just shocked. My sister Daisy called Simon. Did he tell you? She's always managed to track me down somehow. It would be a disaster if she came here and saw me."

"Funny he didn't mention it to me."

"Maybe waiting for some privacy. Apparently, he told her that they were moving. Thank goodness she didn't talk to Vic. He might have talked about me and she'd guess. She'd turn me in, you know."

"I guess she would. And I guess you couldn't blame her."

"I suppose not."

"Simon and I will deal with her, if necessary."

"How?"

"Whatever the occasion demands, we will handle it."

Oh yes? Like I would handle it? Only I'm old and weak now.

"I got take-out from that Italian place you like. Lemon and thyme risotto and shrimp."

"Sounds wonderful. I'll freshen up and be down in a few minutes."

"I'll check to see it's still warm enough."

27

Iris and Justin cooked Christmas Eve dinner after they all trimmed her Christmas tree in the afternoon. Vic had been surprised to see it bare.

"Gran, why haven't you put ornaments on your tree? We did ours ages ago."

"I wanted to have some fun with it. The boxes are behind the sofa. I thought we'd do it all together."

"I like that idea. Can I pull them out?"

"Of course. I'll just get everyone drinks."

"No, Iris. Justin and I can see to that," Simon broke in. "You mustn't overdo."

"Oh, Simon, I'm fine, really. Feeling much better." She liked being spoiled, though.

Vic pulled out the boxes and opened them.

"Where's that star that goes on top?"

"Oh, I forgot. Something new. It's in that box on the bookshelf. Hang on."

Iris lifted the box down, opened it, and unwrapped the tissue. She held up an angel tree-topper with a sparkling silver robe and wings made of white feathers. Everyone oohed and aahed, which pleased Iris to an extent that surprised her.

Iris had acquired an artificial tree that came with lights, which saved a lot of trouble. Soon the tree gave off that magical aura of light and beauty that always uplifted her spirits. Christmas joy was only for other people when she was a child. She'd always made sure to make it special for her children, and now for Vic. Although Simon and Justin seemed happy and feeling the spirit.

Like most older houses, Iris's dining room was a good size and accommodated a table for eight. There were only five of them, but they needed the extra space for all the dishes. It gave Wanda more room to sit close to Vic, always hoping for dropped tidbits, which Vic would make sure found their way into her ready jaws. Iris had prepared some, but Justin had really gone to town. He'd made a platter of hors d'oeuvres that looked professionally prepared, featuring roasted asparagus rolled in smoked salmon, deviled eggs, figs wrapped in prosciutto, and stuffed mushrooms. Then came a roasted crown rib and potatoes (Iris's contribution), green bean almandine, and a salad that seemed to contain just about everything a salad could. Everyone was pretty full when they'd polished off most of that, but they managed to enjoy Iris's special sherry trifle—which she made with Grand Marnier rather than sherry—and Justin's raspberry tartlets.

When they all staggered to the living room after Iris decreed that clearing up was for later, Vic noticed a wrapped parcel under the tree.

"Look, Gran, that parcel wasn't there before."

"Oh, no, it certainly was not. Did any of you leave that there?"

Everyone shook their heads.

"Is there a label on it, Vic?"

"It's for me!"

"I guess Santa paid a sneak visit," Simon said, looking at Iris, who shrugged with exaggerated, wide-eyed innocence.

"I'm too old to believe in Santa," Vic told his father reprovingly.

"We are never too old to believe in the magic of Christmas," Iris said softly.

Vic opened his mouth, but thought better of it. "Can I open it, or should I wait 'til tomorrow?"

"Open it. I'm sure Santa will visit your house tonight with other things. This must be a special early one."

Vic tore off the paper and stared at the box, transfixed. "Wow!" was all he could manage.

"What is it, Vic?" Mandy asked.

"It's a kit to make a battleship. It's got an engine and everything. Will you help me with it, Dad?"

"Let's have a look." Simon moved to look over his son's shoulder. "Wow, that is special. That's going to be fun."

Iris almost laughed at the way Simon sounded as excited as the boy. She glanced at Mandy, who looked similarly amused.

"Coffee anyone?" Justin asked.

"No, thanks, it would keep me awake," Mandy said.

No one wanted coffee. "How about a drink, then?" he asked. "I have champagne in the fridge."

That sounded more like it, and the party became even merrier. While they drank, Vic opened up his gift box and drew out the instructions, withdrawing into a corner where he sat next to Wanda reading them, knees drawn up in the same way Iris remembered his father reading his favorite books. Justin, too. Tears came to her eyes, which she blinked away, embarrassed. Justin patted her shoulder. He'd noticed. He was the only one who would. Why hadn't she appreciated him more as he grew up? Perhaps because she couldn't empathize with one so empathetic. She'd been too emotionally stunted. She was different now. She loved people. Her special people.

Eventually, Simon, Mandy, and Vic left. It seemed that Justin had cleared the table of dirty dishes, little by little, throughout the evening. Most went in the dishwasher, and he put some cooking pots on the counter to soak. The few glasses that didn't fit, he washed by hand while Iris put away the leftovers. She remembered to refrigerate the trifle right after everyone left the table.

"You did marvels, Justin. You are a really talented cook."

"I enjoy it. I find it relaxing. And it's nice when people enjoy what you've made. Your crown rib was really succulent, by the way. They weren't just being polite."

"Thanks. I got it from that new butcher in the Leopold Mall. It cost a fortune, but, you know, special occasion and all that."

"Vic was ecstatic about his gift. I think he's going to become obsessed with it."

"Do you remember that kit your father got Simon one year?"

"Of course. He was just the same. He got me a different one. It didn't interest me at all. Dad was quite disappointed. But I'd asked for a new violin. He was never very supportive of my music. Maybe he didn't think it was manly enough." The saddest look came over Justin's face as he put away the last glass and hung up the dish towel.

"I think he felt it wasn't a reliable way to make a good income."

"But when you are a musician, the music is all that matters."

"I know. I don't think I really understood that at the time, either. But I wanted you to pursue something you were good at, and I did realize how good you were."

"I know," Justin said, kissing her cheek. "That was one of the things I loved about you."

That stunned Iris. Looking back, she'd always thought herself as too distant to be a good mother to Lucy and Justin, even though she'd gone through the motions of cuddles and bedtime stories and all those good things. She and Simon—Andrew—seemed to understand each other at a deeper level. Maybe she hadn't been that bad.

"You're very tired," Justin said. "We should get to bed. What time are we supposed to be there tomorrow?"

"Mandy suggested around noon. We'll open gifts and then eat at around two."

"Sounds good."

They went upstairs, Justin outpacing Iris, who realized how exhausted she was as she toiled her way up. Justin kissed her cheek again before disappearing into his room.

The next day was the usual merry family celebration. Everyone was happy with their gifts, the meal of baked ham and all its accoutrements was a great success, and the day ended with champagne like the evening before.

Iris sighed happily as she and Justin walked down the street toward home. This contentment, this happy family, could it last? She knew better, but her life in Charlotte had been blessed, if you didn't count the cancer. But even that had had its upside. She realized she hadn't thought of Dr. Coren for a couple of weeks. It had just been a silly crush, but pleasant all the same. That was another first for her—losing her head over a man. She'd been in love with Sven all those years ago, too naïve to realize he was gay. So, it never got one anywhere. Well, it never got her anywhere. Simon and Mandy seemed fine. Victor had been a good husband until he got older, but she hadn't ever loved him. She'd liked him at first, though.

Justin opened the gate. "You've been very quiet. Are you all right?"

"Just a little tired. And very happy, but wondering if it can last."

"We can only guarantee the present, and that becomes the past in a flash. No use worrying about it."

"Yes, I suppose you're right."

They enjoyed a quiet and companionable Boxing Day. After a dinner of leftovers, Justin chose a movie that Iris enjoyed, to her surprise. She'd made popcorn, which made it feel like a treat.

When the movie ended, Justin said, "Don't feel you have to tell me if you don't want to, but I'm so curious to know where you were and what you were doing while you were ... gone. I read your journal."

"I'll tell you all about it tomorrow, because it's a really long story. For now, I'll just tell you that I was in Canada. I saw Andrew, well, Simon, in an airport with some colleagues and really felt the need to come back. I felt that my burn injuries and the plastic surgery would keep me safe."

"I realized you'd had plastic surgery, of course, but burns!"

"Tomorrow. Simon asked, too, just before I went into surgery. I promised to tell him, but never did. There was never the opportunity. Mandy would be horrified if she knew the truth."

"I'll get him over here tomorrow on some pretext."

"What did you want to discuss with me, Justin?" Simon asked as he entered the kitchen.

"It was me, actually," Iris said. "Justin asked me yesterday what happened to me after I escaped from that awful place. That reminded me that I'd promised to tell you, too. I guess we never had the privacy. I'd rather Mandy not know the truth about Vic's gran."

"Right, she's very fond of you, but it would come as a terrible shock."

"I've made a fresh pot of coffee. Let's take it into the living room and make ourselves comfortable."

Iris led the way and sat in the recliner. Justin placed a cushion behind her head. She smiled at him. *So thoughtful.*

"I cut off my hair and caught a bus to Syracuse. I'd stashed away money and other necessities, including a passport, in a bag in the Syracuse bus station. I had become Lily by then. I managed to get on a bus trip to Toronto with seniors out to buy cheaper Canadian medications. I rented a room with an elderly English lady, an immigrant, as a temporary measure, but it quickly became permanent. Her best friend, a Hungarian immigrant, lived across the street. They were both widows. My mother was a hateful woman, an alcoholic, as was my father. I think you read about that in the journal I left behind. Anyway, those two wonderful ladies were like having an aunt and mother. They brought out a part of me I thought long dead and buried. I had a job in a bookstore, got caught up in a house fire at some point, resulting in plastic surgery, and had a few other adventures, too. And, it might surprise you to know, I became a successful romance novelist."

Iris took a sip of coffee and leaned back again.

"What about that house fire?" Justin asked. "Was the old lady hurt?"

"No. I was renting a studio apartment at that time, because they had sold their houses and moved into a condo together. I visited often, of course, and ended up living with them in the condo when they became frail."

"What caused the fire?" asked Simon.

"That's a really long story."

"We came ready for a long story!" he replied.

Iris told them about it and many of her other adventures in Toronto (leaving out a few things they didn't need to know), and how she'd spotted Simon and found out he lived in Charlotte.

It took most of the afternoon and another pot of coffee.

"Trouble follows you around!" Justin said. "But it was different, wasn't it? Only for good. Only to help."

"Yes, I changed a lot in those years, thanks to Hilda and Magaly. That rose silk lamp in my bedroom was Hilda's. It was in my room when she showed me around that first time. She was so proud of it."

"They sound like wonderful women," Simon said.

"The best." Iris sighed. "They taught me how to live, they loved me, no questions asked. They healed me."

28

Iris grew even stronger as the days began to lengthen. She walked around the neighborhood every morning, sometimes calling in to pick up Wanda. This winter had hardly produced any snow or ice to hinder her progress, so she had been consistent.

She took an art class every week and painted at home most days. She enjoyed landscapes the most, but had become intrigued by the idea of trying portraiture. She had joined the local art guild and one of their speakers had given a demo painting of a quick portrait from a photo. It looked really difficult, especially the different colors he used on the face. Who would have thought of using green and purple? And yet it had looked realistic. She'd love to paint a portrait of Vic. Maybe the whole family. The presenter taught in a studio on the other side of Charlotte, but she knew where it was. She'd think about it.

CHAPTER 28

Easter would fall in mid-April this year. Only a month away. Vic claimed he was too old for Easter egg hunts, but he'd said that last year, and enjoyed it as much as ever. There was a new chocolatier in Charlotte she'd been meaning to visit. She'd like to get the whole family a treat. They all liked chocolate, as did she.

One sunny Friday, Iris came home from her art class and put away her gear in the small upstairs bedroom she used as her studio. Vic was coming to her straight from school as Simon and Mandy had a date night featuring dinner and a movie. Everyone was happy with the arrangement. Vic loved her shepherd's pie. She could never remember to call it a cottage pie, as she should. Cottage pie was made with ground beef and shepherd's pie with lamb, which was logical. Oh well, what did it matter?

Simon called. "Iris, Harold Cane has been released early."

"Oh, dear. Do you think he'll cause trouble?"

"He was bitter enough. But who knows?"

"He hasn't even served half his time. How did that happen?

"I have no idea. He had a pretty slick lawyer."

"Well, all the best. Have a great evening. By the way, have you mentioned this to Vic?"

"No, I thought it best not to worry him."

"Maybe he should be warned. That guy would stoop to anything."

"You think he'd hurt Vic?" Simon's voice got squeaky.

"Not necessarily, but he should know never to go with a stranger. For any reason."

"We've pretty much dinned that into him. I'll give him a reminder. Well, thanks for giving us our evening."

"You are welcome, and you know I don't see it that way. It's a special treat for me, too."

"I know. Is Justin home tonight?"

"No, performing all weekend."

"I'm glad he's found his niche. Well, see you in the morning."

"Bye."

That reminded Iris that she hadn't gotten the bed ready for Vic. She'd had a crib in the small bedroom for him when he was a baby and given it away when he announced he was old enough for a bed. She'd bought a twin bed and invited him to choose sheets from a catalog. It was no surprise that he'd chosen a space-themed pattern. She'd been thinking of giving Vic Kate's room until Justin moved in. Iris cleared her art books off the bed and shelved them alongside the books Vic liked to keep at her house and stowed her paints in the closet. She moved her easel to a corner. She always laundered his sheets after each visit, but decided to wash the pillowcases again to freshen them up. She should get out a towel for him, too. He still liked the Star Wars one she'd bought him a few years ago. He and his father often watched the movies. They must have the dialogue down pat by now.

When she got downstairs, she set out Wanda's water bowl and poured chow into another dish she left on the counter. Wanda could eat at the same time they did. She'd found it easier to be prepared for a visit from the dog at any time.

Vic burst through the kitchen door at about four, his knees grass-stained, his school tie askew, and his hair like a thatch. Wanda trotted in after him and straight over to her bowl where she slurped up water as if parched.

"Hi, Gran, I'm home!"

Oh, how she loved that. "So I see. Get yourself washed up while I put these cases on your pillows. Milk and cookies are on the counter."

"Thanks, Gran."

Iris came down to find Vic helping himself to more milk and his plate holding a few more cookies than he'd started with. And he would have certainly eaten what she'd set out by now.

"Hungry, huh?"

"I'll say. When I've finished, can I watch TV?"

"Homework?"

"Oh, I've got all weekend for that. Coming to your house is a special occasion. Please?"

"Okay. Dinner's at six."

"Is it shepherd's pie?"

"Of course!"

"I'd better have an early night, Gran. I've got a game tomorrow."

"Does your mother know?"

"I think so."

"Well, is your uniform clean?"

"It's in my bag. I've only worn it once since the last wash."

Iris sighed. "Let's have it. What time do you have to be at school?"

"It's an away match. The bus leaves at nine."

"How are you getting to school?"

"School bus, I guess."

"Didn't you ask? It's a weekend. I'm not sure that school buses run on weekends."

"I guess. I'll just run back home by eight and ask Dad."

"I'll drive you. We'll leave at 8:30."

"Thanks, Gran."

Vic went upstairs to take a shower while Iris threw his muddy and somewhat smelly uniform into the washer. She'd go to bed after she'd put it into the dryer. Boys!

When Iris finally got upstairs, she heard Vic talking to someone. She knocked on the door. "What's up, Vic?"

He opened the door. "I just called my friend, Robert. He only lives one street over. I'll walk over there and ride with them. They're leaving at 8:15."

"When did you get a cell phone? Why didn't you tell me?"

"I'm so used to it now. It's as though I've always had it. I guess I sort of thought you knew."

"Let me know the number, just in case. And I'll wake you at seven."

"Thanks, Gran."

Iris remembered that her own boys had been this frustrating at a certain stage, but a little later, maybe fourteen or fifteen.

Vic got off fine the next morning and Iris texted Simon to let him know where his son was. As Iris suspected, neither he nor Mandy had a clue about the game.

At about noon, Simon called her. He sounded breathless. "Cane came around this morning. He wanted money. Of course, I said no. He threatened to make me pay for what I did. I said I testified and told the truth. What else could I do? 'Loyalty,' he said. 'You have none. I'll make you pay.'"

"Why not call the police?" Iris asked.

"He said if I went against him again, I'd regret it. What time is Vic coming home?"

"I'm not sure. Ask his friend's mother. She's picking him up."

"I don't like him being out of my sight at the moment."

"You're frightening me."

"I'll go over there."

"Vic told me it's only the next street over. His name's Robert."

"I'll ask Mandy. She knows more about his friends than I do."

Iris waited thirty minutes before texting Simon. No reply. She put on her coat and walked over to the house. There was no one home, although there was an envelope taped to the front door. If only she'd asked Vic for his friend's address. Her phone pinged.

[Friend's mother said he wasn't there when she picked up her son. Told Robert he had to go with someone to meet me.]

Iris couldn't quite catch her breath.

[Wait, there's something stuck on your door.]

She ripped open the folded page. She texted Simon.

[It's a note from him. Cane. It says not to call the police if you want to see your son again. He wants twenty thousand dollars.]

Simon's silence brought her to tears.

[I will find him, Simon. I have contacts. Come home.]

She called her favorite P.I. and left a message with the details. She needed to know where Harold Cane was living now. "A kid is in danger. Kidnapping." She paced for twenty minutes until Simon and Mandy arrived.

"I'm waiting for some information. Go home. I'll deal with it."

Simon looked haggard and Mandy wasn't much better. "My darling boy," she wailed.

Simon wrapped his arms around her. He looked over her shoulder at Iris.

"Are you sure you're up to it?"

"Oh, yes. He's my darling boy, too. Go home."

Ten minutes after they left, the phone rang.

29

Iris didn't think she needed to disguise herself to visit Cane. While it was true she had attended his trial, he hadn't seemed to notice her, and enough time had passed that her curly hair would make her seem quite different.

The corner house was detached, but tiny, with a postage stamp of a front yard and a backyard not much bigger, the whole surrounded by a sagging chain-link fence. The front door had once been firehouse red, but had faded to an undulating pattern of dirty pink and underlying varnish, although still sporting a few stubborn streaks of red. She walked up to the front door, rang the bell, and stepped back a couple of paces. The door opened almost immediately. Had he been looking out of the window?

"Yes?"

"Hello, my name is Lucy Bayside. I'm with the prisoner rehabilitation project. I hope I'm not calling too early. I need to ask you a few questions about what assistance you might need to find a job, adjust to the outside world again, and so on. May I come in?"

"How nice of you to ask. Yes, please come in."

And how unlike the glowering, arrogant prick she'd seen in court before his downfall. He was still in his pajamas and robe, his white hair considerably thinner than when she'd last seen him. He led her down the hallway to the kitchen at the back of the house.

He pulled out one of only two chairs from the small table. "Please sit down. I'll make some coffee."

"Thank you. How have you been adjusting? Are you in contact with any family?"

"My wife divorced me. My daughter calls on Sundays, but never visits. My son is in his senior year at Harvard and doesn't acknowledge my existence. It's the education fund I set up for him that's paying for his education, but the concept of gratitude seems to have eluded him."

"I'm sorry, that must be hard."

"Well, sometimes you're better off without toxic people in your life."

"I've heard that, yes." *And you're not toxic?*

"Cream and sugar?"

"One sugar and a little cream, thank you."

He almost slammed the steaming coffee mugs onto the table, heaved a deep sigh as if to calm himself. "I was set up, you know. This ambitious scum of a young lawyer set it all up so he'd get a partnership."

"Oh, no, I'm sorry to hear that. Did he get it?"

"Yes, he got it." He smirked and barked a short laugh. "They say that what goes around comes around."

"That's a good one," Iris said. "What will come around for him?"

"I lost everything: respect, career, money, family. He'll know how loss feels, too."

"I hope you're not thinking of doing anything to harm him or his family."

"Oh, no, I would never do anything like that." His smile as he looked into Iris's eyes was deeply unpleasant, almost like a hyena licking its chops.

Iris drank her coffee while she shook off her anger. He must not suspect. "So, do you need a job?"

"Not for the time being. I got half the value of the house when my wife sold it. It was a wonderful place, worth a lot. But I suppose I'll have to find something, eventually. It's hard for someone like me. I was at the peak of my career. I can't ever practice law again. I don't know anything else."

"Are you a good writer?"

"Well, I've drafted plenty of legal documents in my time. But I haven't written anything people would actually want to read. I like to read thrillers, though."

"So, try your hand at that. There are classes you can go to. Adult education, the library, I think they offer classes." *How can I figure out if you have Vic?* She didn't feel good. Maybe she hadn't gotten her strength back as much as she thought. But she mustn't fail Vic.

"Are you all right?"

"I'm feeling a little dizzy, actually. I had surgery a few months ago. I guess I haven't gotten my strength back yet. It's the chemo rather than the surgery that gets you."

"Did you really think I wouldn't recognize you? That bastard Simon's neighbor. I saw you sitting with him, all buddy-buddy. That time outside his house, too. I had you looked into. You're close to the family. Especially the brat. You came to snoop, didn't you? Thought you'd save the brat."

Forgot about that time outside the house. Careless. "You're a monster." Iris heard her drunken slur, still conscious enough to be horrified.

"You have no idea."

Suddenly he was behind her and dragging her down the hall, pulling her up the stairs, cruelly bruising the back of her legs before dumping her outside a door. He unlocked the door and pushed her into a small room. She fell to her knees. Iris took in what she could in her stupor—a mattress lay in one corner with a small figure curled up on it. The boy's eyes opened and blinked. He raised his head a little before letting it drop back. His wrists were tied in front of him and his ankles were bound, too.

"Vic," she managed.

"Gran?"

Cane pushed her onto her face. "Gran, is it? Happy dreams!"

He left, locking the door behind him. Iris crawled over to the mattress, lay beside Vic, and took him in her arms. "Sorry, darling, I should have saved you."

"S'okay."

They woke when he banged two metal bowls onto the floor next to the mattress, together with two mugs of juice. Iris still felt a bit groggy, but managed to sit up, despite the bindings at her wrists and ankles. He must have done it while she was unconscious.

"How do we eat with our hands tied?"

"I will untie them one at a time. No tricks."

"The boy first."

The juice is probably drugged, judging by Vic's condition. Iris must somehow avoid drinking it, despite her horribly dry mouth. But if he was watching them, what then?

"I really have to visit the washroom," she said.

"I'll bring you a bucket," he answered.

"That's disgusting."

"No more than you deserve."

"What did I do?"

"Interfered."

"You are punishing Simon by hurting an innocent child?"

"Is anyone truly innocent?"

"You certainly aren't."

He slapped her face. "Bitch."

"Gran! Don't hurt Gran. Please."

"You want a slap, too?"

Vic sank back on the mattress, sobbing. His hopelessness broke Iris's heart.

"Let him eat. You can come back to untie me later."

"You think I'm stupid? Finish your food, boy." He yanked him up to a sitting position.

Vic somehow choked down the toast and drank his juice before getting tied up again.

"Now you ... *Gran*."

Iris started with the toast, which tasted normal. How to get out of drinking the juice? She lifted the cup to her lips and looked at him, as he watched her intently. She closed her eyes and thought back to the worst day of chemo, when she had to be half-carried to the bathroom where she let loose from both ends, emitting a horrific odor that she would never forget. It paid off, and she spewed juice and masticated toast all over Cane.

He yelled and jumped up, even more disgusted than she was. She pretended to fall back, moaning and clutching her stomach. Vic started to cry loudly. She'd scared the poor boy.

"I'll be back in a bit, you revolting cunt!" he cried, running from the room and locking the door.

CHAPTER 29

Iris kept up the moaning until his footsteps receded. "Don't worry, Vic, I'm okay." She untied his hands and feet, leaving the rope wound so that it looked as if nothing changed, and did the same to his ankles. She removed the flick knife from its hiding place under the waistband of her pants and concealed it up her sleeve. "Lie still and act sleepy," she instructed Vic. He looked half asleep already, the tracks left by tears a sad sight that filled her with murderous rage. She lay back down, facing the door. When she heard the key in the lock, she closed her eyes and clutched her stomach, letting out soft chuffs of pain from time to time. She felt him lean over her. She pretended to extend an arm as if asking for help, pressed the knife into his abdomen, and released the catch. He screamed and fell backward. She leaped up, twisted the knife, and pulled it out.

Vic was still out. She lifted him under the armpits and dragged him downstairs and into the front hall. She slid down the wall to sit and catch her breath for a few moments. Her incision burned. *Must get on with it.* She dashed into the kitchen, found a knife with a blade about the same length as her flick-knife, and went back up to find Cane had crawled out into the hallway. She kicked him onto his back, shoved the knife into the wound, and twisted it. His scream stopped almost as soon as it started. Iris went into the bathroom and washed the flick-knife before entering the other bedroom and hiding it under the socks in the top drawer of his dresser. Then she went to the landline in the downstairs hallway to call 911. She looked at her watch. 5:30.

She didn't want to be identified, so no 911. Someone would find him sooner or later. How could Vic's sudden reappearance be explained? She couldn't expect him to keep such a secret. It was still broad daylight, too. How would she get Vic home without being seen? Could she? Vic had been drugged. If he said he saw her, it could be labeled as a delusion. Why not wipe her prints off the kitchen table and coffee mug and think it through again? Better still, put the bowls and cups from upstairs and the coffee mugs into the dishwasher and run it.

She worked her way through the house, tidying things up. Including the vomit, fighting through her revulsion and exhaustion. The vomit would contain her DNA. She found some bleach next to the washing machine and went over it, just to make sure. There was only about an hour to go before dark. She could do it. She sat in the hall next to Vic, who was still out, thankfully. She felt as if she hadn't slept all night. She closed her eyes. She wasn't quite asleep, nor was she fully awake, while visions of bloody knives and dead faces of those she'd dispatched years before paraded through her mind. She woke with a start. A dark night was her friend, and there were barely any street lights in this part of town. The houses on either side were dark, too. Maybe vacant. She walked a couple of blocks to get her car, driving to Cane's front gate. Vic was beginning to stir as she raised him to his feet. She draped his arm over her shoulder and guided him to the car, laying him on the back seat. He seemed to drop off again. All the better.

Now, where to leave him? The police would be at Simon's house. She hoped they wouldn't notice her car arrive. She'd better do some shopping in case anyone asked. Justin was spending a long weekend in Boston, thank heavens. Ah, she had it.

She drew up at the corner of her street closest to Simon's house with her lights out. She eased Vic out of the car and sat him against a hedge.

"Wha'..."

"You're near home now," Iris whispered. "Just around the corner. That bad man left you here."

She got back in the car and backed up before continuing on to the supermarket. She lowered the mirror in the car and combed her hair. Her coat covered the streaks of vomit. She didn't pay much attention to what she picked up, just shoving a loaf of bread, some milk, and juice into her basket. *Cake*, she thought. She could do with some cake. She still felt wired, but knew that would fade soon, and she'd better get home before it did.

She pulled into her garage and took her shopping into the kitchen. She put the milk in the fridge and left everything else on the table. Upstairs, the hot shower helped cleanse her mind as well as her body. While still fairly early, pajamas and robe would be comfortable and cozy. Then, a glass of wine and some cake.

She poured the deliciously cold white wine and cut a generous slice of cake. She should be eating a nutritious dinner, but never mind nutrition for once. She took her plate and glass into the family room, lit the gas fire she'd had inserted into the fireplace, switched on the TV, sipped, nibbled, and waited.

She turned on the TV and found an old British sitcom that had her chuckling, despite her depleted state. She fell asleep before it ended, only waking when the message notification on her phone sounded.

[Vic is home! He's a bit groggy, but okay. He seems to have been dumped just around the corner, and managed to stagger home. Talk later.]

[So glad he's okay. How much does he remember?]

[Not much]

Good.

It took Vic a few days to recover from his ordeal. Mandy wanted to take him to the doctor, but Simon nixed it. He told Iris what he'd said. He wanted to hide her part in it, too.

"Let the drugs work their way out of his system. You can tell the school he has a stomach bug. How would we explain the situation?"

Vic could only remember strange dreams. Of course, Iris had told Simon what happened. He'd been questioned about the murder of Harold Cane, but he'd been on a long phone call with an international client at the time. He told Iris how he'd offended his client by being irritable and abrupt, but he'd been out of his mind with worry. He'd apologized, saying his son was sick, and he hadn't had much sleep. The client understood, and got off the phone, saying they'd talk in a couple of days.

Everyone was off the hook. Even Harold Cane.

30

The rest of the year passed slowly. Mandy finally had her knee surgery and was soon back to her old self, although she had to undergo physical therapy for a few weeks. Iris had them all over for dinner every night for a week, which had been exhausting. But she wanted to do it, to keep Mandy off her legs. Iris was happy, but somewhat restless. After that, she put a few dinners in their freezer.

They'd had a cozy Thanksgiving and the usual festive Christmas. She constantly reminded herself that she had much to be thankful for, but why did she have to keep reminding herself? Justin still lived with her and had a lovely girlfriend, Barbara, a violinist from his orchestra. Iris coached him from time to time after she noticed him being too quick to please—agreeing to things she knew he didn't want to do, going along with the political leanings of her father, and so on.

There's a way to disagree without causing offense. And if it does cause offense, that is not your problem. If Mr. Brownlee doesn't like your liberal ideas, so be it. It's his daughter's ideas that matter.

You hate the circus, so tell her why. Maybe she'll understand. Maybe she can go with someone else.

You love the symphony you're working on now, even if she doesn't. Why not simply have a discussion, and listen to each other's point of view?

He gradually got used to standing up for himself and she sometimes heard them having quite heated discussions, but they never ended in acrimony. Barbara clearly liked the new Justin. Iris remembered how abrupt Victor could be with him, because Justin wasn't his idea of a real man. Justin always bent over backward to please him, but never could. That's where it started. And she hadn't stuck up for him.

Anyway, the boy was doing well.

Simon—she never thought of him as Andrew anymore—was extremely successful in the law practice, which had expanded a great deal, and had planned some sort of a special trip as soon as Vic got out of school. He would invite Justin and Barbara to join them, too. Iris was really looking forward to that—wherever it would be. And Vic was doing well at school, particularly in math and science. He'd decided he wanted to be an engineer. What kind of engineer he hadn't said, but he probably was unaware of all the different career paths in that field. He was only twelve, so plenty of time, yet.

And Mandy had surprised everyone by declaring she was going to apply for a master's degree in education. She'd been accepted to a program in translation at the University of North Carolina at Charlotte. She would start the following September. If she was still on campus when Vic got home from school, he would come to Iris, which was something to look forward to for both of them.

So why the feeling that life was passing her by? Especially inappropriate as she had felt death staring in the face only a couple of years ago. And she had made it through. *Be grateful.*

She needed some excitement. A whiff of danger. Not the nasty cancer kind of danger, but a challenge with risks. Surely she didn't miss killing anymore? She remembered the frisson she used to feel years ago before a kill. Looking back on more recent events, she hadn't felt that thrill at all. Only the adrenaline rush of getting the job done without getting caught or hurt. Maybe that's what she was missing. Adrenaline.

She wasn't that strong anymore. The altercation with Harold Cane had exhausted her to the point of needing lots of naps and staying in bed late for a week. Dr. Coren had warned her that the effects of chemo could take a few years to wear off. And she was officially a senior citizen, after all.

It was nearly time for Easter again. Simon had mentioned renting a cottage in Nags Head in the summer, which she would enjoy. That sound of lapping waves as she dozed off at night was soothing beyond anything she could think of. She must order chocolate Easter eggs for everyone. They wouldn't have a hunt this year, as Vic had insisted he was far too old for such antics, and said he meant it this time. She knew he'd harbor regrets, though, so she'd hide a few in the house. They hadn't done it at Simon and Mandy's ever since they got Wanda. Dogs like chocolate, too, and it could make them very sick. Wanda would come with them for lunch, so she'd be sure to hide them high. Vic was getting so tall, she didn't have to worry about him being able to reach them anymore. If she could reach them, he could.

She drove to the chocolatier and made her purchases. The plump little shop owner, Mr. Barker, pointed out the fancy ones before he clasped his hands to his heart.

"Such a fancy treat for the ladies, my dear. How can they bear to tear them apart? Because my chocolate is exquisite!" His drooping mustache seemed to quiver with emotion.

Barbara and Mandy would receive these eggs done up with ribbons and pastel netting, with a little yellow chick perched atop each and a furry bunny peeping over the rim of the basket. She chose more restrained confections with green or maroon ribbons for the big boys.

"Just one more," she said. "He's almost twelve."

"Aha!" Mr. Barker disappeared into the back room, soon appearing with an egg shaped like a spaceship. A rabbit dressed like an astronaut dangled from the red, white, and blue ribboned handle of its basket.

"Perfect, Mr. Barker, couldn't be better," she said. "He's mad about space. He'll love it."

"I haven't had time to set them out," he said. "I've got smaller eggs inside chocolate stilettos for the girls."

Iris wasn't sure teenage girls were into stilettos anymore, but exclaimed enthusiastically how wonderful that sounded. She would have loved one like that when she was a teen, but that was long ago, long before she escaped the ugliness of her home life. Not that there hadn't been plenty of ugliness to follow. *Think positive.*

Easter Sunday was forecast to be rainy and cool, so eating out on the terrace would be out of the question. The night before, Iris enjoyed setting the dining room table, which she'd only had call to do three or four times before. She liked this soft room with its pale green walls and polished cherry furniture, which she'd chosen for its simple lines. She opted for placemats featuring spring flowers, got out her white dinner set with its silver edging, and Hilda's pride and joy, the sterling silverware. Iris placed three white pots containing hyacinths along a runner down the center of the table, then carefully got out Magaly's pride and joy, a set of Czech crystal glasses, and took them to the kitchen to be washed. Every place would have a tumbler, and she would put the wine glasses on a silver tray (also from Magaly) on the sideboard together with one bottle of white wine and one of red.

Justin would help her cook, thank heavens. She found preparing these big meals exhausting and nerve-racking. He was working tonight, but they'd start preparing first thing in the morning.

The luncheon was a great success. The lamb turned out succulent and perfectly done, and the several desserts—her Grand Marnier trifle and Justin's strawberry tart—were practically demolished. Barbara fitted into the family group beautifully. Iris was growing fond of the girl and hoped she was the one for Justin. He certainly seemed happy in her company. She sat back and surveyed the family. Her family. Vic, as always, sat to her right and seemed to enjoy her company. They never ran out of things to talk about. She reckoned that was unusual at that age.

"Would anyone like more dessert?" she asked them all. "If not, why don't we move to the living room and make ourselves comfortable?"

"Just one thing I'd like to discuss first," Simon said.

Everyone turned to him, surprised. Iris felt a flutter of unease.

"I've been looking into a special trip for the summer, as soon as Vic gets out of school. I've always wanted to go to Egypt. Land of the pharaohs and all that. There's a tour I've settled on that has everything laid on. A week in Cairo, followed by a ten-day boat trip on the Nile down to the huge monuments in the south, including Abel Simbel. I'd like to invite you all to come. I had a very nice Christmas bonus this year, and this is a once in a lifetime splurge. After that, it's all going to Vic's college fees!"

"Wow" was a sort of gasping chorus.

"Simon, that's going to cost you a fortune," Iris said. "It's too much. Why don't we all chip in?"

"No, I want to do it. But Justin, what about your schedule? And what about you, Barbara?"

Justin said his obligations would be slowing down by that point and Barbara's, too.

"But I'm practically a stranger. You shouldn't be spending all that money on me," Barbara said.

"I can see you make my brother happy, so I'm more than happy to have you join us."

Iris watched Barbara turn to Justin, her eyes teary. He put his arm around her shoulder and squeezed.

"You're the best Dad ever!" Vic shouted and rushed around the table to hug his father. "I can't wait to tell my friends! And I've got a lot of reading to do."

"It's a very full itinerary, and we will see all that is possible in that short time."

"It sounds like a pretty long trip to me," Justin said.

"Not considering all the wonders of the ancient world," his brother replied.

"Iris, you haven't said a word," Mandy said. "Will you join us?"

"Please do, Gran," Vic said, coming around to squeeze her shoulder.

"Of course, I'd love to. I'm just so shocked, that's all. It's an experience I could never have imagined. It's beyond exciting. And beyond generous. I hardly know what to say." Egypt! Never had she expected to visit such an exotic place. She must read up on it. Make the most of it.

"Fine, it's settled, then," Simon said. "Let's get comfortable. I put some champagne in the fridge when we arrived. Let's celebrate!"

Simon fetched the champagne while Iris got out the glasses. "I'll just give them a rinse," she said. "They haven't been used in a while."

"Allow me," Justin said.

"I'll help," Barbara added.

Iris, a little concerned about Magaly's glasses, settled herself in her recliner. Simon and Mandy sat on the loveseat, while Vic sat in a corner looking things up on his phone. "Oh, cool," he muttered several times.

"Where are those glasses?" Simon said. "The bubbly's getting warm."

"I'm sure they won't be long. I hope the glasses will be all right. I inherited them from an old friend," Iris said.

"Here we are," Justin said, entering the room with the sparkling crystal glasses on the silver tray, with Barbara following close behind. "Let's celebrate."

He set down the tray on the table next to the bottle in its ice bucket, turned around, and drew Barbara close to him. "We have something else to celebrate this evening. Barbara has agreed to become my wife. We're engaged!"

Iris couldn't help yelping in her delight. It wasn't easy getting out of her recliner, but she did it in record time and hugged her son and soon-to-be daughter-in-law, tears streaming down her face. "I'm so happy for you both," she cried.

Simon started to shake Justin's hand, but Justin moved in for a hug. Simon stiffened at first, but relaxed into the moment, before kissing Barbara on each cheek. Mandy hugged them both, too. Iris mopped her tears with a tissue before she noticed Vic hanging back, not knowing what to do with himself.

"You can give them a hug and say congratulations," she whispered to him. "It's okay."

"Are you sure? She hardly knows me."

"I'm sure."

Vic stood in front of them, grinning and pink with embarrassment. "Congratulations. I'm very happy for you. Can I call you Aunt Barbara now?"

They both laughed and hugged him. "Of course you can," Barbara said. "I'd be honored."

An hour or so later, Simon, Mandy, and Vic left.

Justin and Barbara sat holding hands. Justin looked at Iris, opened his mouth, and shut it again.

"I think I'll make sure all the food is put away," Iris said. "Then I'm off to bed. What an evening! I'm exhausted. By the way, Barbara. You are welcome to stay the night."

Barbara's surprise and Justin's relief made Iris want to laugh, so she hurried out of the room. There was only a little piece of pie to put in the fridge. Justin appeared in the doorway.

"When you said spend the night, what did you mean, exactly?"

"She can stay with you or you can tidy up the spare room. Either way is fine with me."

"Oh, no need to worry about the spare room."

"I thought not. Good night."

31

The time between Easter and the end of the spring semester flew by. Iris checked out books about Egypt from the library and pored over them, sometimes with Vic. She'd shopped for chic clothing that would do well in the heat and made a long list of what she should take—bearing in mind she could take only one case and had to leave room for purchases. They left the day after Vic got out of school with an exemplary report card.

They took a flight direct from JFK Airport in New York to Cairo. JFK had proven somewhat chaotic, and Cairo airport surprisingly efficient, late as it was. Their tour company would have a bus waiting outside the terminal, so they rolled their cases out of the sliding doors toward the jumble of traffic. The lighting outside the terminal was strong enough for Simon and Justin to walk up and down, looking for their transport. The air was warm and thick with pollution.

"There it is," Justin cried, pointing to a strip of road three lanes over where a bus with "Monument Tours" printed in scarlet across its side sat idling. To reach it, they had to cross against honking cars and cabs. Simon manfully led, holding up a hand to encourage drivers to slow down. It was a frightening experience, but they finally made it, no thanks to a puny policeman, who stood by yawning as he watched. The bus driver flashed a broad grin as he welcomed them and loaded their luggage into the hold.

"My good wishes to you and welcome to Egypt."

They all gazed out of the windows onto horrendous traffic and blighted palm trees as the bus dodged other vehicles with impressive dexterity, too tired to take much in.

When they rolled up the circular driveway to the hotel, Iris noted lush trees and flowering plants that set off the white building spectacularly. The driver got out their luggage while the doorman, clad in an impressively militaristic uniform, led them to reception.

"The Hale party of six," Simon told them.

"Ah yes, we have been expecting you. Monument tours. Welcome to Egypt."

The young man produced their key cards and summoned a couple of porters to take them and their bags to their rooms.

Iris felt exhausted. She hadn't fully regained her strength after her chemo ordeal, not to mention the Cane incident, and hoped she'd be able to keep up.

"Do we have a tour in the morning?" she asked Simon.

"No, not until after lunch. I guess because the flight arrived so late."

"I might just have breakfast in my room."

"Me, too," Mandy said.

"I want to look around," Vic protested.

CHAPTER 31

"You can look around the hotel, but don't on any account go outside," Simon said.

"I want to see the garden, though."

"That's all right. Just not off the property."

They all went to their rooms, which were next door to each other. Justin and Barbara had separate rooms, as unmarried couples were not permitted to share in Cairo.

Iris wanted to shower after the long journey, but didn't have the energy. Grimy as she felt, she unlocked her case, pulled out a nightgown and wash bag, and went to the bathroom to wash her face and brush her teeth. The bathroom was a wonder of ceramic tile and gleaming fixtures. The pale blue towels were thick and soft, leading her to decide to shower after all.

Iris came out of the bathroom wrapped in a cozy robe. Feeling refreshed, she looked around her room. She spotted a mango in the bowl of fruit set on the coffee table with a plate, knife, napkins, a couple of bottles of mineral water, and an ice bucket beside it. She'd eaten a mango once before at a Thai restaurant where it had been served with sticky sweet rice with a coconut sauce. Delicious. She had to wrestle with this one for a while. She peeled it first, then found that it had a large pit, so carved the juicy flesh around it, sucking her fingers as she went. So sweet and delicious. She poured herself a glass of fizzy water and took it to the bedside table, along with her travel tote, from which she extracted her Kindle. After turning off all the lights save the bedside lamp, she climbed onto a gloriously soft mattress and snuggled in, reveling in comfort. She opened her Kindle and took a few sips of water as she finished her mystery. After visiting London, she'd decided to explore a little more of the British way of life, so had loaded everything Agatha Christie had ever written, which had proved a lot more than she'd expected. She loved the characters and the settings, the way they talked, and their everyday life. The books so far were set so many years ago, she realized life in England had changed significantly if, indeed, it had ever been that serene (apart from all the murders). Probably not. But still, she lapped it up.

Iris turned off the lamp and closed her eyes, wondering what tomorrow might bring.

32

Iris wasn't sure what time it was when she awoke. She'd forgotten to adjust her watch. Maybe her phone might have the answer. She fished it out of her bag. Sure enough, the time had changed. Only eight o'clock. Not too late for breakfast. She had slept well and felt like herself again. She got up, got dressed, and went in search of the restaurant.

The dining room was full of families chatting as they ate, a number of their bored children getting under the waiters' feet. Snow white cloths adorned every table, and a long buffet table was set against one wall.

She spotted Simon, Mandy, and Vic already seated and wended her way over, almost tripping over a toddler who had parked herself on the floor while she played with a couple of forks.

"Iris, I thought you were eating in your room?" Mandy exclaimed.

"I slept so well, I woke up feeling fine," Iris said. "I've never slept in such a comfortable bed."

"I know. They're fantastic, aren't they?" Mandy patted her lips with her napkin.

A waiter came and asked Iris what she'd like to drink. "Coffee and orange juice, please."

"Please help yourself to the buffet, madam," he said, indicating the long table.

"Thank you."

Iris walked up and down the table to see the choices. There were some sort of beans that she didn't much fancy as a breakfast food. There was cereal, some good bread, cheeses, jam, butter, and lots of fruit. *Mangoes.*

She took a couple of slices of baguette, butter, jam, and a dish of mango slices. A small pot of coffee and warm milk, together with what looked like fresh orange juice, was already at her table when she got back.

"What's that in the bowl, Gran?"

"Mangoes. They are so delicious. Have you tried them?"

"No, I've heard of them."

"Try a piece of mine and see if you like it."

He bit off a little before stuffing the rest in his mouth. "Oh, yes. Love it. I think I'll go and get some."

"Can I try?" Mandy asked.

Simon wanted some, too.

"All right, I'll go to get some for myself and more for Iris," Mandy said. "She's right, mangoes are wonderful. Simon?"

"No, thanks, not really my sort of thing." Andrew—Simon had never been a big fan of fruit and vegetables.

"I guess Justin and Barbara ate in their rooms," Mandy said, glaring at Vic when he sniggered.

"Maybe we'll see them at lunch," Vic said. "Maybe."

"Enough," Mandy said. "I want to look at the shops. I've never seen a hotel with so many. Then maybe a stroll around the garden? It's so tropical."

"Sounds good," Iris said.

There was a jewelry store that sold touristy beady necklaces in "Pharaonic" style, as well as ornate pieces encrusted with costly gems. Another store sold papyrus, which appealed to Iris. She chose one with brilliant blue figures going up one side of the sheet and down the other in a sort of arch.

"Are you going to Upper Egypt, madam?" the sales clerk asked.

"Yes, we are, on a cruise."

"You will see this in the entrance to one of the tombs. Only it is painted up one wall, across the ceiling, and down the other wall. It is wonderful. You made a good choice." He rolled up the small painting and inserted it into a tube. "This should keep it safe in your suitcase."

"Thank you," Iris said, happy with her souvenir of something she hadn't even seen yet.

In another store, there were hundreds of scarabs. Dung beetles, as they learned. Sacred to ancient Egyptians, they symbolized the cycle of life.

"I think I'd like one of these on the mantlepiece," Iris told Mandy.

"Yes, I'd like one too. It would look nice in the china cabinet," Mandy replied. "What do you think, Simon?"

"Sure. If you like it, get one."

Iris chose one that looked as if it were made of ivory. For the price, it couldn't be. "What is this one made of?" she asked the owner.

"Camel bone, madam."

Mandy chose a black one.

"I would love to have some scarabs," Vic said. "Look, there's a bag of small ones in different colors. Can I?"

"Of course," Iris said, taking them from him. "I'll pay for them along with mine."

"Thanks, Gran."

They were about to go to the cash register when the owner led them over to a cabinet where pendants made of scarabs were displayed. They both dithered, wondering if they were being too extravagant. In the end, Iris chose a small bone pendant that looked old on a silver chain. It had hieroglyphics carved on the back.

Mandy picked up a large black one encased in a gold rim. "I have a chain I can use with this," she said. "I really like it."

"Get it if you like it," Simon said, a note of impatience in his voice. He was never much of a shopper, Iris remembered. But then, most men weren't, including his father.

They wandered by several more stores without making any more purchases.

"Why don't we drop these things in our rooms, then meet down here again in an hour? We can explore the gardens before lunch," Simon said.

Iris thought that was a great idea. "There's a bench I could see from the dining room. Why don't we meet there? I might bring my Kindle had have a read."

33

Iris didn't spend much time in her room. She looked forward to sitting outside and finishing her book. She settled onto the bench, which had been furnished with cushions since she'd noticed it at breakfast, and leaned back, luxuriating in the gorgeous surroundings. She looked up from her Kindle from time to time to enjoy the riot of color, and felt as though only minutes had passed before the others arrived.

The gardens didn't disappoint. Plants Iris had only seen used as houseplants grew in profusion, birds sang and chattered, and little green lizards scurried to and fro as they ran their frantic errands. Iris and Mandy oohed and aahed, taking pictures with their phones. Vic was happy trying to catch a lizard.

"Lizards might bite," Mandy said.

"Or carry diseases," Simon added.

"Let them be free. Just enjoy watching them," Iris said. "Take pictures."

"I guess so," Vic said, disappointed.

They rounded a corner of the building to find a patio with tables and a bar set up with a bartender.

"Let's have something cool to drink," Simon suggested.

The temperature had risen, and they welcomed the idea. The bartender suggested fresh lemonade with mint.

"That sounds refreshing," Simon said.

The beverage was slightly tart and quenched Iris's thirst. They chatted for a while before it was time to head in to lunch. Their tour would start at the Egyptian museum and the bus would leave at two. Simon told them they'd have an early start tomorrow because they were going to the pyramids and they should be finished before the worst of the midday heat.

They joined a group outside the hotel entrance as they waited for the guide. Iris took stock of their tour group, all milling around the bus, waiting to board. An older man whose shirtsleeves were rolled up to his elbows, stood apart from the others, his wide-brimmed hat hiding his features as he watched his companions. Two middle-aged couples who seemed to be traveling together chatted excitedly about their purchases in the gift shop, their southern drawl, sneakers with white socks, and the women's floppy, flowery hats almost a cliché. A younger couple stood on either side of a sulky girl who looked about Vic's age, each clutching one of her hands as if she might be spirited away. An elderly woman leaned on a cane while a young woman held her bags. The old woman complained loudly and often about the wait. Iris had seen her type often enough in New

York while window shopping along 5th Avenue and its offshoots—rich and entitled. She took an immediate dislike to the woman.

Finally, the guide appeared along with the driver, apologizing for keeping them waiting. Apparently, the driver had been told to come at two-thirty. They all got on, with everyone vying for the front seats. Simon and Mandy managed to sit together, as did Justin and Barbara. Vic sat next to the sulky girl at her parents' urging. The two of them studiously ignored each other. Iris sat alone near the front. The man in the fedora got on last and sat next to her. He removed his hat and nodded. "Michael Sercombe."

"I'm Iris Hall. Is this your first time in Egypt?"

"No, not at all. I just prefer to be in a group so that transportation is laid on."

"I see. You like it here, then."

"It's interesting. Endlessly interesting."

"Indeed."

That was the extent of their conversation. The guide, who introduced himself as Kareem, pointed out various objects of interest as they went. An enormous statue of Ramses II in front of the railway station was a surprise. Michael took no notice of anything. *What are you really doing here?*

They pulled up in front of a red stone building with a white portico.

"The Egyptian Museum is the oldest archeological museum in the Middle East and holds 170,000 artifacts," Kareem announced. "A lot of the collection is in storage because there is not enough room to display it all. We can only hope to see a little of the collection. We will see the King Tut display, the mummies, and a few other items that you will see as you walk around."

He went on to explain that this old museum would soon be replaced with a new building some distance away, as the vast collection needed a lot more space to be appropriately presented. They started with the King Tut exhibit. The sarcophagi were splendidly painted and inlaid with precious stones. They looked as fresh as the day they were created. Kareem kept reminding them of the age of what they saw. Everyone seemed to be speechless, except for Vic and the girl, who whispered to one another a few times. Iris reflected that it was hard for Americans to conceive of this level of antiquity.

The museum was stuffed with so many ancient artifacts that the guide let them wander aimlessly, stopping by one artifact or another as the fancy took them. He asked them to meet him outside the mummy hall at four. They strolled through one hall lined with immense statues. Iris admired a couple before concluding that the best thing to do was to simply feast on the whole rather than inspect each item.

Eventually, Kareem rounded up the group and led them to the mummy hall, where they marveled at leathery hook-nosed faces with a few tufts of coarse hair still sprouting from their heads. The guide mentioned that the museum had temporarily closed the mummy room when the late President Sadat had floated the idea of re-interring the remains. Fortunately, the threat had been forgotten. That was the last item on the agenda. Iris noted that Michael joined them as they filtered out of the museum. He had entered with them and disappeared shortly thereafter.

They got back to the hotel, footsore, and ready for a nap, but it was too close to dinnertime. The return trip had been one long traffic jam. Everyone was quiet during dinner, even Vic. Iris showered and climbed into bed almost as soon as they'd finished and read for a while. She hadn't expected to get so tired from an afternoon of sightseeing. North Carolina could get really hot in the summer, but not quite this hot, although it was a dry heat. And the museum had been overwhelming—they must have walked for miles.

The next day, they boarded the bus to the pyramids. Everyone claimed the same seats, so Vic had no choice but to sit with the girl. Iris noticed them exchanging a few words, so maybe they would make friends. She and Michael greeted each other and remained silent for the trip along roads clogged with traffic that wound through a poor section of Cairo. Balconies that were hung with washing looked in imminent risk of collapse. Ragged, barefoot children already played in the streets, the boys practicing their soccer moves with what looked like tight-bound balls of rags. Some of them looked quite adept.

The pyramids came into view, towering over rooftops. Iris felt disappointed. They didn't look like much behind this decrepit forefront. They finally broke free of buildings and wound their way to a spot teeming with tourists, vendors, guides, camels, horses, and donkeys.

"We get off here," Kareem said. "We will journey to the pyramids on these fine creatures you see here. It's a pity we do not have time for the evening Sound and Light Show."

Iris turned to gaze at the pyramids and the Sphynx. Now she could appreciate their immensity. She particularly admired the Sphynx. It had the look of a soul that had seen everything. Vic and the girl—Iris had yet to learn her name—decided on a camel, as did the others. Iris thought an old donkey looked more manageable and was helped up by an elderly man wearing a blue skullcap and a robe that had once been white. Iris and her donkey trailed some way behind the others. She heard the sound of muffled hoofs and noticed Michael setting off on horseback in the direction of some small stone houses away from the pyramids. *You're up to something.*

Everyone was paired off except her, and she felt a pang of sadness. She thought Vic would have been more of a companion. But that wasn't fair. He was young and should be around young people. She sighed. That was part of getting old.

"I come back in one minute," said her guide. The others had been gone a few minutes before she returned. "We go to Sphynx first," the guide said.

"No, with the others," Iris said, alarmed. She didn't want to be separated from the others.

The old man said nothing and trotted along on his donkey with her donkey on a lead rein. She realized that they were going toward the pyramids in a different direction than the rest of her party.

"Where are you taking me?" she cried out, alarmed.

The old man spurred her donkey to go faster, and she had to hold on to the creature's mane to avoid falling off. Or should she fall off? But there was no one around to help her. They came to one corner of the smallest pyramid—still huge—and rounded some mounded rocks. Three men stood there, laughing as they greeted her guide.

"On the ground now, lady," the guide said, almost pulling Iris off. She stumbled, then regained her balance and struck him in the face with her fist. He fell and struck his head on a rock. He didn't move. The other men advanced on her, their faces angry.

"You have hurt my father," said one.

"He has kidnapped me. I suppose you want money."

"Give me your bag."

He snatched it from her and looked through it. "Where is the rest? You are a rich American. You must pay for hurting my uncle."

"I thought he was your father?"

"All families are close here. Your money."

"My son keeps it for me. In case of pickpockets." Iris glared up at the man, whose fetid breath caused her to recoil.

The sound of a galloping horse made the brute look beyond her. He barked an order to his companion. "You are lucky today," he said. "We must go." He struck her so fast she remembered no more until she came to on a mattress in a stone room. Her head ached horribly. She lifted her head.

"Keep still, now," a man said. Michael came into view.

"What happened? Where's my family?"

"The police have gone to find them. I have ordered a nice car to take you to hospital. You have suffered a concussion and must have treatment. Close your eyes until you can be moved."

"Oh, no, the trip. It's ruined. I don't want them to miss it. We're supposed to go on a Nile cruise the day after tomorrow."

"With any luck, you'll be well enough to make it to the cruise."

"I heard a horse. Was that you?"

"Yes, I saw the guide separate you off from the others and followed with my binoculars. I called the police. They have the old man and will soon find the others."

"The biggest man said the old man was his father. Then said it was his uncle. I knocked him out, so he was angry."

"Did they get your passport?"

"No. They were angry because there wasn't much money in my bag. I told them my son keeps it for me. But it was in a fanny pack under my skirt."

Michael laughed. "Your what?"

"Fanny pack. You know, a small bag you wear around your waist to keep things hidden."

"Oh, I see." He was still laughing.

"Why? What's the joke?"

"Well, in Britain, fanny isn't a word a lady would use. It means something quite different."

"What?"

"Never mind."

"Car's here," an American voice said.

"An American embassy car," Michael said. "They'll take care of you. We will carry you out to the back seat. You must stay flat until you've been seen by a doctor."

Iris felt like a sack of potatoes as they maneuvered her into the car.

"Stay awake if you can," the driver said.

"Michael?"

"Yes, I'm here."

"Thank you. I owe you a lot. My life, maybe."

"All in a day's work." *It probably is.*

The driver kept up a steady rate of chatter as they drove to the hospital, no doubt to make sure she didn't fall asleep. They were met by an orderly and nurse, who got her onto a gurney. She was wheeled into a curtained area. The nurse stayed with her.

"Doctor Rafik will be with you very soon."

"You speak good English."

"It is required."

Iris closed her eyes, tired suddenly.

"Open your eyes."

Iris snapped them open.

"Here is the doctor."

CHAPTER 33

The clean-shaven doctor, a small man, looked young and confident. "Mrs. Hall. How are you feeling?"

"I have a headache and my hand hurts."

"Your hand?"

"Yes, from the guide who abducted me. When I realized what he was up to, I knocked him out."

"Good gracious, I hope I do not upset you in any way. We will give you something for the headache."

He peered at her eyes, ordered a CAT scan of her head, and manipulated her hand.

"Your hand is only bruised. I do not believe the CAT scan will show signs of problems, but it is best to be on the safe side. If everything is as it should be, you can go back to your hotel tonight."

"Thank you, doctor. We are supposed to go on a Nile cruise the day after tomorrow."

"That should not be a problem. There is a policeman waiting to see you."

The young man was in civilian clothes and proudly proclaimed himself a Detective Abdu-something-she-didn't-catch.

"Madam, I have some photographs of men I would like you to look at. If you would be so kind. If you are feeling well enough, of course."

"Yes, by all means. I feel much better now."

He passed her the photos one at a time.

"This one was the guide who led me to the thieves, but you already have him."

"He refused to talk when we found him. He complained that you hit him."

"I did." She looked at a couple more.

"Take your time," he said, as if speaking to a fractious child.

She passed him the last one. "This is the man who seemed to be in charge. He was the one who hit me. I'm not sure I would recognize the others."

The CAT scan was clear and Iris was driven back to the hotel in an American Embassy car.

The family stood waiting in the lobby. Vic almost charged at her with tears in his eyes.

"Hey take it easy, son," the driver said. "She's supposed to go straight to bed."

"I'll take you upstairs," Mandy said.

Iris saw them clustered around the driver, asking him questions.

Mandy helped her into bed.

"Room service will bring up some dinner. What would you like?"

"An omelet and some mineral water. Fizzy. And a mango."

"We were so worried about you. We didn't realize you were missing until Vic raised the alarm. We talked to Kareem, and he ordered some of the guides hanging around to search. Then the police came. They told us you had been hurt, but not badly, and the embassy was taking care of everything. What happened?"

"It's a long story. I'll fill you in later. I've got to rest all tomorrow, so you all go out and see the sights. I've been okayed for the cruise. That's the main thing."

Mandy ordered the food and stayed until it arrived.

"Go to your family, Mandy. I'm fine. I just need to rest."

"If you're sure."

She was safe and drowsy from the painkillers now. She lay back and closed her eyes. Sleep eluded her as she relived the scene. Hot anger filled her. She'd missed the pyramids, her one chance to see them. Maybe she could go when they got back from the cruise. She seemed to remember there was a free day in Cairo before they flew back to Washington. Her headache was getting worse. *Relax, let the anger go. Dream of better things.*

34

They filed onto the boat, which shone white against the cerulean sky as it lay at the dock on mercifully calm water. Its name, “Nefertiti” was written in bright blue along one side. Kareem had taken charge of their baggage as soon as their bus pulled up alongside and a uniformed steward showed them to adjacent cabins close to the top deck. Iris looked around her small space. She opened a door that led into a tiny bathroom. Her room had a tall, narrow chest of drawers into which she placed those items that did not need to be hung, and after poking around, found the closet hiding behind a camouflaged sliding door. A couple of bottles of mineral water and glasses had been placed next to an ice bucket on a side table. She poured herself a welcome icy water and lay on the sofa. There was probably some activity planned, but she didn’t feel like exploring. It would soon be time for lunch, anyway. Someone knocked on her door.

"Your case, madam."

She still hadn't acquired any Egyptian money. "Will dollars be all right?"

"Certainly, madam."

When she handed him five dollars, the porter beamed and bowed his way back out.

She made herself comfortable on her sofa and opened her Kindle. She read a couple chapters of her mystery, finishing at the point where the protagonist had settled herself in bed for an early night. *Bed? Wait a minute, where was her bed?*

Perhaps this sofa was the bed. It was attached to the wall, after all. It was comfortable, but not really sleeping-all-night comfortable. Simon would know. As if summoned, he knocked on her door.

"Iris, are you all right?"

"Yes, Simon. Just relaxing."

She got up and opened the door. Simon stood there, a little anxious crease between his brows.

"The others have gone ahead. I think Vic is taking a swim. It's almost lunchtime and our guide is going to give us a little talk any minute now and show us around the boat. Are you up to it?" He looked excited.

"Sure. I'll just grab my purse."

"Don't forget your key."

"I won't. It's huge! Good thing I bought this big bag."

"I noticed that. Where did you get it?"

"In the hotel gift shop while you were out yesterday."

"You were supposed to be resting."

"The police gave me back the one I was carrying at the pyramids, but it was dirty. I didn't fancy it. I liked the camel motif."

Iris turned her old-fashioned key in the lock and dropped it into a zippered pocket on the outside of her tote. They wandered to a short flight of stairs and came up on deck. The boat chugged along, its flag flapping and snapping in the breeze, a breeze that tempered the blazing sun into soothing warmth. Simon led her to the dining room and to their table, already occupied by Mandy and Barbara.

"Where are Vic and Justin?" he asked.

"Justin went swimming with Vic. They should be here... oh, here they come," Barbara said, pointing toward the entrance.

"That was nice," Justin said, his nose and forehead already red from the visit to the pyramids, somewhat fiery now.

"Did you remember to bring suntan lotion with you?" Iris asked.

"No. We should have," he answered. "I meant to look in the hotel shops, but what with all the goings on, I forgot."

"Maybe there's a little shop on board," Mandy said. "We're going to be shown around soon, so we'll soon find out."

The sound of a fork hitting a glass quieted everyone down. Iris waved her hand discretely at Michael, whom she spotted in the back corner of the room, sitting at a small table on his own. He pretended he didn't see her. Typical. She'd have invited him over if she thought for a moment he'd have welcomed company. He was no spring chicken, but was still good-looking and in great shape.

Kareem talked about the monuments they would visit and some of the entertainment they would enjoy in the evenings. The tours would begin early in the day because of the heat, so they'd be back on the ship before lunch and would have the rest of the day to relax. This evening, they were to have a special treat when a magician, fresh off a European tour, would entertain them with his incredible magical abilities. Iris groaned under her breath. She hated conjurors. Boring and predictable.

She looked around the tables. At the center table—the Captain's table?—two women sat next to an older couple, all dressed to kill. The older couple were not members of her tour group, but she supposed the boat had much more capacity than that and would welcome extra passengers. The wealthy woman who was part of their tour wore too much jewelry to be in good taste at lunchtime. Iris noted her large ruby pendant. Iris wondered again if her companion might have been her daughter. She looked sullen and was carelessly, although expensively, dressed in a rumpled linen blouse and silk pants as if proclaiming her disdain for the trappings of wealth. The elderly woman wore a yellow pantsuit that seemed too much for the climate and clusters of pearls at her ears and throat. Her husband wore an old-fashioned white suit with a straw hat. An ivory-handled mahogany cane leaned against his chair. All four seemed encased in their own bubble, silent and brooding. The captain was not in attendance.

The group all got up to follow Kareem for a tour around the boat. A ship, he'd called it. Iris knew people could be tetchy about calling their ship a boat. It wasn't that big. *Whatever.*

They passed a small swimming pool, a café, and an upper deck with seating arrangements where passengers could sit in the sun or shade and be served drinks and snacks. She could see herself there—in the shade—enjoying a gin and tonic and her mystery. There was a small shop up there, too, where Justin dropped back to buy his suntan lotion. Vic looked a bit red, too, but he'd situated himself next to the young girl and they were chatting animatedly about something. Iris sidled closer to listen. They were talking about ancient Egyptian dynasties and the things they were looking forward to seeing. Iris was surprised and pleased. Another nerd! The girl's parents ambled next to Iris, who introduced herself.

"Hello. I'm Iris Hall. I'm here with Victor's family."

"Oh, how do you do?" said the woman. "I'm Nancy Green, and this is my husband James. It seems our Jennifer and your Victor are getting along famously."

"Nice to meet you, Nancy, James. They seem fascinated by the ancients."

"Yes, she'd been pleading with us to come to Egypt for a year now. She reads about it all the time. How are you feeling? We heard you had an accident at the pyramids."

"Yes, I fell and hit my head on a rock. Fine now, though. Ready to enjoy the cruise."

"Glad to hear it," James said, his accent plummy English.

"Oh, you're English," Iris said. "We were in London last year and had a wonderful time. We didn't spend much time there, I'm afraid, because we were on our way to Switzerland and Paris, but I loved what little I saw. I really want to go back."

James looked sad. "Yes, there's nothing quite like it. Pittsburgh wouldn't have been my first choice, but my company sent me there for two years. Then I met Nancy, and there we are. We did spend a week with my family in Devon, though. My older brother runs the estate now. I love being there, but I was never cut out for farming. I'm a civil engineer."

"Interesting," Iris said. "I was born and brought up in New York City, but love living in a quieter place. The noise and bustle of a city rather overwhelms me now." *You never mention your birthplace. You're slipping!*

"James had a business trip to New York once and took me with him. I felt as if those skyscrapers were looming over me, and it was even noisier than London. We had fun, though, and went to the museums, an opera, and the Radio City Music Hall. Crammed a lot into that week. Where did you live?"

"The Upper East Side," Iris said. "I'd better find my group. Lovely meeting you."

She was behaving like an American. A normal American, that is, one who strikes up friendly conversations with strangers and divulges their life history at the drop of a hat. It felt nice, open, uplifting, but it could never be safe for her. She had too much to hide. Depression drew Iris low for a few minutes.

A gong rang out, resounding long after the last strike.

"Lunchtime!" Kareem called out.

They all hurried back to the dining room, eager to see what delights awaited them.

35

Lunch was a simple offering of grilled whole fish, French fries, and salad. A large selection of Egyptian pastries made up dessert. Iris enjoyed a few, and Vic enjoyed more than a few, she noticed. There were no plans for the afternoon, as it was too hot for sightseeing. In fact, there wouldn't be anything much to do until they reached Luxor, the day after tomorrow. Eating and lazing around sounded good to Iris. She'd never learned to swim and didn't care to reveal that, so hadn't packed a swimsuit.

Iris enjoyed chatting with other members of the tour. Kareem offered a couple of short lectures on ancient Egyptian history and the sights they'd be seeing in Luxor and Aswan, together with slide shows. Vic and Jennifer took it all in with rapt attention. After the first lecture, Vic stayed behind to ask Kareem a question, while Jennifer wandered out onto deck. He hurried after her when he was done, calling her name. She didn't respond. Iris frowned. Trouble in paradise. She followed them, curious to see what was going on.

Vic grasped her elbow. She turned, clearly startled. "You didn't hear me call you?" She gasped and blushed.

"Sorry, I must have been miles away. Thinking about all my friends in Chicago."

"Chicago? I thought you lived in Pittsburgh."

"Oh, yes, silly of me. I mean Pittsburgh, of course. Let's go swimming. I'll go get changed. See you in a few."

Vic stared after her, clearly confused. Iris joined him. "That was strange, wasn't it?" she said.

"You heard?"

"I did."

"Why didn't she answer me?"

"I wonder if Jennifer is her real name?"

"Why would she lie?" Vic looked distressed.

"You know, sometimes people have to get away from something. Change their names and start again."

"Like witness protection, you mean?" He looked excited rather than downcast now.

"Not necessarily, but possibly. I wouldn't worry about it. Don't forget, it's not just her, it's her parents. Just respect her as you know her and let it be." Iris hoped it was that simple.

"Okay, Gran, I guess. I'll get changed now."

"Did Uncle Justin get you suntan lotion?"

"He did. Don't worry, I'll use it. I don't want to look like a lobster."

The conjuror's first show was scheduled to start just after dinner. Iris sat toward the back so she could slip out if she got too bored. She felt bloated, too, as she'd eaten far too much of the sumptuous buffet—lamb, chicken, vegetables in aromatic sauces, rice with almonds and raisins, and more delicious desserts.

The woman with the ruby pendant wore a deep red dress, no doubt to show off the gem, nestling at the top of her cleavage—which was very much on show. She'd sat next to the captain at dinner, and it wasn't always clear which objet d'art fascinated him most. She had an aisle seat, but her companion, probably her daughter, was absent. Michael was there, to her surprise. She would have expected him to hate this kind of thing.

The show began, unbelievably, with a rabbit and hat trick. Iris thought it was long time past giving that one a rest. The magician was a plump little popinjay who wore a tall turban with numerous "jewels" sewn into it, no doubt to give the illusion of height. He spoke with a strange accent. After listening carefully, Iris caught a phrase or two of fairly educated English interspersed with a whiff of Cockney from time to time. His female assistant did not speak, but swanned around in her tights and sequined bodice as if she were the pretty young thing she might have been thirty years before. This ship was rather luxurious, leading Iris to wonder why they couldn't have found someone more sophisticated to perform.

The magician, "Ali Baba" as he called himself, came down to the audience to select someone to come up on stage to assist with the next trick. Iris hoped to high heaven it wouldn't be another boring card trick. He picked Jennifer. Her parents didn't look too happy. They probably didn't want to attract too much attention to themselves if they were indeed in hiding.

The trick involved mind-reading and, of course, cards. Iris sighed and got up to leave, but was transfixed by a shriek that would have put a banshee to shame.

CHAPTER 35

"My ruby!" The rich bitch (as Iris thought of her) stood clutching the front of her dress. Pandemonium ensued as people stood, exclaimed, buzzed, and sat again, not quite knowing what to do. Iris had noticed one of the stewards leaving quickly, no doubt to call security. Jennifer's father beckoned her to leave the stage, which she did, rushing to sit next to Vic again. Ali Baba looked ready to disappear behind the back curtain, but the remaining steward stepped forward and grabbed his arm before raising his voice.

"No one is to leave. No one!" he yelled. "Everyone, sit down. Now."

At that point, a couple of uniformed officers arrived with the other steward.

One of them sounded Scottish and asked a few general questions about who had been near Mrs. Trelawny (AKA Rich Bitch) at the time of the disappearance. He asked a steward to search the floor in case the chain had broken. The poor man crawled around the floor on his hands and knees for some time before he gave up. Iris thought of pot plants and looked around, but there weren't any. She wondered if Mrs. Trelawny's bag might hold the answer. The officer had the same thought and asked her for it. She roused herself from a half-swoon to protest but handed it over when stared down by the Scotsman, whose face had taken on the aspect of a granite block. Nothing to be found there. It could be way down that cleavage, but the officer was in no position to go that far.

"Two million dollars, lots of small diamonds around the center stone, solid gold setting and chain. Two million dollars!" The woman repeated it like a mantra while the officer listened, still stony-faced.

"Everyone can go back to their cabins," he announced when she paused for breath. "Please stay there until notified otherwise. We will not go ashore tomorrow. We will be at anchor until this matter is cleared up. All cabins will be searched, so please do not leave them for any reason."

Iris sat thinking through the scenario just before the shriek. To the woman's right sat the two older couples from their group, who oohed and aahed throughout. Vic and Jennifer sat in front of her, and Michael sat behind. He had seemed to be watching someone—or everyone—rather than the show. He had no doubt seen something useful. Iris wouldn't have noticed some sleight of hand, but she was pretty sure he would. Just what was he up to?

"Madam?" The stern officer stood in front of her. "Is anything the matter?"

"No, not at all. I was just running everything through my head to see if I might have seen something useful. I had a good vantage point here, after all. But I can't think of anything out of the ordinary."

"Thank you, madam. Please return to your cabin."

"Of course."

Iris got back to her cabin to find the bed made up, fresh ice and water on the table, together with a basket of fruit. She thought she'd better stay dressed in case security wanted to search her and her cabin. She went over to the fruit basket. Small plates and forks sat next to it, as well as a sharp knife. She selected a mango, peeled and sliced it, then washed her sticky hands. She set a small table next to her bed and placed a glass of water, the plate with mango chunks and a fork, and her Kindle on it before making herself comfortable. She didn't mind being confined to her room under these conditions. Not at all.

She woke when someone rapped on the door. "Who is it?"

"Security. Officer Brant."

"Just a minute." She swung her legs out of bed and made her way to the door. "Good evening. Do come in."

A younger officer followed him.

"We are here to search your cabin. I'm sorry to come so late. We have many passengers to check."

"No problem. My purse is under the bed." Iris pulled it out. "And my suitcase is..." Iris looked around. Where was it?

"When the steward finds it unpacked, he moves it out of your way to a locked storage room," Officer Brant said, clearly amused, judging by the upward curve of his mouth.

"Oh. How odd that I didn't notice it was gone."

The young man searched her purse before looking through the drawers and closet. He moved on to the bathroom.

"All clear, sir."

"He didn't look under the bed," Iris said. "Or in the fruit basket."

The young man blushed.

"Get out your torch and have a look," Officer Brant ordered.

He got out a small flashlight and kneeled beside the bed. Iris stood hurriedly. "So, you call a flashlight a torch? You had me worried."

"Aye. That's what we call it. What do you call a torch?"

"Something like people used before electricity, a live flame carried on a stick. To set fire to things."

"Och, yes. I suppose we never left off some of the old words."

The young man got wearily to his feet and made for the fruit bowl.

"Hey, not with those dirty hands," Iris said sharply. He jumped and looked to his superior for guidance.

"I'll do it. I wouldn't bother, but I canna waste a good suggestion, can I?" He almost smiled again. "Young Timothy is new to our company and is still feeling his way."

Young Timothy blushed again.

"I will wish you goodnight, Madam. Timothy will wait with you until Miss Leila comes to search your person. It shouldn't be long now. Timothy will leave as soon as she arrives."

Not two minutes after Brant left, Miss Leila arrived and Timothy left. Tired by now, Iris simply removed her clothes and let them drop to the floor before turning in a circle with her arms outstretched. Mis Leila gasped before searching the discarded garments. She didn't even say goodbye before she left. Iris hung up her clothes, wrinkled from falling asleep in them, and pulled a nightie over her head. She checked her watch. Just a few minutes before midnight. It felt later. She read for a few minutes before turning out her light.

A nightmare woke her. She'd been dozing in a deck chair near the pool when the magician suddenly bent over her and shoved the ruby down her throat. His assistant laughed as she choked. Iris put her hand to her throat. All normal. She turned on her side and calmed her breath. Ali Baba had been going up and down the aisles looking for someone to use in his act. Had he passed by Mrs. Trelawny? As far as she remembered, he hadn't come up that far. Could he have an accomplice? He could hide several rubies in that ridiculous turban. Officer Brant would probably have thought of that.

Someone at the door. "Yes?"

"It's your steward, madam. You are permitted to leave your cabin. Breakfast is being served."

"Thank you. Did they find the ruby?"

"I really couldn't say."

Iris had a quick wash at the sink and cleaned her teeth. She'd shower later. She should have asked the steward about having yesterday's outfit pressed. Later. She threw on a flowery cotton dress and pulled on her sandals. Her hair looked presentable after a good brushing. She hurried up to the dining room. The others were all eating already.

"Good morning, sleepyhead," Simon said.

"I didn't get to sleep until well after midnight," she answered. "They came quite late to search my room. And me."

"Oh, that's too bad. They came to us almost right away."

"Who do you think did it, Gran?"

"I have absolutely no idea. I was sitting near the back so I could leave if it got boring, so I had a good view of everyone, but I didn't see anything useful."

"Aw, that's too bad. You could have been a hero!"

Iris gave her order for tea and went to the buffet table. Michael was loading his plate with what looked like the Egyptian options—beans, feta cheese, olives, and pita bread. Iris didn't know if she could accept beans for breakfast. She had a dim memory of her parents eating baked beans on toast for breakfast, but they'd been devoid of good taste, anyway. She hadn't thought of them for years, and didn't want to start now.

"Wouldn't you like to try a typical local breakfast?" Michael asked.

"I don't think I'm up to beans at breakfast," she said. She looked up and down the table. "Oatmeal, that looks good. Toast and marmalade. Maybe I'll come around!"

Michael laughed. "Quite a scene last night."

"Indeed. Did they find it yet?"

"They did not."

"I was thinking it could be hidden in that ridiculous turban the magician was wearing."

"I was watching him. He was nowhere near her."

"Why were you watching him?"

Michael lowered his voice. "He is not who he seems."

"He's not the only one," Iris whispered. "That couple with the young girl. I don't think that's the girl's real name, and I don't think they're from Pittsburgh."

"You're right. Smart of you to pick up on that. They should be more careful. But don't worry about them. They're all right. Take my word for it."

"All right."

Iris took her food back to the table. Should she have trusted Michael? She had a gut feeling that he, while certainly one who was not what he seemed, was probably honest in his own way.

Barbara broke into her thoughts. "I guess we're stuck here still. I hope we won't miss too much."

"It's got to be somewhere onboard," Justin said. "It was apparently a big ruby, but still pretty easy to hide."

"I wonder if they searched the kitchen," Vic said. "It could be in sugar, flour, rice, anything like that."

"I'm sure they thought of that," Mandy said.

Iris looked at Vic. Apart from a terse "Morning" when she appeared, he'd been unusually quiet. Was he upset about Jennifer? Worried about the theft?

Kareem came to the table.

"We have arranged some entertainments for this afternoon and evening," he said.

"Not that so-called magician, I hope. Utterly boring," Iris said.

"No, madam. He will not be performing again. There will be a film about Abu Simbel, and an opportunity to paint some ceramics. In the evening, there will be a show of Arabic music and dance."

"That sounds good," Simon said. Everyone else added their appreciation, including Iris, who felt she'd been a bit harsh in her criticism of the magician.

CHAPTER 35

After breakfast, Simon said he wanted to swim. Everyone else said they'd join him. Iris said she'd walk around the ship, then sit by the pool. She went back to her cabin to fetch her Kindle and sunhat. She ascended to the upper deck and walked toward the lifeboats. Voices seemed to be arguing in whispers. She stopped and flattened herself behind a stairwell. She could only pick up snatches: "Can't keep moving it" … "got to" … "no suspicion" … "I don't know" … "keep your head" … "leave" … "looks bad" … "Shh. Let's go."

Iris looked around frantically. There was nowhere to hide well enough if they came her way. She'd have to brazen it out. She stepped out and walked toward the voices. They had started to walk her way and looked startled.

"Oh, good morning," she said. "I thought I'd explore this side of the ship. Needed to blow away the cobwebs after last night."

"Why, I know just what you mean," said the matron from flyover country. "Isn't this view just too glorious?"

"I agree," Iris said. "I do hope we're not missing too much of the tour. I missed the pyramids as it is."

"We heard you had an accident," said one of the men. "Are you quite recovered?"

"Oh, yes, thank you. To tell the truth, it was more than an accident. My guide took me away from the rest of you. Some men pulled me from the donkey and robbed me. I hit my head when they pushed me over."

"Oh, no, you poor dear," both women said in various ways.

"How wicked," said one of the men.

"Shocking, quite shocking," said the other.

"Well, I'd better get on with my walk. I promised to join the family by the pool. I don't care to swim, but they all love it. I just sit and read my mystery. See you at lunch, I hope."

"By the way, do you know who that big man is? He seems odd. I saw you talking to him at breakfast."

"You know, I think we need to introduce ourselves," Iris said. "I know they went around with names on that first day at the museum, but they've gone out of my head. Forgive me. I'm Iris."

"I'm Julie. This is my best friend Charlene, this is my husband Bob, and this is Charlene's husband Jim."

"I'll try to remember. Anyway, you were asking about that man. I only know his first name, Michael. He's the one who rescued me and took me into someone's house until the ambulance came. He happened to be looking through his binoculars when he noticed what was going on. I'm very grateful to him."

"What a terrible experience for you," Charlene exclaimed. "But you don't know anything about him?"

"No, I don't. Only that he seemed to know the person who owned the house he took me to. He doesn't join in much, does he? I think he's been here before. Well, I must be going. Nice to meet you all properly!"

Iris walked as sedately as she knew how until she was out of sight before increasing her pace toward the pool. She had to be careful about talking to Michael. They were obviously suspicious of him. No small wonder. Too bad she didn't know where his cabin was.

She stood and watched her family for a while. Her spirits rose high as she enjoyed their antics in the pool, laughing and splashing. She could never have imagined this while incarcerated in that awful prison for the criminally insane, then during her years in Toronto. She could die happy. But not yet. She moved to a deck chair in a shaded spot. A steward soon appeared and asked if she'd like a drink. She suddenly fancied a cold beer, which soon appeared at her side accompanied by a dish of nuts and another of chips, or crisps, as he called them. She loved chips. She didn't have to worry about her weight after the pounds she'd lost during chemo. One small silver lining, at least.

She sipped and munched, read her book, occasionally looking up at the family, once catching sight of Bob walking past quickly. She pretended not to see him, and he pretended he hadn't seen her. He'd been checking on her, she was sure of it.

About an hour before lunch, they all got out of the pool. "You must have prune fingers by now," she told them.

"Totally," Vic said, grinning, and holding up his hands for her inspection.

"Well, I didn't have time for a shower this morning, so I'm going to get ready now. I can smell the chlorine from here, so you might all want to wash it off, too. See you at lunch."

Iris went back to her cabin, took a shower, and got dressed. She looked at last night's silk pants, which seemed to have lost their creases after hanging for a few hours. The shirt was a different story. She rang for the steward, who took charge of it. Before leaving for lunch, she scribbled a note about the two couples she'd overheard arguing. And when she thought of it, although she couldn't hear them very well, their accents had sounded different. More New York-ish. Bronx, maybe. She added that they'd asked about him.

When she got to the dining room, the two suspicious couples were already seated, as was Michael. They nodded a greeting with plastered-on smiles, as did she. She said hello to Michael. Her family arrived while she studied the menu. How to pass the note to Michael? The lunch passed pleasantly. Vic had asked to be excused to sit with Jennifer. Iris waved to them. She did full justice to her kebab, as did the others. She mostly listened to the conversations between the two younger couples. Justin and Simon seemed so much easier together than when they were younger. The tolerance of maturity for different interests. Barbara and Mandy were both quiet women, but chatted together easily. They would become close sisters-in-law. Barbara probably wasn't that much younger than Mandy.

The four imposters (which they surely were) got up to leave. Iris stayed where she was in case one of them was spying. She could just see Michael in the mirror on the opposite wall. She hoped he wouldn't be in any hurry.

"I'm going back to freshen up before this afternoon's activities," she told her family. "See you back in the theater. When was it, two o'clock?"

She sauntered out, dropping her note on Michael's plate as she passed.

36

As Iris walked to the theater, she noticed a police boat anchored close to the ship. *Interesting.*

The others had saved a seat for her in the front row. Vic and Jennifer sat at the end of their row, chatting earnestly. *Don't break his heart.*

The captain entered and stood in front of the stage. He waited until all were seated and cleared his throat.

"Ladies and gentlemen, I am sorry for the inconvenience you have all suffered due to the unfortunate incident concerning Mrs. Trelawny's ruby. I won't go into detail, but the ruby has been found, and the thieves apprehended. Our normal schedule will resume tomorrow morning. Enjoy the film."

He walked out to applause. Iris looked around to see who was missing. The four imposters, Michael, and Mrs.

Trelawny. Her unfortunate companion was present, though. Iris wondered how she'd been let off the hook.

The film was fascinating, showing some of the monuments they were going to see, including the tomb from which the artwork for Iris's papyrus had been copied. It started with the Aga Khan's tomb, which they'd visit their first morning in Aswan. The number of steps to get to it looked daunting. But she'd try.

The ship had started to move into port. Iris hoped there would be no more adventures.

A morning's sightseeing, after a 7 a.m. start, left them all exhausted. Iris wanted nothing more than a shower and a nap. She'd picked up some brochures. They'd seen some interesting places, and she'd loved the ride in a horse-drawn carriage, but Luxor and Aswan promised bigger and better things. When she got back to her cabin, she felt as though she hadn't the energy to shower, but she didn't want to get between her sheets all sweaty. She had a headache, too. It had never quite gone away after the assault at the pyramids, and she felt she shouldn't tire so quickly either. She'd been doing so well, too. Well, travel was tiring, and she wasn't used to all this walking, either.

She felt something move on her leg. She lifted her skirt and gasped before freezing. A bug was crawling up her thigh. Too big for a flea, it was a like a cross between a tick and a spider. She raised her pamphlet and whacked it. It fell onto Iris's shoe and lay still. Then it waved its legs. Iris tipped it onto the floor and ground it with her heel. She became aware of a burning sensation on her thigh. Had she been bitten? She peered at it. There was just a big red mark.

She'd not only whacked the bug, she'd whacked herself. She shuddered. She scooped up the tiny remains on the pamphlet and deposited them into the trash.

Iris woke in a panic. What time was it? She looked at her phone. She'd catch the second lunch sitting if she just threw on something easy. She'd showered, after all. She flung on a dress and sandals and combed her hair. No time for cosmetics. Maybe a touch of lipstick.

By the time she got to the dining room, her family was having dessert. Why hadn't they checked on her? Her eyes pricked with tears. *Don't be so weak.*

"Hi Gran! Dad said he didn't want to wake you."

Iris looked at Simon. "How did you know I was asleep?"

"Well, I just wanted to be sure you were okay. So we asked the steward to open your door very quietly. Mandy popped her head around, and reported that you were fast asleep. We know how exhausting the morning was for you and felt we could order something for you if you missed lunch."

Iris smiled at them all, suddenly joyful. "I appreciate it," she said.

She ordered a light lunch of soup and salad and drank delicious sweet and tangy lemonade.

"I guess the program has changed. Do you know what's on this evening?" she asked.

"I think we're going to sail to Luxor very soon," Simon said.

"They had originally planned something for tomorrow in town, but the captain decided Luxor and the rest of the stops were more important." This came from Barbara.

"Quite right," Justin added. "Today was nice, but the biggies are ahead."

"I agree," Iris said. "Wow, I feel as if I need another nap!"

"Rest as much as you can," Mandy said. "There's some heavy-duty walking in the days to come."

Iris wondered if she'd be up to it. She felt a bit off. Not unwell, exactly. Just old, maybe. What a depressing thought.

The rest of the trip was exhilarating and exhausting. Monuments started to blur together in Iris's memory. She bought souvenir books with lots of photos in both Luxor and Aswan, and a slightly heavier one at Abu Simbel. The wonder of ancient craftsmanship never lost its thrill and just the age of what they gaped at and walked through was staggering to contemplate. The Aga Khan's tomb nearly did Iris in. And when she reached the top after a few rest stops, it wasn't that awe-inspiring. When they finally got down to the bottom of that torturous flight of steps, dozens of urchins lay in wait, offering ice-cold bottles of soda. Iris didn't much like sodas, but she enjoyed every last drop of her cola on that occasion. Crafty little sods.

The colossi at Abu Simbel were just that—colossal. Iris realized that she hadn't been very sociable during their sightseeing tours, but she didn't want to talk. She wanted to drink it all in, feel the antiquity, feel the weight of history, her own insignificance—which made her feel more at ease with herself and impending old age. Her own bad deeds seemed diminished in the face of centuries of invasions, conquests, glories, and massacres.

Michael once walked beside her at Abu Simbel. "You must have seen all of this many times," she said on their last tour.

"I have, but I never tire of it."

"It's a good thing that having to keep an eye on people has its compensations," she said with a snarky smile.

"Indeed," he replied with a snarky grin of his own. "I believe you have a free day in Cairo before flying back to America. May I escort you to the pyramids? It would be terrible to go home without seeing them properly."

"Oh, I was so regretting that. Thank you. You're very kind."

"My pleasure," he said before walking on.

The last couple of days were spent on board. Iris was relieved because she'd had more than enough of walking on rough ground in the heat. Even early in the morning, it must have been close to ninety degrees. A winter trip would have been more comfortable, but with Vic still in school, that was out of the question.

The ship offered entertainment, such as belly dancing and a band for dancing after dinner. The family sat at the captain's table one evening. When she asked him what had happened to the magician, he frowned before rearranging his face to a more benign appearance. "A family emergency. He left us in Luxor and flew back to Cairo."

Fired, more likely.

Since they were sitting where Mrs. Trelawny and her appendage usually sat, Iris realized that she hadn't seen them, either. She didn't like to question the captain again, so she asked the steward when he came to turn down her bed. Apparently, they'd flown back to Cairo from Luxor, too. The elderly couple who used to sit with them were at a small table on their own. They'd started out on tours with the group, but hadn't lasted through any of them. Iris usually noticed them sitting on a wall or a bench (if they were lucky) waiting for the rest of the group to finish. They didn't look happy. Actually, they didn't look well. It was probably all too much. It had nearly been too much for Iris.

The morning they disembarked, Vic and Jennifer had disappeared, apparently to make their farewells in private. Her parents, Nancy and James, who had socialized quite a bit with Simon and Mandy, looked worried. "I'm sure they're just exchanging addresses and so on," Iris said, soothingly (she hoped).

"But we have to get the bus back to the hotel. We can't miss it," Nancy fretted. James's frown deepened.

The two miserable teenagers rounded a corner. When their parents told them off, albeit gently, they merely shrugged. Iris wondered why they were saying goodbye so early. Surely they had another day.

"Don't you have another day in Cairo?" she asked Nancy.

"No, we have to leave on a late flight tonight. It was the only one we could get."

"No wonder they're sad," Iris said.

"Well, we don't stay in one place for long."

"Oh."

"Work."

"I see." Iris would ask Michael. He'd know if anyone would.

37

Iris spent most of the afternoon on the hotel terrace, shaded by its awning. It didn't seem so hot after where she'd been all week. Her Kindle in hand and lemonade on a side table, she felt supremely happy. If only she could get rid of that headache. Even though it was mild, it felt like a guest that overstayed its welcome. She was so tired, too. But not the sleepy kind of tired. Maybe she was too old to be gallivanting around the world.

"May I join you?" Michael asked as he took the chair across the table.

"Of course." Iris closed her Kindle.

"I thought we'd leave for the pyramids at about eight in the morning. We should be back here well before lunch."

"Are you sure that's not too much trouble?"

"Not at all. We won't need a guide. I know it all by now. I just wish I had time to take you to the evening Sound and Light show. It's spectacular. I'm afraid I have a rather pressing appointment."

"I'm sure you do." Iris laughed quietly. "How long have you lived here?"

"About fifteen years or so. I started out with the British Council, stayed with them for about five years, then branched out on my own after my contract ended. I love it here."

"You must. And I heard you speak Arabic. What do you do exactly?"

"This and that."

"Ah. A spook. A British one?"

"I wouldn't quite put it that way. My mother was from Malta and my father English. I lived in Malta for a long time, but went to boarding school and university in England at my father's insistence. He felt it was important to meet the right kind of people."

"What was your father like? It must have been difficult for someone who thought that way to live in a different culture with a very different outlook."

"They were both from that kind of upper-class family. You're right, he was never quite comfortable living abroad, but he loved my mother. And they were good parents."

Michael looked sad, suddenly, so Iris changed the subject.

"How many people on that cruise were on the up and up?"

"Not many in your group."

"I'm guessing not the Greens. The girl made a little slip with her name."

"American Witness Protection Program. I agreed to keep an eye on them. They didn't know about me, though."

"The four thieves, of course. What about that so-called magician? He was so amateurish, I could hardly believe he'd been hired by such a reputable company."

"Con man. His last con was in Germany. Interpol tracked him to Cairo. I tracked him to the cruise. He's been dealt with."

"The old couple?"

"Not wanted for anything. Not now, at least. They used to run a brothel in Manchester."

"My god, are all these cruises full of shady people?"

"Not at all. Just a coincidence. People think they are nearly invisible in a place like this. But there are eyes and ears everywhere."

Iris felt a chill run down her back.

"Good thing our family is honest. Well, the boys are brothers. I'm a neighbor, but we've grown close over the years. I babysat Vic from the time he was about nine months. I love him as if he were my own. And his parents have been very good to me."

"Yes, I can see you are close. And I know Simon was once known as Andrew. And about his mother."

Iris fought to keep her composure. "What about his mother?"

"You really don't know? Well, it's not my story to tell. See you tomorrow in the lobby at eight." He got up and left.

He knows! He knows who I am. How? What will he do?

Iris went up to her room to get ready for dinner. She fought to control her breathing, which threatened to become hyperventilation. Would she die in prison? Was this wonderful life a dream that would soon turn into a nightmare?

She managed to engage with the others at dinner. Vic hardly spoke, but that wasn't surprising. She caught a few puzzled looks from Simon. Perhaps she wasn't putting as good a face on it as she thought. She wouldn't tell him. He'd probably feel he had to speak to Michael, and that could only exacerbate the issue. She'd see what happened at the pyramids.

After a restless night of tossing and turning, interspersed with a few snatches of sleep, Iris dragged herself out of bed and got ready. Dread sat heavy in the pit of her stomach. She couldn't bear for Vic to think badly of her. She looked at her watch. Seven-fifteen. Time for breakfast. She wasn't hungry, but needed to get something in her stomach before sightseeing.

Michael rose from his seat in the dining room as he invited her to sit with him. Her family wasn't down yet. Hardly anyone was.

"Did you sleep well? You look a little tired."

"Not well, I'm afraid."

"You know, I will not tell anyone about Simon's mother. It's been too long. No point. It's over. Don't worry about it."

"Thank you. I'm sure he'd have appreciated that if I told him. Which I haven't."

"Good. Our little secret." He smiled at her, clearly amused by her discomfort.

Bastard. You enjoyed that. "Where is the waiter?"

The waiter soon emerged from the kitchen and took her order for juice, tea, and toast. Michael finished up what looked like a hearty breakfast.

"What is all that you're eating?" she asked.

"A typical Egyptian breakfast. Fava beans, feta cheese, Arabic bread, olives. Delicious."

"A bit much for me."

"More than sausages and bacon? Well, I guess so. Especially the full English breakfast."

"Sometimes you sound very English, but just occasionally I hear a little of something else. I'm not quite sure what. Is there such a language as Maltese?"

"There is, but I'm a bit of a mongrel. While I went to school and university in England and was brought up in Malta, we moved to Germany when I was about sixteen, after which I had to spend a couple of summer holidays with a German tutor. I hated it, resented having to study when I should have been messing around with friends. My father was a stickler for good English, too. But I have to admit, these languages have been a great asset."

"And now you speak Arabic, too. What about your mother?"

"She was Palestinian, from a wealthy family who had just finished university at the Sorbonne. She lost her family to the violent years of Israel's founding. My father was working for the British government there and helped her to get out to Malta. They fell in love and married. She died in a car crash when I was eighteen."

"I'm so sorry." Iris sensed the grief that even now hung over him. *So how old are you? How old was she when she had you?*

"Well, we all have our sad stories. Let's go. The car should be waiting outside."

The car was a jeep that Michael had to help her into. The streets were busy, even this early. It took them over half an hour to get to the site.

"Camel or donkey?" she asked.

"Neither. This can take us all the way."

"That's a relief."

They toured and even went inside the Great Pyramid of Cheops, which Iris found a little frightening. There was a handrail to hang onto and Michael led the way, but it was so eerily quiet and dark. Michael talked knowledgeably about the pyramids and the pharaohs they honored before they made their way to the Sphynx.

Iris saw the Sphynx on her first visit, but not up close. She hadn't internalized how massive it was.

"It is generally agreed that the Sphynx was built around the same time as these Giza pyramids, about 4,500 years ago. But some archeologists surmise that at least part of it might be about nine thousand years old. A few years ago, someone compared striations near the haunches that looked as if they were caused by heavy rainfall over the course of many years. Then they researched climate change in this part of the world and found that the only time when there was that much rain here was nine thousand years ago."

"What do you think?" Iris asked him.

"I don't know. It seems farfetched that the statue could predate the ancient Egyptians. And we know that the face resembles that of the Pharoah Khafra because of other statues we have of him. I keep an open mind. That's my approach to most things I do."

Iris looked at him, wondering if that was a dig of some sort. "It's magnificent."

"Are you tired now?"

"Do I look tired?"

"Yes. I hope I didn't upset you yesterday."

"Oh, no, not at all."

Surprisingly, Michael stuck two fingers between his teeth and produced a piercing whistle.

"Wow, you're good." Iris stuck two fingers in her mouth and did the same, only louder. Michael's face was a picture of shock and awe before they both laughed so much they held their sides.

"Sir?" said a confused voice.

Still laughing, they climbed into the Jeep.

"You are a remarkable woman, Iris."

"You have no idea!" *Well, maybe you do.*

When they got back to the hotel, Michael held out his hand. "I have to drive to Alexandria this afternoon," he said. "It's been a great pleasure. You are a fascinating woman."

"Why, thank you, kind sir," she said. "I've enjoyed it, too. Maybe we'll meet again some day."

"Maybe. I'd like that."

He disappeared up the scarlet-carpeted staircase. Iris chose the elevator.

Their flight home was scheduled for very early the following morning, so Iris decided to take a shower and pack before lunch. They'd just hang around for most of the day. As it happened, Barbara and Mandy wanted to go shopping, and Simon and Justin felt they should accompany them. So she and Vic enjoyed a companionable afternoon reading and chatting—mostly about Jennifer. Jennifer was so intelligent and knew so much about history, and she was rather pretty, too. And so on.

38

The flight to London was followed by a three-hour wait for the flight to Dulles, then another wait for their flight to Charlotte. It was long and exhausting. Once home, Barbara and Justin decided to order pizza. Iris grabbed a bottle of water from the fridge and went to bed right away, only just managing to scrape up the energy to change and brush her teeth.

The next morning, she awoke to the sound of crows kicking up a racket outside her window. She got out of bed and parted the curtains. Some circled close to a huge oak near the back of the garden, and others perched on nearby branches and joined the chorus. She looked at her watch. Five-thirty. Jet lag. She shrugged on her robe and padded downstairs. She kept slip-ons next to the back door, so put them on and went to see the cause of the commotion. The sound ramped up as she got closer to the tree. A baby crow lay on the ground flapping its wings in a panic, but unable to levitate itself.

"Now what do we do about you?" she asked it.

"Quaaw."

Iris had seen a fox running through the garden a few times on its way to somewhere else, so this did not bode well for the baby crow.

"What's up?"

Iris spun around. "Justin, you startled me! It's a baby crow that's fallen out of its nest. It can't fly yet. But you know that fox will get it. Or the neighbor's cats. I can't even see the nest, but there's no way any of us can get up there, anyway."

"I suppose we should take it to a wildlife rehab center. I'll do a search on my iPad and see if there's one nearby." He hurried back to the house.

Iris didn't like to leave the chick alone in case it became some creature's breakfast. She sat next to the little bird and leaned against the trunk. She sang it a nursery rhyme. The adult crows had calmed down a little, with only the occasional caw, caw echoing through the treetops. Soon, Justin appeared, wearing jeans and a tee shirt now, with a carton lined with a towel.

"The center is only about a twenty-minute drive away. Barbara is up, too, so she'll come with me. I guess we're all jetlagged."

"They won't be in so early, will they?"

"There's always someone there overnight."

He lifted the chick gently and placed it in the carton. He walked carefully to the gate that led to the front garden. Iris hurried to open it for him. The crows started up their racket again, some of them following Justin high overhead. Iris wandered back to the kitchen to prepare the coffee. She hoped the little bird would make it. So vulnerable, the adults powerless to help. Like she used to be. Her adults couldn't even help themselves.

She went upstairs to take a shower and throw on some clothes. She'd start the coffee when she came down. The others should be back by then. The shower felt so good—it had been almost a couple of days since she'd felt clean. She wrapped her hair in a towel and went across to Justin's room to look out of the window to see if his car was parked in front yet. No, no Justin. But a woman in a broad-brimmed hat was hanging around the front gate. Iris drew back as the woman's eyes raked the windows. Daisy! Iris went to the top of the stairs to listen. The gate clanged, and the doorbell rang. Iris didn't move. It rang again. A car door slammed. Justin's voice.

"Can I help you?"

"Aren't you Justin Hale?"

"Who's asking?"

"Daisy. Your aunt."

"Oh, hello. I'm afraid we just got back from a long trip. It's not a good time."

"That's no way to welcome your aunt."

"You are actually a complete stranger."

"Justin..." Barbara sounded shocked.

"Barbara, I've got this. Why don't you go inside?"

"I'm looking for your mother."

"My mother? Whatever do you mean? We haven't seen her in years."

"There's that woman you live with."

"She's a friend of the family who suffered some ill health. She's not strong. We help her in return for living here."

"Yeah, right. You know you could go to prison for harboring a fugitive? You know she tried to kill me, right?"

"She left a journal. We read it. I understand your anger, but my mother is not here and never has been. Now, please leave."

"I'll be back."

The gate clanged again, and Iris heard Justin open the front door and close it behind him. She ran to the window to make sure Daisy had left. She could just make out her back before she turned a corner. She tiptoed downstairs.

"Justin, was that really your aunt?" Barbara asked

"Yes."

"You weren't very nice to her. You could have asked her in."

"I don't like her and don't want her in my life. And she's obsessed with my mother."

"What's this about your mother being a fugitive?"

"My mother committed a crime, was sentenced to a hospital facility, and wrote a journal while she was there, telling us about her background and why she did what she did. She escaped, and no one has seen her since. They think she might have gone to Florida. That was in Virginia years ago. It was a very difficult time for us all and I don't like to think about it or talk about it."

"Okay." Barbara sounded hurt.

Iris walked into the kitchen and switched on the coffee. "How did it go? And who was that at the door?"

"It was my aunt, who Simon and I hardly know. She's making a real nuisance of herself. I sent her packing. The chick is going to be all right. The center will make sure he's fed and taken care of until he can fly. They suggested that when he's strong enough, we release him here in the garden."

"That's great. I was worried about him. So helpless."

"I know," Barbara said. "He's so cute. We stopped on the way back and got croissants. I've read about that bakery. They're supposed to be authentic."

"Thank you, that sounds like a great start to the morning. A new start, that is," Iris said, laughing. She didn't feel like laughing. Daisy was proving tenacious. Iris didn't want to kill anyone anymore. She'd had her own brush with death, which had proved a shock. Imagining a world without her in it was impossible. Humans are egocentric. They can't accept their own nothingness, so invent religions that promise everlasting life. Could there be something to it? Barbara handed her a croissant. Time to savor what she had.

Iris enjoyed the rest of the summer, despite feeling a little under the weather. Justin and Barbara had only a few concerts to perform, and Iris attended most. She'd never been a music lover, but she started to lose herself in it more and more. Justin was free of his teaching load until September. Simon seemed as busy as ever, but Iris arranged a few lunches and movies with Barbara and Mandy. Vic was away at Outward Bound camp for half of July and most of August. Iris missed him, but he was growing up and following his own interests now. She had to accept that. She borrowed his dog on more than one occasion. She loved her sloppy kisses and panting excitement whenever she sensed there was a walk coming up. Iris liked how it felt when she slept with her head on her feet while she watched TV in the evenings, too. She went to bed pretty early these days. Coughing often woke her, and she got breathless after any mild activity. She tired easily and the headaches were getting worse. The painkillers were upsetting her stomach, too.

"Iris, you don't look well," Justin said one day. "I think it's time you saw Dr. Coren for a checkup. Just to make sure everything is as it should be."

"You mean, to see if the cancer has come back."

"Well, no, I wasn't saying that."

"It's what you're thinking, though."

"No, well..."

"It's best to be sure," Barbara said, gently, taking Iris's hand.

Iris knew it had come back. She was exhausted, headachy, weak, and sometimes nauseated. She should get it confirmed and make arrangements. No chemo this time.

Dr. Coren met her with his widest smile, which sent shivers down her spine. *Too late for any of that.* His examination was not very extensive, although he took blood.

"I can't tell much without further tests, but your symptoms are worrying," he said. "If there is a recurrence, it's important to know where it is and how widespread. But let's not jump the gun. Blood tests might show a completely different issue." He smiled broadly again, a fake cheery smile. Iris knew. She just knew.

"Well? What did he say?" Justin asked. She'd found him pacing in the waiting room.

"He referred me for testing. He took blood. He said it could be something quite different, so not to jump to conclusions."

"I see." He turned away, but Iris saw his cheeks redden and his eyes well. "Let's go home," she said.

It was cancer, metastasized to her other lung, her right breast, and her brain. "Maybe three months," Dr. Coren said. "I'm sorry I don't have better news."

"I expected it," Iris said. The news still felt like a punch to her gut. She realized she was clutching her stomach and bending over as if she had a cramp. She sat up. "What's next?"

"We can arrange for hospice care in your home. That will involve palliative care so you won't suffer pain. You won't need full-time care yet, but that will be available when needed."

"Thank you, Dr. Coren. How is your wife, by the way?" He looked surprised.

"Oh. Well, we are divorcing, actually."

"Well, you won't be single for long. You're too attractive." She grinned into his shocked face and walked out, surprised that her legs still supported her.

She'd kept this appointment from Justin and Simon, as she needed time to process alone. She went to her car, slowly, as she labored for breath after controlling herself so tightly. She couldn't open up. Not yet. She'd parked in a far corner. There weren't many cars in the lot, as hers had probably been one of the last appointments of the day. She climbed in stiffly, feeling a hundred years old. Then she let go. She'd known her good fortune couldn't last forever. She'd been too wicked, too ready to mete out her own version of justice. Were heaven and hell and fate just earthly matters? Her mind collapsed into a whirl of grief and anger, fear and dread as she bawled. When she'd calmed down, she started the car. She looked at her watch. Nearly six. She'd been carrying on for an hour or more. Fortunately, Barbara and Justin had a concert and wouldn't be home when she got back.

She would drink wine and eat cake tonight. She'd make arrangements for her cremation tomorrow. She'd write letters to all of them—Simon, Justin, Mandy, Barbara, and Vic. Then she'd wait. She had pills saved up. Not while she could still enjoy, but when it got too tough, especially for her family. Yes, she had a family. A real family. Good people.

She stumbled up the front path and opened the door, trying several times to get her key in the lock. She turned on all the lights. No darkness for her ever again. She used the washroom and rinsed her face with cold water. Her eyes were almost closed from weeping. She rummaged in the fridge. Champagne! Yes, if ever an occasion called for champagne, this was it. She got out the chocolate cake she'd bought that morning—in preparation, she now realized. She sat at the kitchen counter and spooned up cake until she felt sick, which didn't take long these days. She sipped the glorious fizz slowly, savoring every complex drop.

A knock on the door. She didn't want anyone to see her like this. Too late, Simon opened the door and entered. He took one look at her and enveloped her in a bear hug.

"I was worried when you were out for so long. Why didn't you tell us you were going?"

"I needed time to get used to the idea. Maybe three months, he said."

"Oh, Mom." *Mom.* She cried a little more, but felt a little uplifted. *Mom.* She realized that he was crying, too.

"It's all right, my love. I was expecting it."

"What can I do?"

"Nothing. Dr. Coren is arranging for hospice here at home. I'm not bad enough for a lot of medication yet, but when the time comes, there'll be people to help."

Simon sat down and pulled a tissue out of the box Iris kept on the counter. Wiping his eyes, he said, "How on earth am I going to tell Vic?"

"No need to tell him until I'm bedridden. No need to have him tied up in knots before necessary."

"I suppose you're right."

"I knew my luck couldn't hold. But I'm grateful for finding my family again. You are all very dear to me." She felt strangely calm now, almost as if she were talking about someone else who was going to die. "You'd better get back to Mandy. I'm going to bed early. I don't suppose a hangover is recommended in my situation, but what the hell?"

Simon kissed her cheek and almost ran out. Poor boy. He'd always been a loving son. So had Justin, just not always on the same wavelength. But she loved them both. Loved them all. And Lucy. What about Lucy?

Iris toiled upstairs, clutching the tote armed with the champagne bottle, a bag of ice, a glass, and another slice of cake in a plastic container, a pretty plate, and a fork. She set it all out on her bedside table before undressing and climbing into bed. She'd bought a TV for her bedroom a few months ago, realizing she enjoyed watching after waking up from a nap, or even first thing in the morning. She rarely watched in her room at bedtime, but tonight would be an exception, no doubt the first of many. She looked on public TV first to see if there was a good British show on. There was an Agatha Christie film that had only just started. She loved Miss Marple. An old fuddy-duddy, but so sharp. She was almost happy, lying comfortably on fluffy pillows, sipping champagne, and finishing off another slice of cake. It was strange she didn't feel nauseated. Probably the alcohol was good for her. She might not feel so good tomorrow, though. Never mind, it was worth it.

40

Four weeks went quickly, too quickly. Four out of twelve. A third of her allowance. It had been a rollercoaster of emotions, Vic's reaction the worst. He'd run away for an afternoon after Simon and Mandy told him. They'd decided he should know sooner rather than later. They'd been worried sick until a police officer brought him home. He'd found Vic sitting under a tree in the park, sobbing. Finally, Vic had come to see her, looking wary, as if she might die right there in front of him.

"It's okay, Vic. I'm all right. I've got medicine if there's any pain. I'm ready."

"I'm not ready, Gran," he cried. He ran to her and buried his head on her shoulder. "I'm not ready. Not at all. Don't go."

The episode with Vic had been deeply painful and debilitating, and she had to take a nap on the sofa in the living room after he left. She didn't venture upstairs until bedtime.

The climb was getting too much. How she loved that boy. She hadn't cried, though. She was about cried out.

Later, Simon brought Wanda over. "Vic said you would need her."

The precious girl rushed over to Iris and licked her face when she bent down to pat her. Yes, she did need her.

"I brought her kit along," he added, setting down her dishes and kibble. "I'll just get her bed from the porch."

"I think I'll sit outside for a while," Iris said. "Justin set out a chair and table in case I'd want to. Wanda will like that."

"By the way, why did you pull up your daisies in the pot by the front door and plant pansies? I happened to notice while I was passing."

Iris gasped painfully and sat down hard on a kitchen chair. "I didn't. Think about it. Pansy."

"Dear God, that bloody woman! Shall I stay?"

"No, I'll be fine. I'll be just fine. What can anyone do now?"

Simon kissed her forehead and left. He didn't seem to know what to say to her. No one did. Talk about it? Ignore it? They fell over themselves to avoid upsetting her. She got a bottle of mineral water out of the fridge and led Wanda outside. Her plants seemed to be getting a second wind now the weather had cooled to more reasonable levels. They were cheerful and healthy. She'd take some inside to put in a vase for her bedroom. She had a vase up there, so all she had to carry up were the flowers themselves. She leaned back and reveled in the sun on her face.

"Hello, Pansy."

She felt groggy. She must have been dreaming. It was getting dark.

"I said, hello, sister."

Iris sat up in shock. "Who are you? What do you want?"

"I want to see you in jail. Remember Daisy and all those other friends you tried to poison?"

"I don't know what you're talking about!"

"I've been watching you while you slept. I can see through that plastic surgery. You're Pansy."

"I'm Iris. Yes, I've had plastic surgery. I was badly burned in a fire while living in Toronto. You're bothering me. I'm sick. Go away." Iris thought she might pass out. She started to cough and couldn't stop.

"Oh, quit the playacting."

"Not acting," Iris panted. "I've got cancer. I've only got a couple more months."

"Nice try," Daisy said, her sneering voice ugly and tough.

"What's going on?" It was Daisy's turn to startle.

"Oh, Mr. High-and-Mighty Andrew."

"Simon," Iris gasped.

"Oh, come off it."

"Let's take this inside," Simon said, his words stretching as taut as his nerves.

Simon gave Iris his arm to help her along.

"So, you really are sick?" Daisy said.

"Iris has terminal cancer." Simon almost growled. "Leave her alone."

"Oh, she can die in prison, can't she? Think of all that free healthcare. You'll go to prison, too."

"Get out!" Simon yelled.

"I'm staying in a bed-and-breakfast a few streets away. When I come back, it'll be with a police officer." She turned on her heel and left, slamming the door behind her."

"Car keys?" Simon said.

"There, on the counter." Iris pointed to a dish by the back door.

Simon grabbed them and left. She heard the garage door open and the car leave. She had to go to bed. She wouldn't be able to make it upstairs if she left it much longer. She needed to take one of the strong pills the nurse had left yesterday. She had to sleep without dreams, without care.

She awoke feeling as if she hadn't slept at all. Fuzzy-minded and blurry-eyed. She became aware of Simon and Justin sitting next to her bed, one on either side. A large wet tongue licked her cheek. Then she remembered. "I don't want to die in prison," she murmured, tears rolling down her face.

"You won't," Simon said. "Daisy won't be bothering us anymore. By the way, I'm afraid I clipped the wall next to the garage door. It took out a headlight. Justin helped me wash the car, but we haven't cleared away the debris by the wall. Just in case anyone asks. Sorry about that." He grinned at her in a humorless kind of way. She looked at his pale face, his lips gone back tight now. She looked at Justin, whose white face looked ghastly, with his bloodshot eyes and trembling lower lip.

"My boys," she murmured. "My boys."

She wanted to doze off again, but didn't want to lose a moment, so fought for consciousness. She knew that she was declining rapidly and ready for that stash of pills. Maybe in a couple of days. She still had letters to write. She shouldn't have put it off.

"You are safe, Mom. Quite safe," Simon said, sounding very far away.

That's my boy.

Book Club Questions

1. How soon do you think Simon recognized his mother?
2. How did Kate influence Iris?
3. Why did Iris seem to have an affinity for older women?
4. Were you happy for Iris that she found her family?
5. Book 2, *Lily Transplanted,* was a story of redemption. Has Iris progressed further along that path?
6. What did you think of Justin's ready acceptance of his mother?

7. Was Iris's attraction to Dr. Coren true magnetism, transference, or just a crush? Was it unusual for someone of her mentality?

8. Who do you think Michael (in Egypt) was working for? He seemed to know all about every member of the group, including Iris. Why do you think he didn't expose her secret?

9. Why do you think Iris tuned into Barbara's plight (in Switzerland) so soon?

10. Why did Daisy always go to great lengths to track her sister down, even before Iris tried to poison her?

11. Did the ending surprise you?

Author Bio

D. A. Spruzen grew up near London, U.K., graduated from the London College of Dance and Drama Education, and earned an MFA in Creative Writing from the Queens University of Charlotte. She teaches creative writing in Northern Virginia when not seeking her own muse. She is the author of *The Flower Ladies Trilogy* and the *Sleuthing with Mortals* series. Other publications include a historical novel, The Blitz Business, and a poetry collection, *Long in the Tooth*. Her poems and short stories have appeared in many online and print publications. She resides in Northern Virginia and Southern Maryland. Her faithful companion, a Cavalier King Charles Spaniel named Sam, is always by her side, whether she's writing, painting, gardening, or reading yet another British mystery.

www.ingramcontent.com/pod-product-compliance
Lightning Source LLC
LaVergne TN
LVHW091258150826
845673LV00006B/1459

* 9 7 9 8 8 2 3 2 1 0 2 4 9 *